DISEASE

DISEASE

Second Edition

M.F. Wahl

www.mfwahl.com

Halifax, NS Canada

DISEASE

SECOND EDITION

Edited By: Lance Fling, Loretta Clem ISBN: 978-1-987808-13-1 eBook: 978-1-987808-12-4

First Edition ISBNs: 978-0-9938513-0-8, 978-1-987808-02-5, 978-0-9938513-0-8 Edited By: Jennifer Melzer

For Charles,

   you know why.

CONTENTS

ACKNOWLEDGMENTS

I would like to express how thankful I am to everyone who has supported me throughout this process. It has been a long, tough road, and you helped me reach the end.

To my long-suffering better half, thank you. You, above all others, have made this possible. Without you, the world might never need suffer my ramblings.

To my sons, you are too young to understand that I truly do this for you. I can't expect you to shoot for the stars if I haven't done so myself.

Thanks to my good friend and editor Lance Fling. You have been so encouraging and helpful, this wouldn't be the same without you.

Lastly, I would like to thank my dog.

DISEASE

BY M.F. WAHL

1

Casey's frazzled nappy hair is held back tightly. The elastic has seen better days. A few thick, kinky strands stick to her face and threaten her dark brown eyes. Sweat drips from her brow as she pinches a match between her dark fingers and wipes her forehead with her arm, careful not to drip on the empty matchbox she clutches. Vaguely, her lungs call from somewhere far away, begging for oxygen.

The match flares, but the sound of the strike is lost as a loud crash shakes the wall she leans against. It rattles her teeth and flakes of plaster float down, dusting her shoulders. Her hand trembles, a strand of firecrackers clenched in it. The fuse sparks and then catches as she brings it to the fire.

Casey tosses the explosives into the next room.

She breathes, her chest filling with the stench of decomposing flesh. Nearby lays a rotting body, a lifeless lump, head smashed into the dust-laden area rug beneath it. Grimy, broken pictures of the family that once lived here smile down from the walls. They are frozen, forever grinning approval at all that may transpire under this roof.

Casey is pushed into motion by the roar of gunpowder disintegrating cardboard shells. She grips the door jam and peers into the adjacent room. Inside, a disheveled man roots through a hoarder's paradise of broken furniture, searching for the source of the noise. This is Casey's cue to flee and she reaches for a splintered baseball bat that leans against the wall. Blood slowly thickens on its wood, clotting in cracks and crevices, and tufts of hair cling to it, visible by the early morning light. They're from the dead man. Casey curls her fingers around the bat and creeps toward the back of the room as quietly and quickly as she can.

Aged floorboards creak and broken glass crackles underfoot. She timidly shifts her weight with every step, picking her way around a broken flat screen and a mouse-ridden couch. She skates a foot around a crushed frame on the floor, avoiding the crinkle of a moldering marriage certificate that has escaped.

An overturned desk lays cockeyed in the corner. When she finally reaches it, Casey thrusts her hand underneath and gropes for the small, clammy grip, which grabs hers back. She yanks, and Alex's blond hair catches the light as he soars to his feet. Tears cut deep rivulets through the grime and dirt on his pale, nine-year-old face.

The wall shakes again, raining more plaster.

Casey remembers seeing a back door in the house. It's the only way out that doesn't cross paths with the man they just escaped. They creep through the main hallway into the kitchen. She's holding her breath again, an unconscious reflex.

The man in the other room continues to tear through piles of garbage and broken furniture. Once loved items clang and clatter, hitting walls and falling to the floor. The Tanners used to live here. It says so right out front on their still intact mailbox; bills sitting inside, unpaid for over three years. Credit card applications and sales flyers now a rotting memento of times past. The man with the putrid face does not mourn them. No one does.

SQUEEEEEEEK!

Casey's stomach drops and her gaze ratchets to her foot. Her toe jabs through a thin excuse for a shoe next to two long-abandoned dog bowls where her foot presses a rubber newspaper: The Daily Growl.

"Shit."

The man in the other room peers sharply into the darkness. His eyes are swollen and bloodshot. One orb is so overinflated it bulges from its peeling socket. Rips shroud the dulled cornea and try as it might, the eyelid is unable to close. Black, clotted blood forms dried rings around his neck. Flake by flake, it falls to his chest, as though his jowls are the world's most profane croissant. He peels his lips back in a snarl.

The sound of smashing glass rings through the air.

Back in the kitchen, Casey pushes her arm through the broken window of the door. The damned thing is jammed, of course. Alex stands beside her, thin-lipped and fidgety. She can't get the knob to work from either side.

Casey pulls back her arm, glass nicking at her skin. The only way this door will open is if she forces it. She slams her foot into the wood just beside the knob and lock, driving her heel into the door. Her foot punches through, and for a moment, it sticks. *Cheap piece of shit! It isn't even solid.* She looks over her shoulder just in time to see a shadow approach.

Like the mouth of a hyena, the man's skeletal jaw gleams teeth from the darkness of the hallway. He launches himself at her.

There's no time to think—Casey acts on instinct. She rips her bleeding foot from the piece-of-shit door and shoves Alex into a corner, raising her bat. It makes a sickening thud as it connects with the man's skull. He goes down and, without even a momentary pause, springs for Alex, now at eye level. Alex tries to dart around him, but the man is quick—very quick. He snags Alex's pant leg and drags the boy toward his gnashing teeth. Alex thrashes, kicking wildly.

Casey hits the man again, crashing her bat down on his head. Skin leaks down his face, alleviated from its tenuous grip and the blow knocks him sideways, but he doesn't loosen his grip on Alex. Nothing slows him down. She swings again, with skull-crushing force, caving a dent and causing the man's remaining hair to stand awkwardly askew. He turns his repugnant face toward her. A raspy attempt at a growl escapes his chewed lips.

SLAM!

Casey's bat finds a home. Chunks of bone and tainted flesh splatter the lace curtains adorning the windows. She hits the man again, and again, and again. Finally, he stops moving, his skull obliterated, now twin to the body lying in the study.

Breath tears through Casey's lungs, and she blinks away sweat. Alex is still on the floor, staring with large blue eyes at the pummeled skull inches away from him. *He's seen worse*, Casey thinks, and offers him a hand up. "Are you okay?" He looks up at her but says nothing.

Casey grabs an old dishtowel from the dusty countertop and wipes herself clean of dead skin and bone. Her adrenaline is fading and with it,so is her strength. Her arms feel shaky and weak and her empty stomach spasms, cannibalizing itself. Alex's watchful eyes bore a hole through her. He's hungry too.

Barely able to remain steady on her feet, Casey investigates each cupboard in the kitchen.

Empty.

Empty.

Empty.

She grips the countertop and takes a calming breath; she can't waste energy feeling sorry for herself. Defeated, she slides against a wall and sits on the floor. Alex copies her exactly.

"Sorry, Kiddo. Looks like another night of rock soup."

Alex continues to stare at her. God, is that stare ever disquieting when he wants it to be. No wonder he doesn't speak. There's never any need—everything he has to say, he says with those eyes. She bets someone once gazed into them and imagined his entire life for him. Some mother or father somewhere, a lifetime ago.

There's no way they imagined this.

Casey looks away from Alex and closes her eyes for a moment. Sometimes it's just too hard to look at him. When she reopens them, she focuses on a pile of old, empty cans in a corner, near the dog bowls and that dumb rubber newspaper. *Man Bites Dog* reads the headline. Good one.

Casey pulls herself across the kitchen floor and digs through the pile. A huge black spider shambles away as she sorts through rusted tin, revealing one unopened can, lonely and forgotten at the bottom of the heap. Her eyes brighten, and she snags it, dusting off the label. A smile springs to her face. DOG CHOW. She turns, beaming at Alex. Finally, a little luck!

"Dinner!"

Alex silently opens his knapsack, and Casey watches as he methodically searches its contents, ferreting out a can opener. He holds it out to Casey. At least he understands food. Casey crawls over the dead man lying on the kitchen floor to join the boy.

As she opens the dog chow her stomach rumbles, aching, but she hands Alex the can first. Without hesitation, he jams his fingers inside and pulls out a glob of mush, then stuffs the quivering, fat-laden mass in his mouth. No need to chew this delicacy—just open up and down the hatch. He digs in for seconds, and Casey finally takes some for herself.

She feels as though the tin is polished off before she can blink. Stabbing hunger pains demand more, but they have nothing; haven't had anything in days. Casey hopes the kid is at least partially satiated, but a loud, hollow growl from the pit of his stomach is her answer. The empty rumbling is oppressive in the silence. It would be nice if he could speak, or would speak, who the hell knows? His precious face looks up at her, belly protesting loudly, and she feels each growl on top of her own. It's enough to kill anyone, no bat required.

Casey closes her eyes and leans her head against the bottom cupboard. She once thought the graveyard shift as a paramedic was a grind. The two-week overnight rotations in the city were brutal and especially dangerous. That seems like a vacation now.

***

A monumental hotel looms in the scorching sunlight over a baked and unmanicured lawn. Windows, barricaded with scrap metal, reflect the sun's rays across the huge expanse of field between the looming building and the thick, dark forest resting beyond the grounds.

Through the brambles and low hanging branches is a well-worn path that leads to a clearing. Once, adventurous hotel guests used it as a hiking trail, taking in the natural beauty of the wilderness around them.

The concierge, known by staff as Poppy, used to put apples near the mouth of the trail every winter for the deer. The animals would venture out evenings and early mornings, their bodies shaggy with thick fur, and guests would *ooh* and *ah* and snap pictures. Most would slip him a few dollars for being so helpful and friendly. This attention to detail put his kids through college.

Now Poppy is gone, and many would consider him one of the lucky ones. A heart attack killed him, just after the world fell apart. No emergency number to call, no doctors to save his life, no need to bear witness to the utter destruction of modern civilization. It was quick, unlike the death of so many others. Unlike the fate of those who still roam the earth in some kind of heinous limbo. Only one of Poppy's girls remains in this world now, and it's a blessing her father never lived to see it. Who knows if anything is left of the bright engineering student inside the shambling mess she is now.

Lot, the leader of the community that now lives within the hotel, bore witness to it all. She saw the downfall and the peoples' desperate need for law and order. She quelled their fears and worries, sheltering them from the harsh reality of the New World. Now, she stands in a small clearing at the edge of the forest bordering the hotel's land, feeling the weight of many binoculared eyes upon her. It's dangerous to be away from the safety of reinforced walls, but she must deal with Aaron, the traitor. She clasps her hands before her and wears a solemn expression on her weathered, yet appealing face.

She raises a hand to play with a blue spiral triangle that hangs from a necklace. She's had it for many, many years, before all the horror. The chain lays gently against her throat, caressing her skin as she moves toward the older man before her. He's on his knees.

Accompanying Lot is Marge, a buxom, muscular woman, and her counterpart, the bulging Arnold (or whatever his name actually is). They are both career military, craving the structure and regulation Lot happily provides. Together they head the community's security team. It's up to them to protect the people sheltered within the hotel walls. They hold Aaron down.

In the background lurks Opie, a weaselly looking man. He says nothing as he watches from a slight distance.

Beads of sweat trickle down Aaron's face as he struggles. "You support this? A society where political dissidents just disappear?"

Lot raises a well-groomed eyebrow in mock surprise. "Aaron, you're far from a political dissident. You're a coward, plotting the upheaval of our entire society."

"*Your* society. *Your*—"

"Yes. *My* society. Because of *my* teachings we've survived The Plague. For three long years, we have struggled and persevered because of me. And you are a heretic."

"Amen," comes the sentiment from Aaron's captors.

"Is this what you want? A society where anyone can disappear without a trace?" Aaron's breathing quickens, whistling through his nose with force.

"Without a trace? I think not, Aaron. You're to be an example. A strict warning to those who wish to sow discontent and spread lies, to those who threaten what I've worked so hard to build. You'll serve as the poster child for those who would strike the hand that feeds them."

"You've strayed from your own teachings, Lot! What you're building here is an abomination! You're more concerned with being Queen for a Day than—"

"Can you hear yourself? I've saved the life of each and every person under my roof. What have you done? Become a thug—a terrorist. Death will be my greatest gift to you."

Aaron drops his head and his face softens. He closes his wet eyes, breaking, snapping like a twig. *They always break when facing their inescapable mortality,* Lot thinks.

Her thoughts turn to brave men. False men on a Hollywood movie screen, facing down death with a jaw of steel—standing with bared chest thrust valiantly forward, ready to take the sword. In her mind, the television screen flickers, a smile flashes across celebrity lips, beaming defiantly with the knowledge that he faces a good death, a meaningful death. But it's just acting, and life rarely follows that script.

A smile of triumph lights upon her lips, and she presses them together, concealing it just a little too late. Perhaps she let it slip purposefully, this is a war after all, and they must all go out groveling. There will be no martyrs made on her watch.

"I've been with you since the beginning, Lot."

"And all good things must come to an end, my dear."

"What about my wife?"

"What about her? You can't honestly expect us to keep her here after all of this. After you've corrupted her mind against us, against me."

"Please, don't kill—"

"Don't be so banal. She'll be sent to live with the Castlefield colony."

"*Sent to live?* Is that what you call it?"

Lot can feel the prickling of eyes on the back of her neck. Thick Marge and Arnold are honed in. "You've done this to yourself, Aaron, not I. I'm merely an instrument of justice, and mercy. Your wife could be out here next to you."

Aaron sucks in his breath as though Lot punched him in the gut, "Monster."

Her delighted eyes smile back at him and electric thrill fills her belly. Behind her, Thick Marge clears her throat. "We better hurry this up, Lot." Arnold nods in agreement, his bulging neck muscles rippling under his skin.

They're right, it's time to wrap up this fine piece of theater, Lot thinks. The woods are teaming with disgusting, rotting corpses—The Risen. Out here, it doesn't matter who you are. Murderer or newborn babe, everyone is a walking, five-course dinner.

Lot's dancing grey eyes flick to Opie, cuing him to finish things. He scurries away and she locks her gaze back on her prisoner. "I don't often attend executions, Aaron, but your actions have been so devious I feel it necessary to speak to you, to hear your reasons why. I pray you plan on going to your grave with a clear conscience."

Aaron spits at Lot's feet, a light spray settling back on his quivering lips. Terror leaks from his pores and Lot imagines she can feel it rushing over her like a river current. She breathes deeply, steadying her appearance for the outside world. Aaron's voice trembles. "My conscience is clear, Lot. Is yours?"

Opie returns, shouldering an armload of heavy chains. He drops them near a tree in the center of the clearing. Lot doesn't hide her smile from Aaron this time. It's a smile that can melt the bark from trees. It's a smile that can turn blood to ice pellets. It's a smile no one else can see through. "Perfectly," she says.

Lot can feel the words die in Aaron's mouth as he bites his tongue. She knows he thinks of his wife. He begins to scream. It's the desperate, broken scream of a man beaten. She nods at Thick Marge and Arnold and they drag Aaron, kicking and screaming, to the tree. Arnold smacks him across the mouth. "Quiet down, traitor."

"You can't do this! You can't do this!"

Padlocks click around tight chains. Opie plants a wind-powered noisemaker in the ground nearby.

"Without your support, she has no control!"

Arnold grabs Aaron's face. "Scream all you want. You're only hastening the inevitable."

Lot turns and strides away, quickly followed by Thick Marge and Arnold. Behind them, Opie starts the noisemaker and it begins to whine.

"Opie, stop this, please."

Opie sheepishly casts a glance at Aaron, the doomed man has no clue who betrayed him. He holds Aaron's eyes for a second, and then scurries after Lot and her henchmen, leaving Aaron to face his grisly death alone. "You're just as guilty as she is!" the dead man shouts. "Even more so because you know this is wrong. You know it's wrong, Opie! Those poor children!"

Opie shuts out the screams, as he has done many times before, and is gone from the clearing. Aaron shakes with fear as the noisemaker picks up pitch with the rising wind. It won't be long now.

2

As the wind ebbs and flows, so too does the whine of the noisemaker Opie plunged into the dirt. That damned device. The man who created it may as well be the inventor of the nuclear bomb. It's an instrument of destruction, its sole purpose to attract the ghouls who roam this forest. It allows cowards to lie within the safe embrace of the hotel walls, unwilling to witness the consequences of their actions.

Aaron's wrists and ankles ache. Blood oozes from beneath the tight, rusty shackles, where his skin has rubbed clean off. He leans into them again, groaning with the effort to get free. Although he should be reminded of long ago history lessons about witches burning at the stake, his mind keeps turning to a different abomination.

When he was a boy, he read a book about Native Americans. Of course, everyone called them Indians back then, and he still thinks of them as Indians even now. He can't remember what tribe the book was about, or if it was truly a book and not a movie, or TV show of some sort, but what stuck with him through the years was the sinister torture the Indians doled out.

They'd use leather strips soaked in water to tie an enemy warrior to a stand made of branches, and leave him baking in the sun. The sun would shine and the leather would shrink, slowly cutting through the warrior's skin and muscles, causing unthinkable agony. Eventually, and never too soon, it killed him.

Aaron always imagined some poor wretch, wearing a headband with a single feather poking up from it, left to die high atop a mountain. Every time he thinks of that stereotypical brave, he imagines giant crows swooping in to tear the flesh from his still living body. They would cackle and caw as the man beneath their talons screamed helplessly, then the largest of the sleek black birds would pluck one of the warrior's eyes from its socket. The crow would tug on the tasty morsel until it snapped away, then swallow it in one gulp. This is the image Aaron can't shake as a lumbering, coverall-wearing hulk breaks into the clearing.

The creature's eyes bulge. Its lips are drawn back, exposing chunks of flesh stuck between its teeth. Black gunk leaks from its eyes, down its cheeks, and its coveralls support a huge distended belly. It will eat until it bursts, they all do.

Aaron tries not to move, not to breathe, not to exist. A smaller, rotten creature with half a face suddenly appears from the side. It wears nothing but a pair of saggy, stained tighty-whiteys. Another appears, this one with no clothes and missing an arm. Then a child, who could pass for living if it weren't for its gnashing teeth and ripped corneas.

Aaron presses himself against the tree. Each shallow breath he takes booms like a jet engine in his ears. If he so much as blinks, he's sure they'll hear it.

More decaying figures stagger from the forest, some stop to stare at the noisemaker. Coveralls cranes its head around the clearing, searching. Aaron stops breathing and tries not to sweat.

The monster eyes him, steps a little closer.

Aaron's heartbeat is the only thing he cannot quiet. He silently prays.

Coveralls lunges.

Aaron springs out of the way, straining against his bonds. He kicks the brute, but it has no effect. Coveralls sinks its teeth into Aaron's shoulder. Aaron thrashes and is somehow able to shake the ghoul off, but it's useless. The creatures descend like a pack of wolves, biting, growling, and clawing at his flesh. The mob wrenches him from his feet, struggling against the chains to drag its meal off into the bushes.

Aaron screams. His shoulders pop and snap. Muscle and bone rip at the joint like a chicken wing as his arms separate from his body and fall limply to the ground, raising a plume of dust. His bloodcurdling shrieks are lifted away by the very wind his death rode in on.

***

The sheets are smooth against Casey's face, and the mild heat of morning sun pushes in through curtains, warming the room. The smell of fresh coffee and breakfast fills the air. It's disorientating for a moment, something feels off as she steps from the bed. She looks down at her bare feet, the nails are perfectly pedicured, painted a raunchy red. They are sexy toes. No blisters, no callouses, and no dirt. She wiggles them; they are hers.

This isn't a room she recognizes, but that doesn't matter; it's also hers, she can feel it. She's safe and she smiles. Casey doesn't know why, but she missed this place, has longed for it for centuries, eon upon eon, and now she's finally here. Or has she always been here?

The enticing aroma of food guides her through the house, which is huge, chic, and luxurious. Her feet are soft on the warm hardwood, her fingers velvet against the vividly painted walls. She catches a glimpse of herself in the mirror and touches her smooth, straightened hair. It's perfectly pinned back with a glamorous tortoiseshell clip. A flirtatious silk kimono, baby blue, hugs her curves, allowing the outline of her matching underthings to peek through. Gorgeous diamond-encrusted earrings dangle from her ears.

This is my life, she thinks.

Casey steps lightly into the kitchen. "Hello?" No one answers. "Anybody home? Anton? The food smells amazing!" Casey reaches the stove, her mouth watering as she peers into a skillet.

Frying in oil, skin bubbling and crisping, is a human hand.

Carey crinkles her face in disgust, but her stomach grumbles. She backs away in horror as she spies Alex crouched in the corner. Like a swollen cob of corn, he holds Anton's disfigured head and sinks his teeth into a cheek, tearing off a piece of meat. He chews it slowly, eyeing her, daring her to do something.

Casey's eyes pop open. Alex sleeps soundly with his head in her lap and she takes a moment, the image of the boy chewing on her husband's face still fresh in her mind. With effort, she forces the lingering smell of cooking flesh from her memory. Her stomach growls.

Casey rubs her ring finger where her wedding band and engagement ring once were. From time to time, she still finds herself moving to adjust them, but it's been two years since she wore them. The constant reminder of everything she lost so quickly was too much to bear.

The morning light is bright; it's late. It was stupid and dangerous to fall asleep here. They must find a safer place before nightfall, one where the front of the house isn't nearly destroyed. Casey shakes Alex awake. It's heartbreaking to watch him open his groggy eyes. "I'm sorry, honey, but we can't stay here."

Alex rises. A dirty white button-up shirt hangs on his frame, making him seem thinner than he is. It's a size too large and missing buttons. He squares his pack on his bony shoulders, ready to follow Casey's lead. Casey's throat catches. When she looks at him, she can't help but wonder what her own child would have looked like now.

She had been six months pregnant; the baby was Anton's last gift to her. It had been so hard to be pregnant and on the run. Food and water were scarce, sleep even more so—not as bad as now, but bad enough, and they weren't able to stop driving when the contractions started, it was just too dangerous and too many creatures littered the roadways. The group, spread out between several vehicles, had been twenty people strong, but not a single person could save her baby.

That was about two and half years ago, but she can still feel the clenching labor pains rip through her abdomen. She can still feel the despair as she looked down at the tiny wrinkled face in the back of that station wagon. Blood caked her thighs, her hands, pooled beneath her in a thick puddle mixed with sweat and urine.

He was so small. So pale. And he never made a sound, never cried. The baby only lived for two hours. Now, she hears his ragged breathing, like a buzz-saw on her brain, in every dream she's had since.

She wept over him. Cried so hard she thought all the tears in the world, in the history of worlds, must be pouring through her eyes. She'd clung to his limp little body, clasped him to her chest, and unleashed everything her soul had to offer. But it didn't matter. He was dead. Dead like Anton. Dead like this world.

Casey closes her eyes. When she opens them, she ruffles Alex's hair.

"You ready, kid?" He stares up at her blankly. "Nod, Alex. Do you remember what I told you? I need to know you understand me." Alex continues to stare blankly back at her and Casey sighs. Sometimes it's like talking to a brick wall.

She turns away from him and peeks through the broken window. Outside, a rotting ornamental garden fence runs the length of an overgrown flowerbed. It keeps company with a rusted swing set that stands nearby, motionless in the muggy summer air. There is no sign of life.

Casey reaches her arm out the window. Now that she has a second to think, maybe she can get the door open. She grips the knob from the outside and turns. It screeches, metal against metal, but it still won't open. She pulls her arm back inside. They'll have to get out of here one way or another, and it won't be through the front. Quite a few creatures were wandering around out there earlier, and she would rather avoid another confrontation.

She dances in place for a second, revving her engine and mustering up energy from the dog chow and catnap, then kicks the door, trying not to put her foot through it again. It shakes in its frame. She kicks another time. It cracks. Panting, she kicks it again and the door snaps free of its humidity-swollen frame. *Finally!* Casey reaches behind her and snags her bat, then steps out into the summer sun with Alex trailing right behind.

A gun's hammer clicks back, echoing in the thick morning

air. Casey freezes, "If you fire that thing you'll attract everything around here for miles."

"If I fire it, you'll be dead, and we'll be gone before there's a problem to worry about."

Casey swallows hard. "Run, Alex!"

As the words escape her lips, a tall blond man snags the boy with one hand and tosses him backward, into the arms of three other men, where Casey can't see him well. She clenches her jaw and draws her weapon back for a swing.

"Drop the bat, lady."

"We don't have anything. No food. No water. We've already been robbed, just let us go."

Casey strains her ears. Over the hum of cicadas, she can hear the huffing and puffing of silent struggles behind her. She turns her head slightly, just enough to see the men that have Alex. They wear guns and machetes, but worse than that, they are removing the boy's clothes. Her stomach drops and her heart catches in her throat.

The muzzle of the blond's gun bites the back of her head and Casey cringes. "We don't want your stuff," he snaps. "Now drop the bat." His voice is quiet, but hardened with a razor edge. She slowly begins to lower her bat to the ground, keeping Alex in the corner of her eye. Her chest quivers with her pounding heart.

Behind Casey and the blond, Alex flails like a trapped animal, landing a hard kick squarely on the chest of one of the men accosting him and sending the man stumbling back. Another slaps the boy across the face, the loud smack reverberating in Casey's ears. She can almost feel the sting on her own cheek and it's all she can bear.

She reclaims a hard grip on her bat; it never fully touched the ground, and she turns, swinging violently at the son-of-a-bitch with the blond hair. He reacts instantly with well-fed muscles, catching the bat mid-swing before there's any damaging force behind it. In one smooth move, he rips the bat from Casey's grip and slams her into the side of the house. Her face cracks a windowpane, spider webbing it.

Fear floods her mind. *What do these men want? What're they doing to Alex?* She can't see him now. God, she wishes he would say something! All she can hear is breathing as he struggles against three grown men. Casey swivels her face to catch a glimpse, and the blond man blocks her view. His stubbled, faintly tanned face and blue eyes scowl down at her. She wants to murder him.

"Please. Leave the boy alone," she begs.

"Shut up." He lifts her shirt, pulling it over her head. The tired, dirty fabric rushes by her face and she can smell her own fear-stink. The man tosses her shirt aside and Casey twists away, trying to flip around, to see Alex. Using brute force, the blond slams her back into the side of the house. "Once more and I'll kill the kid, not you. Do you understand?"

"Yes."

"Take everything off."

"Let the kid go, and I'll do anything you want."

"This isn't a negotiation, lady."

"Just let him—"

"Now!"

Casey fumbles as she unhooks her bra. As the worn straps slip from her shoulders and it falls to the ground, she digs her nails into her palms, fighting the urge to panic. She unbuttons her pants and pulls her shaking legs out, biting her tongue. The pain helps her focus. Her hands shake, and after a brief hesitation, Casey slides off her old, droopy underwear. Maybe if she cooperates they won't kill her and Alex. She'll do what she has to—bide her time until she can get away with the boy somehow. She just has to find an opening. *Don't panic.*

"Shoes too."

Casey pulls her bare feet from her shoes. Only after skin touches dirt, does she truly feel naked, vulnerable. The blond man roughly grabs at her, his hands crawling over her body, harsh and prodding. They make her skin want to peel away, make her want to vomit. Big, fat tears well in her eyes, and she bites her lip, blinking them back furiously. This man may rape her, he may even kill her, but he sure as hell isn't going to see her cry. He leans in close, examining her as though she's livestock being prepared for slaughter.

One of the men holding Alex calls out to his boss, "Kid's clear." The blond grunts a response and forcefully flips Casey around to face him. She wants to spit on him, but her mouth is dry. His is the face of a dead man. She will kill him when she has the chance.

Over his shoulder, she can see Alex still struggling with the other three men. Now, they're trying to get his clothes back on. It would be almost comical in another situation. Casey's head spins. Why remove the boy's clothes if...

"Woman's safe." The blond steps back and, for a split second, looks over his shoulder at his men. It's all she needs. Casey drives her knee between his legs. He pitches forward and Casey darts for his handgun, tearing it from his belt. His men clamor for their own weapons, surprised and clumsy. They've grossly underestimated her.

Casey kicks the blond in the spine, sending him sprawling onto his hands and knees, wheezing. *Good. Fucker. He deserves it.* She forces the gun against the back of his head, and he stiffens. "Throw your weapons into the woods," she shouts.

One of the henchmen glances toward Alex.

"If you so much as look at the kid one more time I'm gonna blow this fuckin' guy's head off. Do you hear me?"

They don't drop their weapons, but they don't move either. The one in the middle licks his lips. He has the pudgy, freckled face of someone who eats four squares a day. "Just hold on, lady," he says.

Who the fuck does this sack of shit think he is?

"I said, throw your goddamned weapons in the woods!" Casey jams the barrel of the blond man's handgun against his head. He winces.

"Do it," he barks.

His men don't move.

"How do you think Lot will react when you come back with some half-concocted story about what happened to me?"

The henchmen pass a look between them. Dissension in the ranks. *Good*, Casey thinks. Maybe it'll help her and Alex get away.

The fat one is the first to lower his weapon. He throws his gun and knife into the woods behind him and the others follow his lead. Casey takes a step back and prods the blond with her bare toe. "You too." She will kill him soon.

Kneeling, the man slowly removes the machete from his belt and tosses it in the woods with the others, never taking his eyes off of Casey.

She motions with one hand. "Alex, come over here, honey." The kid stares at her, unblinking, pants on but unbuttoned, rumpled shirt at his feet. "Alex! Come on!" He gawps, scared of the men next to him. Exhausted, Casey lets her attention slip, closing her eyes in frustration, for just a split second, and the blond grabs for his gun.

BAM!

A shot rings out that sends the birds flying from the trees. Everyone jumps as the bullet whizzes harmlessly into the brush. The blond wrenches his gun from Casey's hand and shoves her fiercely to the ground. "Great," he scoffs. "Now everything within a mile of this place knows we're here." He belts the gun as Casey scrambles to her feet.

The blond's men stand around dumbly. "What the hell are you waiting for?" he growls at them. "A mass of flesh eaters? Go find your goddamn weapons!"

"Sorry, Danny," the brigade hustles to obey, no hint of their opportunistic mutiny left. It seems the alpha male is back, for now. He leaves Casey and stalks over to where his machete lays in the dirt, near Alex. The boy still has yet to put his shirt back on. He ignores the child and leans down for his knife.

Casey throws on her clothes as fast as she can. Her voice wavers with the effort, "What the fuck do you want from us?"

"To be sure you weren't bitten."

"You could have just asked me, you bastard."

"I could have, and you could have lied."

"And, if I had been bitten—*Danny?*"

Danny stops and looks at her, his cold expression saying it all. They stare at each other and Casey wonders if there's even a human being beneath those icy blue eyes. He obviously has some weird Rambo complex, is a man, or more accurately, a boy not far out of his teenage years, who gets off on being a survivalist or something.

"What're you, the bite police or something?" Casey asks.

Danny rolls his eyes. "Take your weird little kid. He's freaking me out." He shoves Alex toward Casey. Just as Alex steps forward, a creature crashes through the bushes, leper-like face and snapping jaws gunning for him. Casey searches frantically for her bat, but it's too far away. She whips her attention to the ghoul as an inarticulate scream escapes her throat. She can't reach them in time!

Alex takes a step back, almost trips as the creature lunges. Machete drawn, Danny steps directly in front of the boy and sinks the blade through the creature's eye. With expert precision, the thing is dead, and it drops to the ground like a lump of dog shit.

Casey grabs Alex, falling to the ground with him and clutching him to her chest, nearly crushing the wind from him. She can barely find her own breath—that was too close.

Danny wipes his blade on the grass then tosses Casey's bat at her feet. During the commotion, the other men found their weapons and are now anxious to leave, "Come on, Danny. We've wasted enough time here."

Casey stands, gripping her bloodied bat in one hand and protectively holding Alex close to her with the other. Danny's blue eyes find hers. "There'll be more any minute. I don't think you and that kid stand a chance by yourselves. Let's go."

"You point weapons at us, strip our clothes off, and now give orders?"

"I also just saved the boy's life."

"He wouldn't have needed saving if it weren't for you."

"We're not interested in hurting you."

"Why should I trust you?"

Danny shrugs. "You don't have to."

His nonchalant attitude is a real piss-off. Casey keeps Alex close as the blond man joins his brigade. Between them lies the creature, dead and rotting in the sun, flies already landing. She watches the group of men trudge away on a well-worn path. It would be dumb to join them. Who knows what kind of men they really are, or what their endgame is. They're assholes, too, especially the leader. All piss and vinegar, her mother would have said, lifetimes ago.

Casey's a trained paramedic. She saves lives for a living, at least she did, before the end of the world came to stay, and she isn't into playing house with ragtag bands of men who fancy themselves God's gift to everything. She and Alex haven't been killed so far, haven't died of exposure or infection either. They're doing just fine.

As they watch the blond and his men leave, Casey's stomach growls. The empty aching tugs at her bones, a persistent hunger that never goes away. Until now, she'd always been able to keep their heads above water, and their bellies full; but the truth is, they're in bad shape. She wonders if the men have food where they're going.

3

Lot places both hands on the polished mahogany in front of her and peers at the maps spread out on it. Candles leak wax onto the table, doing little to pierce the gloom, their flames flickering as the group huddled around breathes. Outside the sun burns brightly, but in here, barricaded windows suck the light from everything.

It's been about three years since Lot and her surviving band of followers took over this hotel. It was overrun with creatures, their fetid bodies bouncing off one another, forever doomed to be locked inside. Most were shut in rooms, this one included. They'd been huddled masses, too scared to leave when alive, unable to escape in death.

Lot thinks of her people. *Where would they be without her? Alone, starving, dead? Probably*, she nods unconsciously. Every single person in this room, in this community, owes her a great debt of gratitude. They've come so far since those first days.

A thick finger with a dirty fingernail smears across the laminated lands of the map. "The Risen tend to accumulate here," Thick Marge, standing next to Arnold, informs the group. "The terrain forces them through this pass."

Lot's gaze sweeps the eight faces that crowd the room. She points out a line on the map, "Then the best way around is probably Wallard."

One of the faces, Habib, a true cowboy, grumbles. He always has something to say and always wants to do things the hard way. "That'll add over an hour round trip."

Lot stands straight. "We have a substantially higher risk of casualties if we try the pass." She rolls up the sleeves of her thin, tan blouse. Her jeans stick to her legs. They've been in here for almost an hour and between the candles and the people, it's uncomfortably warm. "Do you have another suggestion, Habib?"

He sucks his teeth, glares down at the maps, shakes his head. "Addin' over an hour to our trip is dangerous in its own right. We're already fightin' against the sun."

"You're right, but what would you have us do? Fight through a throng of The Risen?"

"We can do it!"

"The chances of being overwhelmed, of being surrounded, are extremely high."

"But if we clear it, we have a straight way through."

"For now," pipes in Cindy, a black-haired beauty. "But they'll just accumulate there again." She's a steadfast loyalist and has been around almost as long as Opie.

"Over time," Habib counters.

Arnold shakes his head. "There's no telling how many are there now. It's a bad idea."

Habib's face hardens. "I can do this. Give me the right men, and I can do it."

"Are you crazy?" Cindy asks. "Who do you think you are, He-man? It's not worth the risk!"

Habib slaps his hand on the table. "It's not worth the risk of being stuck outside at sunset when we can't see shit, like sittin' ducks balancin' solar panels on our backs! We can't get vehicles through those roads, how quickly do ya think we'll be able to move? The less time we're out there, the better."

"It's a suicide mission," Arnold adds calmly.

Habib's passion is unaffected. "It's not, not with the right people. I know it can be done."

Lot leans in to analyze the maps and carefully weighs the options. Finally, she looks up at Habib. "How many men would you need?"

Around the table, eyes pop open wide with surprise. Arnold turns to her. "Lot, their chances of survival—"

Lot flicks her wrist. Arnold closes his mouth and rubs at a tattoo on his forearm. It's a fierce bald eagle clutching the earth and an anchor between its talons. Around it, in beautiful lettering reads "USMC Death Before Dishonor." He's a good soldier and knows when he's been outranked.

"Habib has a good point," Lot says. "Night isn't the time to be stuck outside and if he's successful, this could save lives. How many people would it take?"

"Minimum? Five."

"You can have them, *if* they volunteer. Make sure they understand how risky this is."

"I will."

"And I'd like you to take Danny with you."

"He's not even back from his last mission yet. He'll be road worn."

"He's young, he'll be fine, and you'll need him. He's one of our best."

Habib sighs with annoyed resignation and nods agreement.

Lot nods back. "It's settled then. Now, if you'll excuse me, I have a date with some children." She grabs a candle and steps into the hallway. As the voices in the room fall away, Opie scuttles after. He passes her a folded map. "The information you requested."

"Thank you, Opie."

***

Lot smiles at the group of children sitting at her feet. The two oldest girls, who are eleven and thirteen, watch after the very young. Both are pretty and will soon be desirable. If married to the right men in neighboring communities, alliances will be strengthened, and power will be solidified. They're good assets.

The youngest of the group is a baby, just shy of a year. Her mother begged Lot for permission to have a child. After the woman proved herself worthy, Lot gave her blessing. People here understand the need for population control, that more mouths to feed mean less food to go around. They understand that, if allowed to procreate, they must pay back the burden on the community two-fold.

The baby squirms and plays quietly, as babies do. It's almost inconceivable to think this child was born into a world so different than the Old World. Her mother's world no longer exists. In fact, most of these children will never remember how things used to be.

Lot turns the page of the book she's reading out loud. They're lucky enough to have an extensive library with over one hundred books here. Many were on the premises already, in staff quarters, but members of the community also salvaged books from their former lives. There's even a handful of children's books. Lot keeps them in her room, just to be sure they aren't lost. The world has changed, but children are still children. Will they even be able to relate to this story in a few years?

"The dirty little puppy peeked his powdery head out of the pink and purple pail. Was he ever in a pickle? Just how was he going to clean this mess before Boy got home?"

Henry, a redheaded three-year-old with striking green eyes, pulls softly on Lot's pant leg. He was born at the beginning of this new world. Lot peeks over the top of the large book with a big blue puppy printed on its front. "Up," says Henry, in his tiny voice, stretching out his arms. Lot swoops him into her lap and flips to the next page.

**

It would've been dumb to stay there alone and starving, sleeping with one eye open and praying for a stray can of dog food or a thick, juicy cicada. Casey's afraid to think of how many parasites are probably living in her gut from drinking contaminated water and eating whatever she's been able to kill—squirrels, cats, groundhogs...

Not that she'd caught anything lately, the ghouls that now roamed the earth were decimating the wildlife population. Two weeks ago, she even taken Alex to dig in a creek bed, flipping rocks, hoping to find salamanders, crayfish, or earthworms. They hadn't found much, and, thanks to other bad circumstances, they had no way to cook the hapless little animals they did find. Casey thought of smashing them into a slurry, but that was even less appealing than stuffing the wiggling bodies down their throats.

She has to hand it to Alex though; she was sure he'd turn his nose up at such delicacies, but he took to them quite well. That's why she isn't surprised now when, huddled next to her in a tree, he shoves some sort of beetle in his mouth. It crunches as he chews, slowly savoring the gooey insides. Danny raises a disgusted eyebrow at Casey and she shrugs. "So, where are we going anyway?"

"Somewhere safe."

"Is it far?"

"Yes."

"How far?

"A while."

"Well, aren't you the chatterbox?"

One of Danny's men, Morgan she heard them call him, with the freckles, snickers at their exchange.

It's been a long time since Casey's been in the company of other adults, or anyone who can talk, for that matter. The other two manage to play a game of cards, but no one else says a word. She thinks on just how odd it is that she's trying to come up with conversation starters while they sit in a giant tree, hiding from a drove of flesh-eating monsters. But beyond conversation, she needs answers. Real ones, and Danny hasn't exactly been forthcoming.

The freaks pass below one after another, moaning and growling, dragging broken limbs and trailing strings of their own intestines behind them. They're mindless, killing machines that never stop, spreading death and disease everywhere they go. Most look exactly like what they are: walking corpses, their rotten bodies in a never-ending crusade to destroy life itself. A true plague, if there ever was one. They're deadly, but they sure aren't smart. Sit quietly above, and they never even look up. Case in point.

"Is that something you do a lot? Eat bugs?" Danny asks.

Casey isn't sure who he's speaking to, her or the boy, but she answers. "When it's necessary."

He nods. Is that a glint of empathy in his eyes? Casey's not sure. She strokes Alex's hair lovingly as he scratches at the red, swollen bug bites that pepper his arms.

"So how far away is your community, Danny?"

"Another day."

"And there are other women and children there?"

"Yes. This is the third time you've asked."

"And, it's the first time you've answered."

Danny pauses, thinking, then nods acknowledgment. "Fair enough."

"Am I gonna have to ask every question three times to get an answer?" Casey grins, hoping to soften the blond man's shell. He blinks at her, doesn't even crack a smile, and she sighs, annoyed.

Danny turns his attention to the kid. She knows he must be wondering why Alex doesn't speak, and she hopes it's not an issue. Some people are hesitant to deal with anyone who could be considered a burden. She studies Danny as he studies the kid. Eventually, he loses interest and stares into space, deep in thought. She can feel his wheels turning, his face set in an unconscious frown.

Minutes pass without anybody saying anything, mosquitoes whine in her ears. Finally, Casey can't take it anymore. She waves her hand in front of Danny's face. "Helllloo. Anybody home? You all right there?"

He focuses on her, casting an annoyed look her way. "Yeah," he snaps. "I'm fine. What do you want?"

Casey curls her toes inside her shoes—maybe this is a bad idea. This guy seems to be in a permanently bad mood, and she really wishes he would stop skirting her questions. It's like he's purposely coy and that makes her nervous.

Her trepidation must be showing, because Danny looks

quickly away, shamefaced. He clears his throat and rubs his chin, a few days' worth of whiskers bristling under his hand. He rolls his shoulders twice and then looks at Casey again. This time he's softer, more affable. "Why are you and the kid alone?"

Casey relaxes a little. The guy is obviously making an effort, and she can forgive anyone for being stressed when hiding from walking corpses. She smiles. "If you ask three times, I'll tell you."

Behind Danny, Morgan chuckles again. Danny whips a deadly glare in his direction and the laugh sours in the man's throat. He turns back to Casey.

"Wow, you really take yourself seriously, don't you?" she asks.

Danny shrugs. "So? Why are you alone?"

"That's twice."

He grinds his teeth. It's clear he's not used to anyone poking him, and it makes Casey want to do it more, to break the rigid ice between them. She smirks, waiting for him to ask a third time.

"Are you serious? You're not going to answer unless I ask a third time?"

"Turnabout is fair play."

"Fine, have it your way. Why?"

"Why what?"

"Oh, come on!"

"Ask."

"Why are you and the kid alone?"

"Because we don't have anyone else."

Danny stares at her—she stares back at him. After a few tense moments, she's relieved to see a tiny smile touch his face. "Okay, I deserved that," he says.

"Yes, you did." Her playfulness fades. It's almost fun to goof around with him, but it can't cushion stark reality. "Everyone one else is dead."

"How?"

"Another group. They ransacked us. Took everything, every last drop of water and piece of food. All our weapons, all our supplies. The only thing they left us with was our lives. Then we died, one by one."

"How long ago?"

"Months, almost a year."

"Not many people could've survived that long alone, especially with a kid in tow. Are we the first people you've met since then?"

"No. But, no one wants an extra two mouths to feed."

Danny nods and they fall into silence. He glances at his men playing cards, and then back at Casey. His eyes hang on her a little too long, she can feel them all over her body, almost the same way his hands had been earlier that day. He's undressing her with his eyes. "Having yourself a nice look?" Casey crosses her arms defiantly.

Danny looks away fast, his face flushing red. Dennis, one of his men, gives him a knowing nod and a sly smile and Danny glares back. Dennis rolls his eyes and returns to his card game.

Danny peeks back at Casey. She marshals her most threatening look, gripping her bat tightly. It seems to do the trick. He can't look her in the eye, and his mouth runs of its own accord, stammering. "I… you…" He stares down hard at one of his hands. It twitches nervously, a momentary expression of weakness, and he rapidly balls it into a fist. "You've got a spot on your shirt," he finally manages.

Casey looks down at her t-shirt. It's covered in dirt, blood, and sweat. Once it was a dark pink. Now it's mostly a light grayish brown, with pit stains and black smudges of who-knows-what all over it. It's threadbare, just a rag. A far cry from Danny's nearly clean T-shirt, pale yellow, with a faded graphic splashed across the front. Oh well, pink (or gray) isn't really her color anyway. She prefers green, a pastel, retro, sea-foam green.

As she observes the mess her shirt is, she smiles. Danny's cover-up has to be one of the lamest excuses she's ever heard. EVER. "Really? I don't see it," a giggle escapes her lips before she can stop it. It softens the rock façade of the man sitting before her. He looks much younger when he's not glowering at the world.

Casey's mirth is short-lived. The herd of creatures below drags on, seemingly endless. She'll give Danny a pass this time, but if he stares at her like that one more time, he's going to lose an eye. She glares at him.

Danny reaches into his side pouch and fishes around. Casey watches as he lifts a piece of dried jerky from the bag and thrusts his hand out toward her. It's not exactly a bouquet of roses, but it's a fair apology. He keeps his eyes locked on the ground far below, careful not to look at her anymore.

Casey snags the jerky from his hand. Her stomach screams, insisting she gobble it *now*, that she stuff it down her throat without taking the time to chew. Holding her bat between her knees, she snaps the jerky in two. Sure she can't fight the urges much longer, she thrusts the bigger piece at Alex and then she finally gives in, tearing off a chunk from what's left. It's tough, like leather, the most delicious leather she's ever tasted, and it's heads-and-tails above a can of dog food. Food of the Gods.

Alex snuggles up beside her. She feels like hunger is playing tricks on her mind, and it's so hard to decide if Danny and his crew are the good guys or the bad guys. The blond man watches the creatures below, his leg jigging up and down nervously. He's definitely temperamental, but he's not really that bad. He's young—maybe he thinks he has something to prove. His men don't seem to like him very much, but they trust him enough to be out here with him, to take orders from him.

Casey swallows the chunk of jerky. "My name's Casey. This is Alex." Danny looks up at her, a dark cloud momentarily passes across his face, a sadness that's shuttered so quickly she wonders if she really saw it. He looks away, down at an old wristwatch. Casey can see from where she sits that the seconds are ticking by much too slowly to be an accurate gauge of time.

The group falls into a pervasive, dragging silence.

***

The horde of cadavers finally passes, and when they're sure it's safe, Casey hands Alex down from the tree to Danny's waiting hands. The boy is light, so light it worries her. They're starving;

she can see the hollows of Alex's cheeks starting to form and knows she probably looks the same. It's no wonder Danny feels the need to bring them back to his home base. The jerky and bit of water from his canteen have done little to ease the hunger pangs.

As she lets go of the boy, Casey's struck by how similar he looks to Danny. Same blond hair, same blue eyes. It's not hard to believe the fragile, emaciated, child could grow up to become the solid, healthy man below her.

She swings down from the tree without help, managing the descent with her bat in hand. The second her feet hit the ground, Danny shoves Alex toward her. "Hurry up."

So much for pleasantries, she thinks.

Much farther ahead, the brigade pushes through the underbrush like well-seasoned woodsmen. Danny walks with Casey and Alex, his face set on scowl, and she wonders why he feels the need to put on this tough-guy act. "Where're we going?" she asks.

"Somewhere safe."

"I thought we were past all this now."

There's a rustling in the grass nearby, but Danny is annoyed and doesn't notice. "What do you want me to say? Does it matter? We're going somewhere where there's food and shelter and lots of other people. Do you want me to draw you a map?"

"Will you at least tell me why you're out here?"

"No."

Casey stops walking.

"What are you doing now?" Danny steps toward her. Casey lifts her bat, knuckles growing lighter with her tight grip and biceps flexing, preparing to strike. Danny throws up his hands, his hot temper getting the best of him.

"Fine, suit yourself," he turns away nonchalantly.

"Watch out!" Casey yells as a grotesque, nearly skeletal hand reaches up from the weeds at Danny's feet. It wraps around his ankle, and he tumbles to the ground, landing mere inches from a horrifically rotted face. He squawks in surprise and flinches back, just avoiding teeth that snap shut like a gator that's been lying in wait.

A face and arm are almost all that's left of the creature, but that doesn't stop it from being deadly. One bite is all it takes. It digs its fingers at Danny's ribs while weeds slip down in front of his eyes. He rips a handful away from his face and scrambles back, the thing's teeth just missing his face a second time. It drags itself up using his clothes, scaling him.

Casey's foot streaks through the air and catches under the creature's chin. The sheer power of her kick rips the thing's head right off and catapults it, sending it arching through the sky. It lands a safe distance away bouncing off a rock and coming to rest near scraggly water starved bushes. Danny struggles comically to shove off what remains of the creature. He stumbles to his feet and kicks the corpse for good measure. Casey raises an eyebrow.

"Uh… Thanks," Danny brushes himself clean.

"Yeah, no problem, are you okay?"

"Yeah."

"Should I strip you to see if you're bitten?" Casey knows it's a cheeky remark, but she can't help herself.

A half-pleased look washes over Danny's face. "If you like."

Casey smiles slyly. "Maybe another time, soldier."

"Another time then," Danny turns back toward his men. They nod, he nods. Nods all around.

"They seem concerned," Casey says.

"Yeah, they're real sweethearts."

She snorts amusement and Danny motions for her and Alex to follow him. "You coming?"

Casey nods; it seems the thing to do.

4

Hours pass. Insects bite and sting. Brambles and bushes pluck at exposed skin, leaving it tender and itchy, and the infrequent stops take their toll as fatigue becomes the new norm. Night descends rapidly while the brigade chats in hushed whispers, gossip mostly. So-and-so did this or that, water cooler chatter that would almost make this world feel bearable, if not for the occasional reference to "The Risen."

Casey gabs eagerly with the other adults. She doesn't care if she barely knows these men. It's been months since she's had the opportunity to converse with anyone, and despite the circumstances, it feels good, almost normal. Besides, she's learning quite a bit.

They're headed to a fortified hotel, which sounds like paradise. Security, food, and community. The kids go to classes and the leader of the place is a woman named Lot—a great person by all accounts. The brigade men have warmed up quite a bit to their visitors, and they're more talkative than Danny, who hasn't said a word in hours. He'll get along with Alex just fine, Casey thinks.

The group falls into another quiet lull, everyone is tired. Casey's feet ache terribly, but the thought of getting a hot meal pushes her forward. Her mind wanders in the silence, and she thinks about the first few weeks of The Plague, when she still thought there was hope.

She and Anton had holed up, boarded the windows to the house, and kept to themselves. They had a well-stocked emergency supply kit and cupboards filled with non-perishables. Careful rationing sustained them for almost two months.

Things outside were bad. More than once they had to defend themselves from looters. Worse were the infected. They wandered the streets, attacking everything that moved or made too much noise. Casey and Anton watched helplessly as a horde pushed its way into their neighbor's home, breaking windows and pushing down doors. She'll never forget the screaming.

She and Anton listened to the radio every day. It was just emergency broadcasts with no real information, nothing about what the disease was, or how it spread. Still, they clung to hope, staying quiet and hidden. Eventually, the radio transmissions stopped, and they lost all contact with the outside world. It became clear help was not coming.

As a strategy to keep their sanity, and their lives, they began working on a plan for a more sustainable set-up and better protection. The world became a new frontier they could conquer together. Despite daily horrors, they felt they could triumph. They thought they could create a new Eden. The world had gone to shit, but at least they had each other—it was almost romantic.

They started with limited trips away from the property to collect supplies. When Anton scraped his arm badly on a nail, they didn't think much of it. They'd been raiding a neighborhood garden for tomatoes, and the rusty little dagger was jutting out of a fence. Casey had been keeping an eye out for the infected and heard him swear. Later, when they got home, she cleaned and bandaged it, concerned about infection.

The wound was healing nicely when Anton began experiencing lockjaw. After that, the tetanus progressed quickly, soon affecting every muscle. Anton hadn't been up-to-date on his vaccinations. She didn't realize it at the time, but she would beat herself up for that fact every day for the rest of her life. She was a paramedic, for God's sake, she should have been on top of that kind of stuff.

There was nothing she could do. No medications could help him, no doctor could have saved him, and the worst part wasn't even watching her husband suffer and die of a preventable disease right before her eyes. The worst part was watching it alone.

No one else was with her as he lay on the bed screaming in pain. No one else was there when she covered his mouth to stifle the screams. No one else cared when his muscles spasmed, breaking his back and tearing his tendons, or while he fought for air, unable to breathe through the attacks. No one else was there when the last convulsion subsided, taking Anton with it, and no one else was there when she used Anton's autographed baseball bat to defend herself from him when he rose again. She had known abstractly, but that was the day she truly came to understand what the "infected" were.

Casey wipes away tears, the dark memories getting the better of her, and she's surprised to feel Danny's awkward hand pat her shoulder. He doesn't ask why she's crying, just uncomfortably thumps her back.

A chuckle escapes her lips. "You don't do this much, do you—comfort people?"

"No, I guess not."

She smiles, and he smiles back briefly.

Casey feels Alex slide his small hand into hers and squeeze. Just when she thinks the kid has totally shut off, or that maybe she only imagines the connection between them, he goes and does something so lucid, so touching—so needed—that it bowls her over in surprise.

"Thanks, Alex."

***

Lot sits behind a large, polished oak desk in an opulent office. It's one of the few rooms in the hotel that remains essentially unchanged from its glory days. There's a fireplace set deep into a sidewall, but no fire burns there today. Candles and lamp oil are becoming scarcer by the day, but despite this, Lot works by candlelight.

Search parties rarely return with much anymore and trade

routes are in their infancy. Lot has done her best to hoard the community's gasoline and other fuels, but those supplies are only used under extreme circumstances, and it won't be long before they start going bad, if they hadn't already. Lot thinks light may become an exercise in creativity if she's unable to secure the solar panels before winter begins.

Above the mantle hangs a painting of the hotel's exterior, when it was in its prime. The façade of the building is huge and overwhelming. Faceless guests arrive in luxury cars and forgettable doormen guide them inside. It's like looking at the shiny side of a penny. Now the hotel has armored windows and an overgrown field. One day, she thinks, she'll see this place reverted to its former glory, but right now she has other priorities.

Spread out on the desk is the map Opie gave her. Its worn creases threaten to break apart under her hands. Lot contemplates a circle drawn on it with red marker, the ink spotted and dying. Written next to the circle is one word: children.

Entire colonies of children litter this ravaged world—just like in the Old World, when bombs leveled cities whose names have now been forgotten, it was the children who managed to survive. Their parents gave up everything to ensure their offspring lived. They fed them when they themselves starved, clothed them from their own backs, and laid down their lives to spare the lives of their young.

Now hordes of these children live in squalid conditions, hiding in just about every nook and cranny. They scavenge and steal, their agile young bodies carrying them quickly out of danger's path when needed. They live only to lament the loss of YouTube and selfies. They are animals, uneducated and unhygienic. They are rats, holed up in walls, squirming out to root through garbage and spread disease. But those who have survived are tough, and they're strong, a ready-made labor force.

There are many communities that need bodies to till their soil, cook their food, and fill their beds. *The children*, Lot thinks, *should be grateful. Many will find their new lives in servitude more satisfactory than living like wild beasts.*

Lot touches the red circle with her finger. It's dangerous work to corral feral children, but fortunately, there are a trusted few in her inner circle that can handle such matters. They see eye-to-eye with Lot when it benefits the community and betters their own lives within it. Opie has a real knack for identifying such individuals.

She sits back in her chair, its still-supple leather supporting her gently, then folds the map and drops it into a drawer. It won't be long before there isn't any need to round up children from the wild—they'll only be young for so long, but they can work, and breed, for a lifetime. She's put plans in the works that will concentrate their efforts solely on the distribution side of the business, facilitating between the haves and have-nots.

Lot slides the drawer closed, her touch lingering on the dark polished wood. Years ago, she sat at a humbler desk in her home office. It was functional, and not much else, made of cheap particle board and plastic-coated veneer. Lot was sitting at that desk, working on her laptop and creating the monthly budget for her doomed commune, just a few years old back then, when Danny first came into her care. She'd just come into a large sum of money courtesy of his father, Oliver.

The man was a mess. Wheelchair bound, barely able to get around. He had some vague hope that relinquishing everything to Lot's cause would garner him mercy in the eyes of the Lord. That somehow, against all odds, a miracle cure would be found, and he would rise, healthy and vital, from his rolling coffin.

Oliver was a wilted and disgusting man with bedsores and a catheter, a man who relied on his son to feed and clothe his disease-ridden body. It was no life for a seven-year-old boy, watching his father waste away. What kind of person would do that to his own child?

The day Oliver relinquished his son to Lot, a soft knock had come at the door, and Opie slithered across the carpeted room to open it. On the other side sat the decrepit man, lopsided in his wheelchair. Behind him stood Danny, then a quiet boy with a mop of blond hair and striking blue eyes.

"Come in, Brother," Opie smiled. In the Old World, he'd always been relaxed and upbeat. Oliver offered back a labored smile, and Lot could see it was an effort to control his muscles for even such a simple task.

The boy tried to push the wheelchair through the doorway, but Opie stopped him. "I'll take your father. You wait outside in the corridor and keep still." The boy looked to his father, but he twitched his hand, motioning for Danny to comply.

Once Opie had guided the boy into the unadorned hallway, he shut the door and pushed Oliver to face Lot. Inwardly she cringed, but outwardly she smiled warmly. "Brother Oliver, thank you so much for seeing us."

Oliver gummed every word out of his wasted mouth. "It's... a pleasure."

"Nonsense, the pleasure is mine. I trust you've found the other members accommodating to both yourself and your son so far?"

"Quite."

"Good, good. I'm glad."

Lot paused to look gravely at Oliver. She closed her laptop and folded her delicate hands in front of her, holding the silence a few moments and intentionally allowing the ailing man before her to become uncomfortable. It was amazing, the power a little silence had, and it was a trick that still served her well.

Oliver's head shook with the tremendous effort it took to speak. "Is... everything... alright, Sister?"

Lot sat back, calmly assessing the situation. She knew her cool calculation was usually taken as thoughtful repose. "Oliver—I hate to speak with you about this, but I haven't a choice."

Lot waited again, forcing the cripple before her to respond. Every word was a struggle for him, and soon he'd have no voice at all.

"What... is... it?"

"We don't feel that Danny's adjusting to life here very well."

A bright sheen of panic glazed over Oliver's eyes. Lot was

surprised by how quickly it happened—she'd been expecting to push harder—but the man was desperate.

"He's... adjusting. He... just... needs... a little... more time."

"This isn't a judgment, Oliver. It's very hard for a boy his age. You've moved across the country, uprooted him, taken him away from everything he's ever known—his home, his friends. His mother is already gone, and now he's facing a future without a father, too."

"You... have to... give us... more... time. We've... only been here... a month."

"He doesn't participate in services, doesn't obey his elders, and overall, he seems unhappy."

"Please! I've... given... you... everything!"

"Oliver, listen to me, I know this may be hard to digest, but sometimes the miracle we want isn't the miracle we need."

"What... do... you... mean?"

"You're dying, and there's nothing we can do about it. Your ALS has progressed so far, you'll be lucky to see next year. Isn't that why you came to me in the first place?"

"Yes... but—"

"Listen to me. Nothing is going to stop your disease. Not begging, not prayer, not good will. Soon, you'll no longer be with us. Meanwhile, your little boy not only has to watch his father waste away in front of his eyes, but also has the added burden of caring for him. It's no wonder Danny can't adjust to life here, you're preventing him from having a childhood."

Oliver's face crumpled in dismay; it was so easy. Lot had seen a perfect opportunity several months back when he'd first made contact with her, and now she was sure he'd hand her the keys to the city, no questions asked. Tears began to leak from his eyes.

"Opie, get him a Kleenex, would you?"

Opie appeared from the side with the tissues, almost too quickly. It was as if he'd been waiting with his hand on the box the entire time. Lot knew he was always quick to please and stayed loyal because she made sure the commune looked after his every need. Many people were easily blinded by the furnishings of an easy lifestyle, and Opie has no problem not seeing many of the things that took place in front of his nose.

"Oliver, I think it's time you allowed me to take Danny under my wing. I'll look after him the way you would if you could. It pains me to see the boy so distressed, and his lack of acclimation is a warning sign of things to come."

Oliver blew his nose, soaking the tissue with snot, while his head bounced up and down. He opened his mouth, trying to form another word, but Lot cut him off. The time for fishing was done and she was ready to reel in her trophy.

"I know you've been resistant, but we will provide for you. You'll receive care from your fellow brothers and sisters. You needn't suck the childhood from your boy any longer."

Oliver's head shook involuntarily, raw emotions playing across his face. Finally, and with great effort, he spat out the word Lot had been waiting to hear.

"Okay."

Lot sat back in her chair. She'd been prepared to pull out the big guns, but things had gone so smoothly she couldn't have planned it better. She smiled reassuringly at Oliver. He smiled weakly back.

"It's important that Danny understands this is your decision. For his well-being, he needs to know that you want this."

Oliver nodded agreement.

"Good. Now, compose yourself, and we'll let the boy in."

The sniveling cripple wiped his eyes and blew his nose again. The deal was done.

Danny struggled with the decision at first but quickly came around to the idea. As much as he loved his father, he was an over-burdened child faced with the prospect of relief. It was obvious he felt guilty, and Lot knew he would struggle with that guilt for many years to follow, but with heavy-handed reassurances, he gave up control of his father's care—not that he had a choice.

"Come over here, little boy." Lot motioned for Danny to come close. He shyly stepped around the desk to face her. Although she was petite, she was still large compared to the child, who was small for his age. His round blue eyes dared to have just a glimmer of hope in them, and she smiled at him, warm and comforting. "Why don't you pull up the chair over there, and I'll show you what I'm doing. I can teach you how I run this place."

"Okay."

Opie quietly wheeled Oliver away; the wheelchair-bound man didn't say goodbye.

Lot tenderly ruffled Danny's hair as he leaned closer to the computer screen. He had smiled openly and easily at the matronly woman he sat next to. He knew computers well and had been keen to know if Lot had some sort of shoot-em-up game. She promised him if he stuck with her lessons, she would get him anything he wanted.

From that small, meek boy grew the moody man that Danny is today. Those around him fear him, but Lot knows the truth: he's a groveling servant, starving for scraps.

There's a knock on the door.

"Come!"

Thirteen-year-old Tyson pushes his pimpled face through the door.

"Can I help you?"

Tyson steps timidly into the office. Danny had been a late bloomer, but this kid is a vat of pubescent hormones, the candlelight accentuating his awkwardness. The boy's voice cracks as he speaks and a brief swell of nausea rides over Lot's spine. "Hannah sent me in to tell you that the traitor has been confirmed deceased."

"Fine. Thank you."

The boy smiles, a hint of the man he'll become peeking out from under sour skin. Lot can't look at him anymore without vomiting, and she averts her gaze, seeking refuge in the large painting on the wall. "Please tell Hannah I no longer wish you as her messenger. Tell her to assign you different duties and to send Isaiah from now on."

Tyson's throat catches. God, she hopes he doesn't start bawling.

"But—but, he's only seven!"

Lot steels herself, and then she looks back at the man-child. "Yes, that's true. Don't worry, Hannah will find some way for you to contribute your many assets in a position with more responsibility."

Tyson's eyes light up. "Really? I can't wait to tell the others! This is amazing. Thank you!"

"Go now, and tell Hannah to send Isaiah. I don't want to see you here again."

Tyson sprints out the door, and Lot jumps as it bangs closed behind him. Free of the adolescent, she breathes a sigh of relief.

***

The moon hangs in the sky, nearly obliterated by thick, low-hanging clouds that crowd it. Danny scowls up at the group's only source of light. Casey and Alex follow behind the brigade, carefully picking their way along the road. Side-brush and weeds once tended to by the city of whatever the hell hick town this used be, have grown back with a vengeance. Thick roots push up slabs of broken concrete and vines choke out everything.

"Maybe we should stop for the night," Casey pulls an invisible spider web from her face, annoyed.

"Yeah, I think she's right, Danny," agrees Jamal.

"No."

Danny's men roll their eyes in the inky darkness.

"Why?" Casey asks.

"We're over a day behind already," Danny replies.

Casey hears Jamal and Dennis giggle—something about Danny being Lot's errand boy. She knows he can hear them too and wonders why he says nothing. Maybe it doesn't bother him.

"Oof!" Casey almost trips, walking straight into Alex's back where he has stopped dead in his tracks. Danny whips around, not a moment's hesitation. His voice is quiet but searing. "What are you doing back there?"

"Alex stopped," Casey gently touches Alex's shoulders. "What's wrong, honey?"

Danny's men keep walking.

"This is ridiculous. They're slowing us down, Danny."

"What's wrong with the kid anyway?" Jamal whispers to Dennis.

The two chuckle and continue their secret conversation. Casey can't hear what Heckle and Jeckle are getting on about, but even by the dimmed light of the moon, she can see Danny's demeanor changes drastically. *He* can hear what they're saying, and it looks like he's had enough.

The moon casts dark patches over Danny's eyes, and his jaw moves slightly as he grinds his teeth. She's seen body language like this before, often actually in high-stakes situations on the job, and she bets he's about to explode. Casey thinks she might not want to be around for that.

Dennis laughs. "Think the rumors about her are true?"

Danny turns to face him, his hand tightening around the handle of his machete. "Shut up."

"Nah, I think that's crazy talk."

"I said *shut up*, you two."

"Cocksucker," one of them whispers to the other, afraid to say it directly to Danny.

Guttural snarls pierce the quiet night. The attention of the group snaps toward the sound where nearby, a pride of shadowy figures hunch over something, grunting and growling, unaware of the fresh meat platter standing in the middle of the road.

Danny, his anger forgotten, reaches out and pats Alex on the head. The small sign of approval blooms warmth in Casey's chest. Pride.

She motions to Danny that they need to go around, who knows how many of those things there are. Danny nods his head in agreement and signals his now silent men.

As they pass, the clouds open briefly, revealing dark forms that surround a carcass. Creatures push and pull, batting at each other for scraps, locked in a disgusting dance. Casey shivers.

Two forms break loose from the huddle, both have an end of the same intestine. The string of gut stretches and slides between their greasy, decaying hands as they fight. Screeching like vultures, they tear into each other's corrupted flesh, attempting to secure the hard-to-grip prize.

The scene reminds Casey of the nature shows Anton used to like—African predators gorging on some unfortunate zebra. She always had a hard time watching, but this is worse-much, much worse. It's as if the King of Hell directs this scene personally, just for her. Casey looks at the faces around her and sees that fear paints them all.

Only the stupid and the dead are unafraid in this world.

5

Opie isn't a particularly good man, but he had once been a God-fearing man, long before the plague of The Risen, when he was young. A better man doesn't need God to guide his hand a righteous way, and he supposes a man such as himself doesn't need a lack of belief to ease a burdened conscience. Despite this, it was like scratching an itch to finally acknowledge God didn't exist. No heaven, no hell, just this, only this.

Opie thinks of all the mindless sheep that follow their shepherd. Where one goes, they all go. Wasting their lives, living for other people, and unaware the shepherd only leads them so she may use them as she sees fit. Maybe it had been like that since the dawn of time, or maybe it only seems that way because shepherds mercilessly beat down anyone who isn't a sheep.

The key grinds in the padlock. He wiggles it, but it jams anyway. Lot has the only other key, but it has the same problem. The tumbler is cheaply made, and frankly, Opie is surprised the thing has lasted this long. With a little more elbow grease, the lock gives. He pockets the key and then swings open the door.

With a sleeve raised to his nose against the stench of piss and body odor, he coughs. It isn't the children's fault, not really, chained in this stuffy, walk-in cooler that hasn't worked since the electrical grid went down. Still, he can't help but feel revulsion, as though they enjoy living like this.

He sets a jug of water and a loaf of bread on the floor then slides them toward the huddled group. There are eight boys and girls in total, ranging from three to thirteen-years-old, plus Aaron's wife, all scared out of their gourds. The oldest child is a pretty girl whose teeth are still in great shape. She's a special order, soon to be delivered upon—not Opie's cup of tea—he prefers women, not girls—but she sweetens the honey pot, so to speak. Lot even went so far as to have the girl examined, ensuring the men who sold them the merchandise hadn't fouled it.

Opie tastes bile. He feels a little sorry for Aaron's gagged and blindfolded wife, as she sits next to the virgin. The children are too scared to help, and she's too scared to do anything but cry. Oh well, he thinks, it's not his problem. Aaron shouldn't have poked his nose where it didn't belong.

He licks his lips, swallowing acid.

Opie's fairly confident that even if the larger population finally discovered the atrocities taking place beneath their very noses, most would look the other way. It's hard to convince anyone today of a strict moral code, and like most people in Opie's position, he assumes everyone is just like him: ultimately out for themselves.

He closes the door on the sniveling and crying. The rancid smell lingers in the air as he wipes sweaty palms on his pants. Tomorrow night, under cover of darkness, the children and woman will be traded. They'll be gone, and he'll never need to see them again.

The gargantuan hotel kitchen echoes as the lock clicks back into place. Regardless of what he tells himself, Opie always has trouble sleeping before merchandise is traded off. The emptiness in the kitchen accentuates the feelings that keep him awake nights. He tries to soothe himself, tells himself that wherever the kids end up, it's better than being outside and alone, and pushes down the whispered thought that outside, at least, they'd have a chance to live free.

***

Lot relaxes by candlelight in her bedroom, the armchair she sits in engulfing her slight form. The room is cozily decorated with bookshelves lining the walls, holding an array of children's books, games, and tempting toys. It's a collection hard to come by.

On a side table beside her steams a hot cup of tea—pure comfort. She picks up a novel, feeling it's heaviness, and runs her hand down the front. Its jacket is glossy and the artwork gaudy, with the author's name—no one she's ever heard of—scrawled prominently across the front. She cracks the cover, her nose filling with the scent of printer ink and paper. On the title page someone has scrawled a note.

To Aaron, the love of my life. Happy Birthday!
    -Marguerite ♥

Lot runs her finger along the lettering, written with a ballpoint pen—a rare commodity. Slight dents in the paper kiss her fingers as she takes a sip of tea and flips to the first page.

There's a knock at the door. *Never a moment's peace*, she thinks. "Come."

The knob turns, and Isaiah steps inside. The boy's tall for his age, and painfully skinny, though Lot's sure he'll fill out eventually. The child keeps his gaze glued to his feet, intimidated. No doubt Tyson, or one of the others, filled his head with all sorts of nonsense. Children are still cruel, even after civilization's collapse.

Lot hears mumbles from the boy.

"Isaiah, is it?"

The frightened child nods.

"Come over here."

He shuffles over to her. This behavior is going to have to change, she can't have him tongue-tied with pertinent information, some messenger he would be then.

Lot taps her foot impatiently. "What is it you have to say? Speak up this time, please."

"Danny is home," he whispers. "He brought people with him."

Lot puts down her tea, a few drops spill onto the side table. Danny isn't known for picking up strays along the way; he knows she keeps a tight control over the population. She smiles at Isaiah and thanks him. He looks nervously from his feet to a catcher's mitt and ball on her bookshelf.

"Why don't you borrow that for a while?"

"Really?"

It's almost comical how some children will drop all pretense of apprehension when faced with rewards, just like their adult counterparts. "Yes, take it and go play."

Isaiah can't contain his eagerness. He snags the glove and ball and dashes out, leaving the door ajar.

***

The candle Opie carries flickers. His mind wanders aimlessly as he walks along a darkened hallway. Without prompting, it always brings him back to his darkest days. He thinks now of "The Center" and the day he stared down at a melted electronic control panel. Inside the panel were the master switches for everything: alarms, front and back gates, sprinkler systems, all of it. From there, every facet of the vast compound's computerized grid could be controlled.

They were in big trouble. All the gates were open, and their defense systems were completely down. Those that had survived until that point were unprotected, with the exception of the weapons they could carry. The brief tapping of gunshots from an automatic caught his ear, walking corpses were pouring into the compound through the open gates, and now it looked like he wouldn't be able to close them.

Opie scrunched his face. The key for the control panel hung loosely from his fingers. Hard plastic from the buttons and switches had melted away and newly corroded metal swam in a pool of liquid. Acid, thought Opie, and the only other person with a key was Lot. He rubbed his hands together a moment while chewing on his lip.

Now what?

He left the control box and crossed the room to peer out the window. About fifty yards away was another building. Between him and it, a gauntlet of living dead. Opie sighed—every dog must prove his loyalty once in awhile.

On top of the building stood a seventeen-year-old Danny and three other shooters. Their gazes were trained at the door, waiting for Opie's signal. He gave it through the window and a hail of bullets began. One after another, the creatures dropped to the ground. Opie took a deep breath to harden his nerves, but they remained jelly. He swung his gun around to the front, counted to three, then dashed for the next building.

Above him, the shooters on the roof did their best to keep him covered. He leaped over bodies and weaved around corpses that lunged for him. It was only seconds until he reached safety, but it seemed to take much, much longer.

Opie slammed the door behind him. The guns outside ceased firing. He closed his eyes for a moment, panting, his mind swimming. *Why?* He couldn't wrap his head around it. It would be months until he understood.

He stepped away from the heavy door and marched down the hallway, his face a little paler than usual. An unfamiliar burn caused him to pause as his stomach threatened to turn on him. They never had the same relationship again.

Opie swung into a room on the right. Sitting around a small table was a handful of survivors. No one else from the group of fifty plus made it. Lot gently consoled those around her. "We will get through this. We've been chosen to carry on."

A few around her nodded, and one woman cried helplessly. A man shot her a dirty look. "Stop crying, Beulah!"

"How can you say that to me!" sobbed Beulah. "They're all *dead!*"

"They died because they were unclean. They were diseased. They—"

Lot placed a hand on the man's shoulder and he spun around to look at her.

"That's not untrue," she said. "But, we may still grieve for the fallen."

The man's face screwed up, pink and embarrassed. Lot left him and embraced the distraught woman.

Opie caught Lot's eye while she smiled reassuringly at Beulah. After a few moments, she joined him.

"What did you find, Brother? Were you able to close the gates and stop this onslaught?" The others gathered around. Opie could taste bile and swallowed hard. "No, I'm sorry. The controls seem to be… malfunctioning."

***

Casey didn't know what to expect when they entered the fortified door of the hotel, but this certainly wasn't it. The entire group—her, Danny, his men, and Alex, stand stark naked and at gunpoint. Goosebumps run along her skin. They are trapped in a wire and scrap metal cage that has been retrofitted to create a "foyer" at the front entrance.

She seems to be the only one worried. Danny's men chat, unfazed, but he is agitated. Casey's beginning to suspect it's his default demeanor. Alex can't separate his attention from his knapsack that's now in the hands of a guard, being inspected.

This is like some fucked-up version of the TSA.

Casey peers through the cage wires into the dark lobby. She didn't notice them as they entered, but now she sees that balistraria line the reinforced windows. Men and women stand on duty at each one, ready to dispatch enemies without ever needing to leave the safe confines of the building. This hotel is a fortress.

Huge, hardwood walls and ceilings loom over a few small fires. The light of candles and lanterns bob in the distance as people pass by, their torn, smoke-choked coughs bouncing around the chasmic room. Dusty chandeliers made of deer antlers dangle above, as though decoration for some macabre, doomsday ball. Not a single person is interested in what's happening at the front.

Another day, another group of naked people.

A large woman, and an even larger man, roll by on beaten office chairs. They examine their captives one by one with behemoth, square magnifiers, searching for bites. Warped by the glass, their eyes look giant and alien.

The guards surrounding the foyer remain silent, vigilant, with shotguns trained at the heads of each group member, even Alex. Casey's bare feet stick to the floor where the cold marble is stained thickly with blood. Her heart pounds and she looks up at Danny, only to catch him staring at her disrobed figure. He turns away quickly, blushing, and says nothing.

Casey purses her lips. She's not sure whether to be flattered or annoyed. This is twice he's seen her without her clothes. At least the playing field is level now. Even in this surreal environment, with death lurking around every corner and hunger gnawing at her ribs, Casey finds she can still appreciate a well-made male form.

It's not long before everyone is deemed safe, and the group is allowed to clothe themselves once again. Dressing Alex, however, is difficult. He could care less about modesty, and all he wants is to get his knapsack back. Taking it from him in the first place was a challenge because he's so obsessive and rarely lets anyone else handle it.

Once dressed, they step away from the foyer and into the lobby. Casey wonders if Alex has ever been in a hotel before. Certainly, he's never seen anything like this—*she's* never seen anything like this.

Danny speaks briefly with a tall, weasel-like man who's been watching from the sidelines. He's unimpressed and shakes his head at Danny while the two mumble quietly. Eventually, the man crosses over to Casey and Alex.

"Hello," the weasel extends his hand. His grip is surprisingly strong. "I'm Opie, and you are?"

"Casey," she says. "And this is Alex."

Casey turns Alex to face Opie, but the boy has other ideas. Opie takes it in stride.

"Well, Casey, please come with me."

He and Danny lead them into a quiet area of the lobby and show them where to sit. Opie offers to bring Casey coffee and the boy a hot chocolate. She can't believe her ears; it's been over a year since she's had a cup of coffee, and hot chocolate just seems unthinkable. Opie promises to have it sent quickly, and then he melts into the darkness behind them.

Danny drops onto an overstuffed armchair. It's a bit frayed, but still in good condition. The blond man seems out of place on the posh furniture. He traces his finger along the top of the designer coffee table before them. Outside, he was a man in his element; in here he's awkward, or nervous, or both? Maybe he's worried about having picked up tagalongs. Casey notices he's staring at her again.

"Stop doing that, you're making me uncomfortable."

"Sorry."

He looks at the kid instead. They sit in silence for a while, Casey beginning to feel a little guilty for snapping. Alex peeks over the high back of his chair and they watch the strange scene behind him. Two children, a bit older than him, kick a ball in the middle of the lobby as adults mill about on their day-to-day business.

"You two look like you could be brothers," Casey says.

"Pretty sure I'd know if I had a dumb, mute brother."

"He's not dumb."

"Oh."

Danny glances over his shoulder, waiting for someone. "Lot should be here soon."

"So, she's your leader, right? That's what your men said."

"Something like that."

The ambiguity isn't comforting, but Danny is unwilling to elaborate. Casey can tell he's on edge.

"How old are you anyway?" she asks.

"Why?"

"Just curious."

"Twenty. How old are you?"

"Old enough to know better," Casey cracks a smile, trying to ease the weird tension coming from him. Danny stares a moment before a shy smile touches his lips. He relaxes slightly and Casey's glad. She thinks they've been building a rapport, maybe even an attraction, and she would hate to lose it now.

She's struck by how kind Danny looks when he lets his defenses down—young too, when he's not mad at the world. She would even go so far as to say he's handsome, but only in the classical, blond-haired, blue-eyed, tall, muscular, and broad-shouldered way. As if anybody would go for that kind of thing. *God, he's only twenty!* Twelve years younger than her.

Danny suddenly tenses as an older woman's hand slides over his shoulder. His half-shy smile drops away in an instant and his face hardens, darkens, ages. As his defenses come hammering back up, Casey is thrown out. The beautiful young man who sat before her transforms instantly into the hardened and grizzled killer she first met. The change in his demeanor is so drastic it raises Casey's hackles.

"I hope Danny has been treating you well," the woman says.

Casey doesn't answer immediately, pausing to take stock of the tiny woman with wavy gray hair pulled back from her brow with bobby pins. This woman with the power to mutate men. This woman from whom confidence and mettle ripple away in waves.

"Of course," Casey finally responds.

The woman seems curiously surprised, only for a split second, before it's covered with a warm smile. Casey notices Opie is back, lurking in the background, listening and watching. Her stomach begins to knot.

"You must be Lot," she says.

"You've heard of me!"

"In brief."

"I'm afraid you have me at a disadvantage then. What may I call you?"

"Casey."

An older man with a withered face arrives, holding a tray with two steaming mugs. He quietly sets the mugs on the table and leaves without a word.

"And the boy?"

"I call him Alex. He doesn't speak, or even write for that matter."

But he sure knows what's going on, Casey thinks, as Alex snags up the mug of hot chocolate with no attempt at politeness.

"He's touched," Danny pipes in.

"Interesting. Touched children are rare for this new world," Lot says.

"Casey will more than make up for the kid's burden here. She's strong. She's already saved my life—"

Lot shoots Danny a nearly imperceptible look, and it shuts him down, silencing him. He's like a puppy at her feet, Casey thinks, *a beaten puppy.*

"You'll have to forgive Danny. He can be presumptuous, but I'm happy to see you were able to make it to us safely. Despite his—standoffishness, you and Alex could not have been in better hands. Ultimately, Danny always does the right thing, but he's had trouble with people ever since his father died when he was a child. I raised him myself, did he mention that?"

Danny is on his feet the second the words leave Lot's mouth. Instinctually, Casey reaches for her bat, and then remembers it was taken from her when they entered the building.

"She doesn't need to hear that!" Danny says, raising his voice.

Lot raises an eyebrow. "Stop being so temperamental, Daniel, and sit down."

Danny crosses his arms like a pouting child. Alex jumps from his chair, suddenly interested and already finished with his hot chocolate. He copies Danny move for move. Danny turns and shouts at the boy, his anger finding a convenient outlet. "Stop that, would you?"

Alex continues to look fixedly at Danny, doesn't bat an eye. It's as if Danny's yelling at a rock. Casey gently takes Alex's hand and pulls him to her. "Quit that, honey. It's not nice."

Lot lightly laughs, completely ignoring Danny's outburst. She reaches over and tenderly pushes Alex's unkempt hair from his eyes. There's something about the way she does it that sets Casey's teeth on edge. Her eyes fall on Lot's necklace, a blue, spiraled triangle. It makes her uneasy, but she doesn't know why.

Lot smiles at her, catching Casey's gaze. "Children are such treasures, aren't they?"

Danny furrows his brow; he's high-strung, and Casey wonders how much of his bad attitude has to do with Lot. The woman seems cordial enough, but there's something that doesn't sit right. Maybe it's the way everyone around the place kowtows to her, even Danny—especially Danny. Casey hasn't known him long, but it's odd to her that for all his macho grandstanding, he's like a starved, neutered whelp when it comes to this woman.

The creeps leak down Casey's spine, and she curls her toes inside her shoes. She's beginning to have serious second thoughts that can't be soothed by the promise of a hot meal, conversation, and a safe bed to sleep in.

Voices rise above the low hum of activity in the hotel lobby. Shouting. There's someone in the caged-in foyer, soaked in blood. Casey can tell, even from where she sits, that he's panicked, calling for a nurse. The guards are jittery, the stocks of their guns held tightly to their shoulders.

The man in the cage is beside himself. Two guards take off, sprinting in different directions to find a nurse, *the* nurse, somewhere in the depths of the building. Judging from the panic of the caged man, someone outside has very little time.

Casey's instincts as a first responder kick in and she jumps to her feet. It's impossible for her to sit back and watch an emergency unfold without doing something about it. Lot and Danny both shoot her quizzical looks.

"I can help," she says.

Danny shakes his head. "They'll find the nurse."

"I'm a paramedic. They need someone now."

Casey is running for the foyer almost before the words fully leave her mouth. If this is a true emergency, and it certainly appears to be, then seconds count to save a life, and she isn't going to have Danny, or this woman, tell her what to do.

"Watch Alex," Casey shouts back over her shoulder at Danny.

Danny ignores Casey's command and follows her, leaving the boy behind with Lot. Alex attempts to follow but is held back gently. Lot strokes a calming hand down his cheek.

"Don't worry, Alex, everything's going to be okay."

Casey and Danny dash for the front entrance.

6

Casey bolted up a down escalator. It was utter chaos. She and her partner had stopped to eat lunch in the food court (he had excused himself to go "drop the kids off at the pool"), and then the screaming started.

People ran, shoving each other, stampeding like a herd of mindless animals. Casey's feet pounded at the folding steps as they passed by. At the top, a little girl in a pink dress crashed to her knees and began crying. The girl's panicked father wrenched the child to her feet and attempted to drag her away, but it was too late—the seemingly possessed man was too fast. A paper shopping bag was still wrapped around his wrist and his clothes were drenched in blood. Casey couldn't get there fast enough—running toward what everyone else was running from. She pushed through the glut of bodies panicked to get away.

The bloodied man had tripped over a bench, and as he scrambled for the girl her father kicked him square in the face. The man's head snapped back with the blow and his nose exploded, but there was no reaction to the pain, and it didn't slow him down. Damn tweakers. Meth, maybe bath salts, or some other drug. They were all bad shit, as far as Casey was concerned. Why couldn't everyone just be content to smoke a little dope? The only thing a stoner ever attacked was a hoagie.

The rabid, drug-addled man lurched again for the girl as she sat on the floor, crying. A man from the crowd suddenly jumped into action. *Finally,* Casey thought, *a Good Samaritan.*

She felt like she was moving in slow motion.

The Good Samaritan tackled the tweaking son-of-a-bitch, and

the two struggled. They hit the glass railing, and a druggie sailed over the side.

People screamed as the meth-head flew through the air, hitting a silvery, hanging decoration. *Sloosh*. One of its long, thin barbs impaled him. His heart and half his ribcage clung to the top of it as he slid down the shaft. The giant decoration swung in the air and the skewered man thrashed like a hooked fish.

Casey couldn't believe her eyes. He should have been dead. There was no way he could survive, but contrary to all that was good and sane, he *was* alive—and angry.

The Good Samaritan dripped blood from several nasty bite wounds. He stared over the side with the rest of the crowd, in shock. Casey finally reached the top of the escalator. Good thing she was in great shape.

She yelled into her shoulder radio for her partner.

The Good Samaritan turned to face her, blood from teeth marks dripped down his cheek. He was going to need a lot of stitches. Casey reached into her pocket, then snapped on a pair of blue rubber gloves.

"I didn't mean to—," he whimpered.

"It's okay." Casey fell back on her training. "I'm here to help."

***

"HELP! SOMEONE PLEASE!" The man in the foyer is covered in blood and desperate. Casey turns to the head guard, the overly muscled military man that ran the foyer inspection. He swings his gun around to meet her. "Open the cage!" she shouts.

"Back away, lady, we have this handled. The nurse is being located."

Casey doesn't lower her gaze, doesn't back down.

"I'm a paramedic. I can help, *right now*."

Danny steps up behind her. "Just open the damn door."

The man's eyes turn to slits. With a grumble, he opens the three padlocks that secure the gate. The surrounding guards tense with itchy trigger fingers.

"Don't move a muscle, Abel," someone says to the man inside the foyer.

Abel nods compliance.

Danny turns to the military man and holds out his hand. "Gun."

Sourly, and with true disdain, the man shoves his rifle into Danny's hand. Danny points to a pouch on the man's hip containing extra shells. Those are also handed over with displeasure. Casey raises an eyebrow at Danny.

"You want backup, or not?" he asks.

"Sure, no problem."

They step into the foyer and sprint after Abel, who dashes outside.

The light of an oil lamp glows in the middle of the field surrounding the hotel. Nearby, a behemoth of an apple tree rises over the flatlands. It must have grown there unchecked for decades, its massive, leaf-burdened limbs stretching toward the sky. Casey's feet pound the ground. Something about the tree reminds her of an elderly nun casting desperate prayers to her Lord. She wonders what the hell people are doing out here in the dark anyway.

Incoherent yelling drifts toward them. As if it isn't already bad enough to be out here at night, the yelling is bound to attract all sorts of unwanted attention.

Casey skids to a stop as they reach the tree where a man is pinned under a thick branch. The man screams as she throws herself down next to him, inspecting the situation. "I'm going to die!" he shouts. "I'm going to die! They're going to get me!"

Abel slides in next to Casey and covers the man's mouth with his hand. "Shhhhh, Lawrence! Shhhhh! You'll get us all killed!"

This only panics Lawrence further.

Danny shoves Abel to the side. "You're not helping."

"Danny! Thank God!" Lawrence is genuinely relieved, and it quiets him some.

Casey grabs the nearby lantern and holds it closer, assessing the damage—just like riding a bike. "It's okay," she says. "I'm here to help."

"Who are you?"

"My name is Casey, I'm a paramedic."

"Thank God! Praise Jesus!"

Casey looks over Lawrence's injury. He's in bad shape. Skin and thigh muscle bulge out around a spear of broken tree branch and there's blood everywhere. The artery is probably nicked. What wouldn't she give for a proper medic kit, or hell, even a crappy first aid kit?

"I need a belt."

Abel snakes off his belt and tosses it to Casey.

Danny stands sentry, his rifle steadily trained on the night. Locked and loaded. "Hurry up."

"I'm hurrying."

"Faster."

There's far off movement in the field, near the woods. Casey slides her hands under Lawrence's thigh. She loops the belt around it and pulls, straining her muscles. Warm blood squirts from his wound, making the leather hard to grip. She digs her knees into the soft ground and pulls again.

Lawrence is crying. "Hurry up. Oh my God, hurry up."

"We need to push this branch off of him," Casey shouts at Danny, without looking up. She ties the belt off and hopes it will hold.

More figures appear in the distance as Danny reluctantly lowers his weapon. "Alright, let's do it."

Casey fumbles around the massive, leaf-laden bough. She wedges her hands under it, and on her count she lifts with Danny and Abel, trying to roll the branch off Lawrence. It doesn't budge.

Lawrence screams at the top of his lungs. "Hurry! Hurry! Hurry!" He flails his arms, beating the ground as though he were whipping a horse.

Danny smacks the screaming man across the face. "Shut-up!" But it's too late. The figures in the field hone in on their strike position. They pick up speed.

Casey counts to three again. Her back cracks, her arms waver, but the branch moves. Wood tears away from Lawrence's thigh and his blood-curdling screams fill the night air, a beacon for the encroaching enemy.

Casey jumps over the branch, back to Lawrence. Despite the Macgyvered tourniquet, blood pours from his wound.

Danny raises his rifle.

BAM!

A moonlit figure flies back and hits the ground.

"Let's GO!"

The ghoul climbs back on its feet, despite missing a good chunk of head.

"He's bleeding out!"

"No time!"

Abel rips off his shirt and tosses it to Casey. "Here!"

More figures appear from the night.

BAM!

Danny braces himself against the recoil of the gun and a second bullet explodes the skull of the closest marauder. This time, when the creature hits the ground, it doesn't rise again.

Abel dances around Casey worthlessly as she jams his shirt into Lawrence's gushing wound, moves the belt over it, then jerks tightly around it. Still more blood.

"Let's go!"

Casey ignores Danny.

"NOW!"

"One minute!"

Danny fires his gun again. Another figure drops. More rotten faces are in the distance, many slow and stiff, but others are fast and agile, very close, and undeterred.

Danny can't keep the monsters at bay any longer. He shouts over his shoulder. "Abel! We're out of time!" He fires his gun, dropping another creature.

Abel grabs Lawrence's wrist and rips Casey's patient from her hands, dragging him toward the hotel. Lawrence screams as a creature attacks them from the other side of the tree. Abel dodges, pulling Lawrence away from its menacing teeth. The thing's spoiled face and bulging, oozing eyes crank toward Casey. It's time to run.

Casey jumps up and a jagged burning sears her arm as the spear-like wood from the broken tree tears through her flesh. *Damn it!* It's deep, bleeding, but she has no time for pain. The wasted corpse lunges for her, and she scrambles backward. Moldy, froth-covered teeth specked with blood click shut mere millimeters from her face. Skeletal, decaying fingers seize her clothing, and the thing drags her to the ground. She can't get away.

Casey screams. Since the time she understood what these monsters were, she knew this was how it would end: with one of them. But she didn't expect to be so scared. When one imagines their own death, it's always with a certain amount of disconnection. It can be believed the end will be met with stoicism, or even with a modicum of benevolence. Everyone thinks they can meet The Reaper with head held high, but in the end, few do. Casey thinks she may meet him having soiled herself.

Danny slams the butt of his rifle into the creature's face, and it keels to the side. Unadulterated relief threatens to overtake every ounce of Casey's being. She watches as Danny kicks the thing to the ground and wallops its skull until it resembles a grotesque, smashed watermelon.

The scene is terrible, and violent, and wonderful.

Danny gives Casey his hand. She grabs it, and he hoists her to her feet without effort. Half a second later, they are running, horror on their heels, and he still holds her hand. Ahead of them, a delirious Lawrence struggles against Abel.

Danny and Casey close the gap and she releases his hand—dashes for Lawrence. She grabs her patient's arm and tries to sling him over her shoulder, but he bucks, swatting her off. His eyes bug in fear and he topples himself and Abel to the ground.

"She's been bitten!" he shouts.

Casey's shocked. What the hell is this lunatic talking about? His accusing finger points directly at the torn flesh on her bicep.

"What? No, I'm not!"

Abel lifts Lawrence to his feet, and Casey steps toward them.

"She's bitten! She's bitten!"

Creatures close in from all sides. Casey bites her tongue, restrains herself from screaming back at Lawrence. They've run out of time and need to move.

BAM!

The sound is ear splitting. A beast flies backward, shot in the face. It's not a kill shot, and even without eyes and a mouth, the thing still attempts to find prey.

CLICK.

The sound of an empty gun is enough to send waves of sickness through Casey.

A second creature flies out of the gloom and tackles Abel, tearing into his flesh. Another attacks, and Abel's oil lantern flies from his hand, smashing to the ground, it's fuel flaring up and igniting the area around them. He screams.

Casey darts for Lawrence and grabs an arm, trying to pull him away. Abel wails in pain as ghouls rip the flesh from his bones. Casey fights against the dying man for Lawrence, but he won't let go of his friend's wrist. Flames rise around them, attracting more creatures, like moths. She shoves one away and dodges another.

BAM!

Music to her ears; Danny is finally reloaded, and a ghoul's head explodes like an over-ripe cantaloupe. Abel continues to scream as Casey tightens her grip on Lawrence's arm and pulls. She leverages all her strength, groaning with effort, but Abel just won't let go.

BAM!

The screaming stops. Abel's head caves in from the front and surges out the back. His hand goes limp, sending Lawrence and Casey flying backward. She stumbles to her feet and scoops Lawrence under the arms, dragging the wounded man from the pile of creatures that feast upon Abel. Danny lowers his gun and grabs Lawrence's legs. The growing fire illuminates eyes, too many sets to count, quickly approaching in the dark.

"Run!" Danny shouts at her.

They dash madly for the hotel, lugging Lawrence. He swings between their arms, a delirious dead weight, while the creatures pursue.

The door of the hotel slides open as they approach, revealing a bank of armed guards beyond the caged foyer. Danny and Casey rush through the entrance with Lawrence dangling between them. They're sealed safely inside as the door slams, leaving the monsters behind them to claw at it, growling and screeching at the top of their decayed lungs.

Outside, the fire from the broken oil lantern burns on the lawn, attracting more and more of the horrid walking corpses that populate the surrounding area. The creatures gorge on Abel's flesh, even as their own chars without notice.

7

Opie rubs his hands together. It's not cold outside, but that doesn't matter with a nervous tick. His stomach churns slightly, a delicious dinner of roasted rabbit and potatoes not sitting right. He knew better than to eat, had hardly eaten in fact, but he's sweet on the head cook, Odette, and she gave him extra at dinnertime.

Odette is a plump lady, not too heavy, not too thin, just the way you would expect a cook to look. She has two children, a little boy and a teenage girl, both of whom adore Opie. Their father is presumed dead, or worse, and Opie can really see a future with them. He's never played house before, but recently the longing has hit him. He thinks it's time to share his prosperity with an official family. Lot's thirst for power and control has served him well, and it's only a matter of time before there's more than one community under her thumb. With her influence, Opie's own will grow too, and he could give a family the world.

He rubs his hands together again, watching Aaron's wife and a train of shackled children stumble by. The nurse, Julie, stands next to him, arms crossed, face set in stone. If she has any reservations about what they're doing, she has never shown it.

She examines each child as they come into her care and vouches for their health as they leave it. They may be filthy and scared, but they are disease free. A few cry quietly, but most stare at the ground and trudge forward; their spirits were already broken long before Opie ever laid eyes on them. This test run has been much easier than dealing with ferals—maybe Lot's right about getting into the middle-man business.

A very short, pudgy man with a well-groomed mustache herds the children into the back of a fortified pick-up truck. There, a machine-gun-wearing woman locks their manacles to the inside. One of the little boys suddenly summons the courage to speak. "Please," he cries. "Please help—"

The woman kicks him in the stomach and locks him into place as he blubbers.

Opie looks away, the rabbit stew rolling violently in his gut.

The mustachioed man reaches into the back of the truck and wraps his hands around a crate that he heaves to the ground. It plops at Opie's feet, followed by a second one. Opie squats next to the first one and pries open the lid with calloused fingers. He peers inside at a swarm of yellow chicks. They peep and cry, piled atop each other in one pulsating mass of feathers. Lot went to quite a bit of trouble to secure this deal. Livestock is valuable indeed, and Opie never needs to remind himself why. During their first winter at the hotel they had a small amount, but bad circumstances and worse weather nearly destroyed everything. There hadn't been enough food to go around.

When supplies began running out, people got restless. There were whispers of revolt; the situation uncannily reminiscent of the first weeks of The Plague. Opie remembers being nervous a similar disaster would strike this community, as it did the original compound, and it wasn't long before people began disappearing.

Maybe, as was the pervasive theory, those people just set out on their own in search of food when their ribs began showing, and they never made it back. All Opie knows is that the meager stockpile of supplies in the hotel somehow lasted until the spring, and when the snow thawed, people stopped disappearing. Many felt it was a miracle.

Opie knows better. He knows in his heart what choices Lot made to ensure the survival of the community, and her position of power, but he tries not to think about it. He's just happy to be the only true person Lot can't do without.

With the merchandise loaded and payment made, the

mustachioed man jumps into the cab of the pickup. He leans out the window and smiles with perfectly capped teeth. Opie wonders briefly what this man did in his previous life—lawyer, investment banker, politician?

"Give my regards to Lot," the man says.

Gunfire sounds from around the corner.

Opie jumps, they all do. Mustachio shoots a suspicious look from the driver's seat as Opie nervously rubs his hands together. For all the times he's done this, he's never heard a peep from the lookouts at the front of the hotel.

The woman leaps from the back of the pick-up, weapon pointing at Opie. Next to him, Julie cries out softly in fear. Opie swallows hard, and his stomach seesaws. He waves down the armed woman. "Go, get out of here."

She looks at mustachio, who nods. Without a word, she slams the tailgate closed then jumps into the truck's passenger seat, shutting the door. They're driving toward a back road seconds later, raising a cloud of dirt.

Opie coughs and squints his eyes against the dust. The taillights are gone quickly. He turns to face the nurse, a touch of sweat standing out on his brow. It's always nerve-wracking to stare down the barrel of a gun. More shots are fired, and Opie's heart skips a beat. He grabs a box and, with one arm around it, hurries through an emergency exit. Julie runs behind him, carrying the other box.

Opie pushes through the propped-open door, back into the hotel, then drops his box on the floor. His stomach loosens a bit and he breathes, relaxing enough to clear his head. He closes the door, and chains it shut. With a wave, he beckons the nurse to drop her box on his, and together they shove a few crates back in front of the emergency exit, concealing the fact it was ever opened. Just as they finish, a shout comes down the hallway. Candlelight bounces off the walls as someone approaches, yelling randomly into the dark. "Julie! We need you! Emergency!" It's a guard.

Opie waves at Julie. "Go, deal with the situation."

She's gone in a blink, jogging down the corridor to meet the candle-carrying man. After a brief back and forth, they take off toward the lobby. The guard never once questions what she was doing in the hallway alone, in the dark.

Opie feels around and finds the oil lantern he stashed in the corner. It's turned down low, a cloth over the glass hiding the flame. He brushes the cloth to the side, then turns a knob and a warm glow leaps to life. He sits back on the crates, blocking the door, and reaches into a pocket to pull out a battered green-and-gold package of *Jack Hatter's* cigarettes—one of the many perks of being Lot's right-hand man. Every once in a while, he shares his stash with his most trusted men, as a reward for keeping their traps shut. He fishes a smoke from the pack with his long fingers and lights it off the lantern, then sits back with the first inhale. He closes his eyes and enjoys the fuzzy warmth of smoke in his lungs.

With every drag, he tries to blot out the memory of whimpering children.

*****

Casey and Danny lean against the wire of the foyer cage, catching their breath. Lawrence screams deliriously from the floor, writhing in pain and white as a sheet. Casey's makeshift tourniquet isn't doing its job.

A crowd, attracted by the commotion, is gathering around the entrance, but parts as the nurse pushes her way through. Every guard is at full attention, their guns drawn; itchy trigger fingers. "She's been bitten!" Lawrence screams, and the people around gasp.

The head guard's booming voice cuts through the noise. "STRIP!"

Casey grips the cage side. She stares at the overly muscled man with the Marie Corps tattoo. What is he saying? It doesn't make sense.

"STRIP!"

"You can't be serious! This man needs medical attention, *right now*!" Casey shouts.

Faces press in, their garbled voices growing louder, more excited.

The guard glances at the nurse. "Julie?"

Julie crosses her arms. "Him too."

Danny drops to his knees next to Lawrence and starts ripping clothes from the blabbering man's body.

"She's bitten! She's bitten! She's bitttttssssstttt—"

Lawrence convulses in Danny's arms. Foam bubbles from his mouth and his eyes roll back. These people are crazy! This man is dying before their very eyes!

Danny struggles with Lawrence's clothing, fighting a seizing arm out of its sleeve. Casey can see him grinding his teeth again. He turns to her, his eyes lined with stress. "Help me!"

She has no choice. Lawrence is probably going to die for all their effort, but he has no chance at all if these loons won't even let him inside.

"Jesus Christ!" Casey kicks the side of the cage then bounces in next to Danny. Lawrence flails against the marble floor and as she reaches for him, Danny leaps away as though hit with an electric shock.

"Get away from him!" he shouts at her.

"What?"

Danny hooks his rifle with one hand, his eyes don't leave Lawrence. Someone in the crowd screams. The guards look at each other, unsure of what to do.

"Get away from him!" he shouts again.

Then Casey sees it. Her eyes zoom in on Lawrence's waxen skin where deep red teeth marks are gouged into his wrist.

Danny aims his gun at the man's head.

"Stop!" Casey screams.

"Lower your weapon!" commands a bellowing voice.

BAM!

The blast is deafening. Blood showers Casey, and the seizing stops. Lawrence's limp body hangs in her arms. He's dead.

Someone, somewhere, demands Danny drop his weapon and he lowers his gun.

Casey grips Lawrence's shirt. She tastes blood in her mouth—her own. Her tongue aches, yet it isn't enough to steady her anger. She springs to her feet, baring her teeth. "What the fuck, Danny!" she screams.

"He was bitten."

"Maybe he could have been saved!"

Danny opens his mouth but Lot's calm, smooth voice interjects before he says anything. "I'm sorry, Casey." Alex stands next to her. The crowd falls eerily quiet and Casey can feel people hanging on the woman's every word.

"The fungus spores were already in Lawrence's bloodstream. There's nothing that could be done to save him."

Casey clenches and unclenches her hands. After a moment of unsuccessfully trying to calm herself, she flips around to face Lot, glaring through the wire mesh of the caged foyer. *Heathens!* They could have given Lawrence a chance. Her body shakes with anger.

"Fungus spores? Are you nuts? You don't know that! No one knows what causes this. We could have tried amputation!"

"No, we couldn't have. I'm sorry, but there was no other option. Anyone bitten *always* turns."

"You don't know that! He could have been the one that was immune!"

Casey feels Danny's hand on her shoulder. Just knowing it's there makes her blood boil. "It had to be done," he says.

Who the hell does this ogre think he is? Judge, jury, and executioner? She spins around and screams in his face. "What's the matter with you? You can't just do that to people. You have to give them a chance!"

"I HAD TO!" he screams back.

Casey brings her hand quickly through the air, slapping Danny across the face, leaving finger-shaped red marks on his cheek. She glares angrily up at him, shoulders rising and falling with each shallow breath. He reaches up, touches his skin, his blue eyes wide with shock and hurt. The lobby is as quiet as death. *This must be better than daytime TV to these psychopaths*, she thinks.

"Danny." The head guard's voice is gentler this time. He doesn't want to stir the pot. "Your gun."

Danny looks down at his weapon, dazed, as though just remembering he's holding it. Without a word, he hands it through a slot in the cage and, staring into space, begins undressing.

One of the guards points at Casey. "Strip."

Casey's rage-filled eyes slide over Danny as he removes his t-shirt. All around them, guards point guns. On the floor lies a man with a belt around his leg and a bullet in his head. The gathered crowd in the lobby waits with bated breath to see what will happen next, and at the center of it all is the petite, gray-haired woman who runs the whole show.

Watching everything, held back by Lot's hand and silently gripping his knapsack, is Alex.

It's too much to take.

Casey growls at the sum. "No. No! I'm leaving. Fuck you all. Give me Alex. Alex, honey, come here."

Alex tries to step forward, but Lot stays him. He looks from Lot to Casey, unsure. Casey thinks she sees something in Lot's eyes, an impending threat like a viper about to strike. The woman plays with the necklace around her throat. "Casey," she says, "I cannot allow you to take custodianship of the boy until it's known you haven't been infected."

Casey digs skin from the inside of her palms with her fingernails. She wishes she could make this woman's head explode. She wishes she had never come here, had never met Danny, had never been enticed by food and security. She begins to tear her clothes from her body, her voice vicious and grating. "You want to see I'm not infected? Huh? You want to make sure I'm not bitten? Fine!"

It's more than raw anger coursing through her veins. It's bitter disappointment and a crushing sadness. The dashed dreams of safety and a future where she and Alex could live, not just survive. Casey whips her bloodied shirt to the ground, casting it off as though it were her poisoned hope. Immediately a guard, the large woman, points a sausage finger at the torn flesh on Casey's arm. "What's that?"

Casey angrily follows the line of the fat finger with her eyes. A chill overtakes her body as she looks at her arm. She swallows hard with the realization these people all have hammers, and that to them, every wound looks like a nail. One by one, she feels the hairs over her entire body as they stand on end. "It's not a bite, if that's what you're thinking."

"Lawrence said you were bitten," says another guard. He hasn't lowered his gun—no one has. A pit of defeat bobs in Casey's stomach, and her knees feel like Jell-O, but she wills them to stand. Words stick in her throat. "I got it caught on the tree."

"It's true," Danny speaks up at long last. There's a small movement as a guard moves his finger to the trigger of his gun. "Lower your weapon!" Danny shouts. The guard ignores him and shifts his eyes from Casey to Lot.

"I'm not bitten! This is clearly not a bite!" Casey stares down at her arm, tears of anger blurring her vision.

Danny locks eyes with Lot.

"Lot," he begs, "Please, don't."

Standing behind Alex, Lot nods, and the guard fires his weapon. Casey collapses to the ground.

Dead.

8

"No!" Danny's voice cracks. Casey's body lies at his feet, and she stares straight ahead, her spark extinguished. Her forehead gapes, leaking grayish jelly onto the bloodstained marble. The world buzzes around Danny as though he's on a different vibration—he doesn't feel like this is reality.

Inside the lobby, Alex bursts free of Lot's grip. Tears begin to stream from his blue eyes, soaking his cheeks. He throws himself at the foyer, knapsack dragging on the floor behind him, and reaches his thin arms through the cage. He grips one of Casey's fingers.

Danny stares down at the child. Utter horror stains the boy's face and scratchy, inarticulate moans of sheer anguish escape his lips. The moaning is more disturbing than if he were crying normally.

Danny turns his moonlike eyes to Lot, his world wavering, as though he's moving through thick water. The guards still have their guns raised, fingers on the triggers. There are already two dead bodies decorating the foyer, what's one more?

Danny's gaze is drawn to Casey once again. He stares at her face. Her large, brown eyes are lifeless, and her mouth is slightly agape. He's seen so many dead bodies in his life, but this is more horrible than any other. The boy grips Casey's hand, his body curving around it, cradling it through the cage. He drops his face into her dead palm and sobs rise from his body in huge, noiseless gasps. Danny chokes back a rising feeling of dread.

"Strip!"

The word slices like a whip. The swish of pounding blood

overtakes the buzz in his ears and he clenches his jaw so tightly it's a wonder his teeth don't crack.

He grips the cage wall and shakes it.

"SHE WASN'T BITTEN!"

Thick Marge crosses her arms and glares back defiantly. "I'm sorry, Danny. Not even your preferential treatment around here extends that far."

If there weren't a cage keeping him in, Danny would punch her square in the jaw. He would knock all her goddamn teeth down her fat throat and then use her face as a stomping ground. He grips the cage so hard his fingers begin to bleed. His body shakes with rage, and he pins Thick Marge down with hateful eyes. She looks worried for a split second that the cage won't hold, but it's solid.

From the corner of his eye, Danny catches Lot as she kneels next to Alex. His chest tightens, and he lets his arms fall limply to his sides as he turns to face them. Lot rubs the boy's back as she gently tries to pull him from Casey's body. Danny's shoulders slouch forward, every ounce of grief and anger suddenly turning inward on him. His insides feel rotten.

Lot looks up at the blond man trapped in the cage. "I'm sorry, Danny."

He's seen the look a million times; it's an elaborate mask she wears, making her seem as though she cares deeply, but for the first time in his life he sees cracks, and he knows she's anything but sorry. The buzzing returns to his ears, and he thinks for a moment this must all be a dream.

"STRIP!" Arnold commands.

Danny's fingers feel like rubber as he unhooks his belt.

Lot gently tries to guide Alex away from Casey's body again. The child resists. He claws for the cage, refuses to release Casey's hand. The guard that shot Casey grips the boy's shoulder firmly and pulls. Alex turns violently and kicks the guard in the kneecap as hard as he can. The guard sprawls onto the floor and barely has time to lift his hand in defense as the boy attacks like a wild animal, growling.

Alex sinks his teeth into the guard's flesh. Blood stains the boy's lips and leaks down his chin. The terrified guard howls and rolls around, as though he's on fire. He screams at the top of his lungs, panicked. "Get him off! Get him off!"

Alex threatens the crowd with his teeth. His mop of matted hair bounces and wild eyes peer out from a dirty face. He jumps and darts around people as they dive away from him. Uneasiness and fear are palpable.

CASEY IS DEAD.

The boy spins in place, unsure where to go. Unfriendly faces hover all around him. Guns are everywhere.

CASEY IS DEAD.

The gray-haired woman glides closer. She reaches out a hand. Alex steps back. Won't let her touch him. Won't let anyone touch him.

CASEY IS DEAD.

He clings to his knapsack, hot tears leaking down his face, and then jets off into the darkness, disappearing into the bowels of the hotel.

***

He doesn't know how he was able to do it, but somehow Danny managed to drag himself to his room. He knows he should feel upset in some way, but instead he just feels numb. He lights an oil lamp in the corner and sits on the end of the double bed. The sheets are clean but dingy, just like the rest of the room.

The lamp burns brightly, its dark smoke staining the ceiling of the hotel bedroom. Almost everything in the room that could be removed and used for another purpose has been, save for the bed and a full-length, inset mirror Danny now stares into.

He barely recognizes himself. The disheveled hair, the unshaven, bloodstained face, and the haunted, sleep deprived eyes that stare back can't be his own. This day can't be his life.

He looks down at a worn water jug at his feet. Somewhere, he is vaguely aware of being thirsty, but the urge to sleep, to shut down and leave this world behind, is much too powerful. He flops back onto the neatly made bed and closes his eyes.

***

Opie stares out a viewing hole at the horde of living corpses decorating the front lawn of the hotel. The fire in the grass is burning lower than before, but it's still bright enough to attract The Risen.

Abel is only blackened bones in the dirt now. With nothing left to feed on, The Risen wander aimlessly. Occasionally, they snap and swat at each other, but somehow, they recognize the living from the living dead. Some may appear to be slow and stupid, but many are fast. All are dangerous.

Frustrated, Opie clicks shut the peephole and surveys the lobby. It's a total mess, with pools of blood clotting on the floor. The larger population must be protected at the cost of the individual, but this feels different to him. He watches as Lawrence's and Casey's bodies are extracted from the foyer.

Opie can't remember a time when Lot was so invested in what happened in the foyer cage. She always trusts the judgment of the guards on duty and she certainly never has a direct hand in the death of anyone bitten. She leaves that dirty work to others; this was a rare public display.

Opie knows Lot better than most. He knows everything that happened tonight has some sort of end game, and he can bet what it is. He knew *something* was going to happen the second Danny showed up with that woman and boy. Lot is an expert at seizing opportunities, at manipulating those around her, and she doesn't waste time.

This plays a big part in her influence, but also in the growing whispers surrounding her. It's become a regular necessity to deal with "political dissidents." Opie has an ear for this sort of thing and tonight's events are sure to start up the underground gossip wagon. Already, he has heard three different recollections of what happened here tonight.

What really sticks with Opie is Alex. He isn't shocked to see Lot's interest in the child (she certainly has a type), but it's been a while, years in fact, since Opie's had to cover her tracks. Now, that child is running loose in the hotel, and there's much unwanted attention on the situation. Opie's stomach burns.

All of this uncomfortably reminds him of when his many suspicions about Lot were confirmed. He hadn't known, not for sure, not until that very moment when Danny, then a distraught little boy, reached out. Opie felt bad, but not bad enough to stop it. Besides, it was the way of the world, and it was better the child learn that quickly than harbor a delusion someone would—or should—save him.

He had scolded Danny, acted as if he didn't believe a word the boy said. Opie had shamed him so badly that Lot's secret remains well kept to this day. It was then he realized he had never needed to sell his soul to the devil. His soul, he thought, had been slowly and willingly leaked away day by day. Finally, it was just gone, with barely a shrug of the shoulders.

Opie rarely allows his mind to drift near Lot's true nature. He knows her for what she is and knows he will never do anything about it. Not as long as it benefits him not to, that is.

Acid bubbles in his stomach. The residue of Opie's humanness often has trouble mixing with his need to put himself first. He can't stop thinking about the new blond-haired, blue-eyed boy, but it doesn't really matter how he feels—it will be what it will be.

***

Darkness blankets Alex. It's comforting, and if he could, he would fade into the wall pressed against his back.

CASEY IS DEAD.

His muscles are stiff and his joints ache from hours of crouching, wedged between long forgotten janitorial supplies. The smell of cleaning fluid, spilled ages ago, itches his nose. Still, he refuses to move, won't gratify himself with a sneeze. It's unsafe.

The doorknob turns. He can't see it, but he can hear it. It scratches. It booms.

CASEY IS DEAD.

The door opens, just a crack, not enough to escape. Alex stays still.

CASEY IS DEAD.

He breathes heavily as the door opens a bit more, and candlelight reaches its fingers into the closet. The pulsating light ricochets off the walls, distorting everything. Alex squints, his eyes adjusting slowly. A face floats behind the glare of flame, he's seen it before: Lot.

She lowers herself to sit cross-legged in front of the door, her body blocking the way out. In her hand is a plate that she shoves a short distance into the closet. On it rests a sandwich, crusts cut off.

Alex stares at the plate. His heart pounds furiously in his chest, and his knees creak as he readjusts himself for a better view of the food. His belly aches so deeply it's hard to remember that CASEY IS DEAD.

He sways on his feet slightly, rocking.

The sandwich, just an arm's length away, beckons him. Thick slices of bread leak globs of dark red jam onto a bright white plate that seems almost phosphorescent. His stomach rumbles. It's all he can hear.

Alex shoots a dirty arm out of the darkness and swipes the sandwich, leaving the plate wobbling on the floor and crams the sandwich into his mouth. The bread is warm, heavenly, fresh. Sweet, sticky strawberry jam coats his eager tongue. He barely chews, can't take the time to savor, his stomach demands food.

And then it is gone. Eaten. And he is still famished.

Alex, squatting like a true Tarzan-child, grabs the plate and licks the crumbs and leftover jelly from it. It isn't enough, his stomach screams, he can't get enough.

"I made that just for you, Alex." Lot is speaking. It's supersonic. Her mouth is moving, her head is shaking, and it's so loud Alex thinks his eardrums will burst. He jerks his head to the side. *Try a little harder, Alex,* he thinks as he squints at her, stares at the words coming from her face.

"Don't be afraid. You won't be punished for what you did to the guard who shot Casey."

CASEY IS DEAD.

Alex's vision washes black, just for a second. He feels the bullet in Casey's head, the searing, unbearable pain, as if it hit his own. Hot tears threaten to corrode his eyes. He fights them, jerks his head to the side. *Try a little harder, Alex.*

Lot is still talking. *Casey,* he hears, *Casey.* The words slur together, a blaring, off-beat orchestra. It's too hard to focus as his stomach growls.

Alex stares at Lot, rocking slightly, not blinking. She stands and steps aside, leaving an opening. Alex ignores the pain in his screaming muscles. It's time to go. Lot holds up a hand. Her nails are clean, round, not ragged. Her hands are washed, soft, cared for.

Alex looks up at her, and she flashes her teeth. Her hand invites him to pass and he pushes by. Beyond the blaring candlelight, the corridors are dark, long, open mouths—unending black holes that lack the comfort of the tiny closet. His stomach growls again.

Lot approaches the hesitant boy and crouches next to him. He is scared, exhausted, and beat to dust. "Why don't I make you a nice hot dinner, with all the trimmings, just for tonight, and I'll help you on your way tomorrow."

Alex looks at her. *She has sandwiches.* Her hand extends. After what seems like eons, he slowly gives her his own small, grimy paw.

She stands, gathering up the empty plate as she does, then hand-in-hand they walk away from the closet, the thick abyss eventually swallowing everything, even the guttering light of Lot's candle.

***

Danny lies on his bed, unmoving, staring blankly at the ceiling, his mind lost in the yawning catacombs of deep thought. He doesn't know how long he's been lying here or even if he's fallen asleep. He traces his fingers along his wristwatch, not even noticing he's doing it. All he knows is the dark spinning of his mind, then suddenly, he is aware again.

A pang of guilt shoots through his core. What did he think he was doing anyway? He wishes he could rewind, wishes he never brought Casey here. He wants to stop thinking, wants to move, wants to do something.

The watch ticks, its seconds going by too slowly. On its side is a small knob that winds it, but he always forgets. The watch was his father's, and his grandfather's before him, and he presumes, his great-grandfather's. The waning noise makes the night's events even more unbearable.

Danny thinks back to when he was a few years younger than Alex. He was only seven then, at his father's funeral. With the watch hidden in his pocket, he sat alone in the front pew, where he could see his reflection in the shiny black veneer of the coffin. Next to it stood Lot, preaching to the small congregation. No one came to comfort him as he mourned quietly, tears streaming down his face.

He remembers feeling each tick of the watch as the long hand swung around the dial, the space between each second causing his heart to seize up. He was deathly afraid the uneven beat would stop, that the watch would die. All it really needed was to be rewound, but in his grief-stricken state, it felt like a living thing with a pulse, as though the watch were his father, and if the watch died, his father was really gone, for good.

Danny could think only of the watch as Lot preached to the congregation. She used to be more "fire-and-brimstone" then, and less "rebuild in our vision." The eulogy was mostly about the wicked world and had little to do with Danny's father. How could it? She had barely known the man. The end would come soon, she said. Soon was relative, but she was right.

There were fewer people following her in the beginning. Just a handful, about fifteen, including himself—if a seven-year-old counted. Now, she has over one hundred followers.

Back then people came to her because they thought she was a prophet, some still do, but these days most come for protection.

Since The Plague, and the sudden influx of a secular populace, Lot has toned down much of the sacerdotal side of things, but that doesn't stop people from fervently asking "how high" before she can even say "jump." Besides, she falls back on the religious mumbo jumbo when it suits her.

Technically, Danny isn't even allowed to have this watch, but somehow, he was able to keep from Lot over the years. When his father joined her, he was supposed to give all his worldly possessions to the "cause." He sold the house, the car, even the furniture. Every stock, every bond, every disability check was absorbed by Lot's influence. Every little boy left orphaned by a desperate father.

With a huge breath, Danny sits up and rubs his face with his hands. They're stained with dried, flaking blood, and his clothes are dirty and wrinkled. He pushes himself to the side of the bed and reaches under his mattress to pull out a creased, worn picture.

The picture is of Danny; he's about six years old in it. Next to him is a tall, fit-looking man with a cane. Father and son smile and wave at the camera, standing in front of the entrance to Disneyland, not a worry in the world.

Danny closes his eyes and breathes deeply, trying to steady himself. He stands, needing to get out of the room, needing to move, needing to escape the torrent of emotions that threaten to carry him away.

***

An overhead lamp brightly lights the bathroom where Alex sits on a closed toilet, wrapped in a white hotel towel. The boy has been scrubbed thoroughly; there's no more dirt on his face and no trace of old tears. For once, he looks like any other little boy, save for being on the extremely skinny side.

Lot brushes his freshly trimmed hair. The child, completely uninterested in grooming, is endlessly fascinated with turning the handle of the sink faucet, although nothing comes out of the tap. He lets his fingers touch the dirty water held in the sink basin, then goes back to turning.

Since Lot brought the boy to her room, he has shown a total lack of interest in anything remotely human. He wolfed down his supper without a hint of appreciation and was then content to explore her bookshelves without acknowledging another person was present. He had spent a good amount of time looking at a picture book upside down, but when Lot corrected the way he held it, he tossed the book on the floor as though it had become uninteresting.

Alex is easily distracted and unconcerned with anyone else. It made it difficult to get him cleaned up. He continuously finds inconsequential things appealing, like the tap he now turns on and off. He demonstrates little-to-no recognition in Lot's direction, making her feel like a ghost. Was this how it was for Casey? Being an automaton caring for a child operating in his own world? No, Lot saw Alex listen to her, pay attention to her. In his own way, he had a connection with her. Maybe this is how it was at first, but Casey found a way to break through to him. Lot's sure this child would have followed her into the fire.

She watches him play with the faucet. After what he's been through, he'll need his world to be reset, to be stabilized. It will only take a few right moves to slide into Casey's void. "Alex, now that dinner has settled, what do you think about having some dessert?"

Alex continues to play with the faucet, ignoring Lot. She places her hand gently on his, stopping the incessant squeak. For the first time in over an hour, the child looks at her, his bright blue eyes firing up. They take her breath away. He's annoyed, but it's something. She smiles. He stares.

Lot guides the towel-clad child from the bathroom into the

bedroom. The bleached white of the fabric stands out against his fresh pink skin. So clean, so pure. She reaches out to touch his golden hair; it's soft and beautiful. Her heart swells.

Alex fiddles with a small ring of keys that sits on a side table, as Lot crouches down to reach under her bed. "As luck would have it, I have something special for desert, just for us." Lot feels around under her bed. Her fingers graze a polished wooden box pushed far in back. She fishes it out.

Kneeling on the floor, she wipes off a thin layer of dust. Suddenly, Alex's attention is caught, and he leaves the keys to race to Lot's side. With the politeness of a rhino, he tries to rip the box from her hands. She gently blocks him, motions for him to sit. He kneels on the floor beside her, riveted by the box, his towel forming a huge terrycloth pool around him.

"I need you to promise me that if I share this with you, you'll never tell anyone about it. Can you promise me that?"

Alex's eyes flick briefly toward Lot's face, he doesn't quite make eye contact, and then they're on the box again. Lot lifts the lid slightly, teasingly, just enough to show off a gleaming, maple-leaf shaped glass bottle, full of pure maple syrup. Alex reaches for it, but Lot snaps the box firmly shut. "Alex—Alex, look at me."

Alex continues to be fixated on the box. Lot carefully lowers it to the floor and takes Alex's face in both hands. A small fire kindles under her skin. She gazes into icy blue eyes, but they remain glued to the box. "Before I can open this I need to know you understand me; otherwise, I can't share this with you."

With great effort, the boy rips his eyes away from the box. Instantly, his attention is diverted, the box seemingly forgotten. He reaches up his hand and touches the blue spiral triangle that hangs at Lot's throat. He traces a finger along the lines. Lot draws his face up to look at hers, her gray eyes shining. "Do you know what this is? It is the *very last* bottle of maple syrup. It's far too dangerous outside to collect the sap to make it, so there will be no more after this. You can't tell anyone about it. You saw what happened to Casey when she was only trying to help…"

Alex flinches. He pulls his face from her hands and tears well in his eyes. It's as though Lot threatened to hit him. She takes his hand. "Imagine what would happen to me, and to you, if anyone else found out I had this, or that I shared it with you. You don't want to be responsible for that, do you? You don't want me to be hurt like Casey. Killed like Casey?"

Each time Lot mentions Casey's name, Alex jolts. A fat tear rolls from one of his eyes. Lot wipes it away from his soft cheek, and he crawls onto her lap, his towel falling away. Her pulse quickens as he curls there, a newborn babe. She strokes his hair comfortingly.

"It's okay to be scared. Casey protected you—" Alex jolts in her lap, "—looked after you, kept you safe. I can do the same for you, if you stay here with me."

Lot wipes more tears away from the child's face, then lifts the box and opens it for him to see inside once more. He timidly reaches out and touches the bottle.

"Remember, this has to be our secret, Alex. Casey would want it that way."

With Alex still cradled in her lap, Lot removes the maple syrup and unscrews the cap. She dramatically smells the syrup inside as though it were a fine wine.

"Oh, no! Oh, darn!" Her words are sharp and dramatic. Alex looks up, concerned.

"I don't have any spoons in here. Now, what are we going to do?"

It's surprising how quickly the boy responds. For a child that, for the most part, seems as thick as two short planks, he sure smartens up when it comes to getting something he wants.

Alex grabs the maple syrup and tips it upside down over his open mouth.

"No!" Lot snags the bottle back just before the thick liquid blobs out the neck. "That will make such a mess!" She pauses to think hard, her actions overstated and theatrical for the benefit of the boy. Suddenly, a great new idea dawns on her. "I've got it!"

Lot holds out her hand and tips a small amount of syrup out into it then neatly licks the syrup from her cupped palm. Alex immediately holds out his hand. Lot tips the bottle over his tiny palm, but just before the contents can escape, she rights it. The boy is crestfallen.

"I just got you all cleaned up and this is very, very sticky. I have a better idea."

Lot pours a small amount into her palm then holds her hand up to Alex. Alex hesitates, unsure of what to do. Lot smiles kindly. "Go ahead. You'll like it."

Reassured, Alex grabs Lot's hand. Still sitting on her lap, in the nude, he licks the syrup from her palm. A delicate shiver traces Lot's body. "That's a good boy. Remember, this has to be our secret." She smiles to herself, her malevolent grin lost on the child before her.

9

Calm takes hold of Opie as he steps into The Library. Although just a boardroom called "The Library," because this is where books are stored, it's still a place of rest. Before everything changed, he often enjoyed afternoons in the museum. It was one of the few things he took true pleasure in. The quiet hum of people coming and going and the company of ancient art helped him to think.

The Library is the closest thing Opie has now to a museum. And why not? The books—quantum physics 101, money market investment strategies, celebrity memoirs, government conspiracy theories—are now but artifacts. Their aging pages will eventually turn to dust and take with them the memories of starlets and Wall Street.

Opie lowers himself onto the cushions of a well-worn chair. It may look a little battered, but it's comfortable and he's been looking forward to this moment. He can already feel tonight's events sliding away from him, and he closes his eyes, trying to imagine Odette's supple rump. He always liked a woman with a little meat on her bones.

The hinges of the door creak, and he begrudgingly opens his eyes. Odette's blissful rear end is replaced with Danny's blood-specked face. It's been hours since the commotion in the lobby, and he still hasn't cleaned himself up. Opie ticks his tongue in irritation. Here is the source of half of his daily stress staring him in the face.

"Why haven't you cleaned yourself up, Danny?"

Danny shrugs his shoulders. Opie pushes his chair back and

stands; he hates it when Danny hovers over him like a giant gorilla. Danny steps back as he unfolds. Opie's just shy of Danny's height, but wiry. He rubs his face absently with one hand, scratching the light dusting of stubble that has sprung to his cheeks, and braces for the hurricane.

Danny paces. "Did you see what happened tonight?"

"Not with my own eyes, but I know what happened."

"And?"

"And what, Danny, what are you looking for?"

"I'm not looking for anything. I just—"

Opie holds up his hand. "Listen to me. It's best to just forget about everything. Clean yourself up, get some rest, and forget about it."

"Yes—I—but—"

"But nothing. You've no one else to blame for tonight but yourself."

"But, Lot—"

Opie curtly holds up his hand again. "Stop. It wasn't Lot. It was you. You brought that woman here. You let her get herself bitten. You're responsible. It's that simple."

Danny's face crumples. Lines of guilt stretch around his eyes, aging him instantly. It's easy to do, old habit. Opie has been reeling in Danny for Lot for many years. A spark smolders in the pit of his stomach, and he shifts his weight uncomfortably.

Danny runs a blood-caked hand through his hair, leaving strands standing on end. Opie shakes his head in disapproval. He wishes he didn't have to deal with this… situation.

He takes Danny by the arm and guides him from the room.

"You're a mess, a terrible example for others in the community. Go take care of yourself, and get yourself under control. This is unacceptable."

Finally, Danny slinks away into the darkness, and Opie breathes a sigh of relief when he's gone.

***

It's been years since Lot and Danny shared a room, shared a bed, shared a life—but the memories are still painfully vibrant. To say he's scared would be to imply the wounds have healed. Instead, they lay open and festering, necrosis eating more deeply into his heart and soul every day.

Early on, Danny somehow managed to build a thick wall around himself. The wall protected his mind from the nightly demands his body knew and hindered the view of his dark reality, twisting it into something more palatable. It protected him as many a blind eye looked his direction, and it protected him as power-hungry monsters facilitated the obscene. The wall was the only thing that allowed him to survive.

Now, it's crumbling.

Danny's lantern illuminates Hannah's face.

After his talk with Opie, he wandered the hallways until he found himself here. They stand in a boardroom turned infirmary-morgue. Faux-wood panel tables are pushed against the wall. Once they sat business people for meetings and held rows of sparkling champagne glasses for weddings. Now they're burdened by two shrouded bodies. Basins of water, strips of cloth, and homemade rope lay to the side; they are the meager supplies of the defense lawyer-turned-undertaker.

Hannah always liked Danny. They've known each other since she and her son, Jamal, took refuge under Lot's merciful wing. They were in bad shape when Lot saved their lives, both ill from drinking contaminated water. Hannah had sat on the side of the road, sweating and green. They were out of gas, food, everything, and they were as sick as dogs.

The open flaps of the winter coat Hannah wore swayed with the chilly breeze. She had pulled it from a child's body a few weeks previous. It was too small, her shoulders stressed the seams, but it was protection against the harsh winter soon to come.

Jamal crouched on the ground next to her, shaking. Vomit speckled his layered sweaters. Hannah knew they should have boiled the water before they drank it, but everything was still soaking wet from the pissing autumn downpours and they had needed water desperately. They hadn't had a drop to drink since the rain took a break almost two days before. Now, it looked like they would still die of dehydration. Her bowels cramped, and she clutched her stomach.

Hannah heard the vehicles before she saw them. This road was a busy one, and they'd seen five cars in the past day; this would make six. She desperately tried to wave all of them down, but not one so much as slowed.

Three old-as-dirt pickups, easy to fix and easy to keep running, rounded the bend, not a computerized part in sight. She expected them to blast on by just like everyone else had, but she waved her arm at them anyway.

When the convoy of trucks pulled over, Hannah finally dared to hope. A petite woman swung open the driver's side of the lead truck. She wore jeans and a red flannel shirt, and her gray hair fell in loose curls around her thin face. She seemed comically tiny, much too frail to command a pickup, yet her flat-soled, black leather boots hit the ground agilely as she jumped down from the cab.

It was hard to stand. Hannah had thought she might need to pop a squat any second and she sure as hell wasn't going into the woods where those—things—were. Forget about modesty, it was bad enough trying to stay safe on the open road, let alone when you had your pants around your ankles.

The pixie-like woman floated toward her, guns cocking from the convoy behind her serenaded each step. Hannah nervously awaited her approach as she helped Jamal to his feet. "Thank you for stopping," she said.

The woman halted about ten feet away, wisely cautious of people she didn't know. "Are you in need of assistance?"

It was one of the happiest days of Hannah's life. She would be forever grateful for the amazing kindness Lot performed that day and she soon came to realize it was par for the course for her hero. It seemed every single person Hannah knew had a wonderful story about how Lot saved them, body or soul. The small woman that stood before her that day was a true savior.

That had been at the very start of the community. There were only about fifteen people then, in the huge empty hotel, but Lot had a vision: to create a paradise where everyone would work for the common good and live in safety and security.

They grew quickly in those first months. Every mission out of the hotel for supplies brought back more survivors, but the winter had been cruel. Hannah remembers the talk of revolt as food rations became meager. Soon, discontent began to swirl about the woman who controlled their flow. There was fighting, and plotting, and turmoil. Snow fell, and the supplies dwindled as the cold and uncertainty ate away at everyone.

Lot caught the first person that tried to steal red-handed. He tried to deny it, but Hannah knew he was guilty. He had been one of Lot's biggest naysayers for quite some time. They voted. Exile. He was put out, snow up to his thighs, wind tugging his beard. He begged, but no one wanted a thief, a food thief, in their midst. It was hard, but it had to be done.

Over the course of the winter, quite a few people jumped ship. They would disappear during the dead of night when no one would hear them pilfering supplies. It was sad to know how many selfish people this world had created, but there was always a little relief when there was one less mouth to feed. It meant a few more spoonfuls of rice and beans for everyone else.

Jamal had been a district manager at a nationwide coffee shop prior to The End. Worrying about sales projections for his stores didn't exactly prepare him for the apocalypse. On the other hand, it felt like Danny was meant for catastrophe; he seemed to thrive in it.

Over the course of that winter, Hannah insisted Danny train Jamal. He was still only a teen then, seven years younger than her own son, but to her, Danny always seemed older. He trained Jamal to defend himself, to survive, and although her son complained often about Danny, Hannah never once worried. His gruff nature and short temper didn't bother her. It was because he was hard on Jamal, and countless others like him, that they could now fend for themselves.

Of course, in a cloistered community like this, rumors spread like wildfire, especially when people are rubbed the wrong way. The current erratic look in Danny's eyes makes Hannah wonder if the whispers about him are true. Not until this moment had she ever considered giving them credence.

She has to admit Danny's relationship with Lot is a strange one. He may be her adopted son, but he has an odd intimacy with her that raises eyebrows. It's even stranger that she simultaneously has him on a pedestal and treads on him like a doormat. Hannah always chalked it up to normal, dysfunctional family dynamics, but rumors still persist.

Hannah had heard that, before everything changed, when Danny was about fifteen years old he tried to rape Lot. The story goes that one night he just went crazy and snapped. Lot, being the kind person she is, just couldn't bring herself to get the police involved, but things were never the same.

Hannah always felt the story was unlikely, that it was just one of those insidious rumors bored people spread, but now she wonders if she's being naive.

"Like a dangerous dog..." Danny mumbles under his breath.

"What?"

"Nothing." He responds, barely noticing her. "There was a woman brought in here, not one of our people."

Hannah extends a finger to point at one of the bodies. Danny puts his hand on the woman's shrouded head. Misery leaks from his face, encompassing his entire frame and he closes his eyes, grips the table to steady himself.

Hannah watches, feeling sorry for him, and counts herself as one stupid old bat. How could she doubt this young man for even a second? He saved Jamal's life numerous times over the course of their countless missions together, and it's obvious he's now in pain. She scolds herself for allowing gossip to color her worldview.

She steps closer to Danny and places a comforting hand on his arm. He tenses, flicking open his eyes, and she nearly jumps out of her skin. She may or may not believe the rumors she's heard, but she can certainly tell a wild tiger when she sees one.

"Did you know her?" A soothing voice to calm the beast.

"Yes. No... not really."

"Sometimes we find that instant connection in life and, no matter how brief it was, we're lucky. Just because it was only for a moment doesn't mean it can't last a lifetime, and we should be grateful for what we had."

Danny's face remains dark and solemn. He nods acknowledgment. "Have you heard anything about the boy that came in with this woman?"

"I heard Lot found him; he's safe now."

Danny's brow furrows, and Hannah wonders if she senses jealousy.

***

Danny is so far outside his comfort zone he thinks his skin may slough off and drop to the floor like one of the creepers outside. He feels like he's drunk about ten cups of strong coffee with a straw and he can't hold still. He paces in the hallway, trying both to work up his nerve and calm himself down.

He raises a hand to knock on the door, *her* door. His entire arm trembles. Maybe it would be better to leave. This is none of his business; there are worse things that can happen in life, especially this life. His stomach is in knots, then suddenly he is rapping his knuckles on the wood. His heart jumps into his throat, twisting around and turning inside out. Time seems to span a century, and then finally, the door opens, revealing a surprised Lot.

She frowns and crosses her arms. Danny is nearly buried by her displeasure and he fidgets like a schoolboy, can't look her in the eye. So much for grand confrontations. "I need to talk to you." The words blurt from his mouth as he looks at the ground. Lot has a way of making him feel like a helpless child in a matter of seconds. She doesn't even need to speak.

"I'm sure it can wait until tomorrow." Lot pushes on the door, but Danny blocks it with his foot. She clicks her tongue and sighs, vexed. He cringes guiltily, as the breath escapes her lips and mumbles something at the floor while rubbing his arm nervously.

"Speak up, Daniel. I haven't got all night."

"Why did you have Casey shot?"

"That woman who followed you home?"

A tide of anger rises, emboldening Danny. He looks up, his eyes burning with rage. "She wasn't a stray cat! Why did you have her shot?"

"She was bitten."

Danny puts his hand on the door and shoves his way into Lot's bedroom. He stares angrily into her light gray eyes as she rolls them. Even through his anger, the gesture hurts. Poking her head into the hall, she peers down the corridor both ways and then shuts the door. Danny glances over at the sleeping child under the covers of Lot's bed. Lot whispers crossly at him. "I had to make a decision. It was the right one, whether you like it or not."

"No, it wasn't."

"You've made the same decision many times yourself. In fact, if I recall correctly, you shot Lawrence without a second thought. Did anyone question you? Did *I* question you?"

"She wasn't bitten, Lot!"

"So says you, but I saw what I saw."

"Since when is my word not good enough for you?"

Lot pauses, keeping her eyes steadily locked on him. They push on his resolve like lead weights and he squirms. "Danny, listen, I'm sorry if you had a connection with this woman but how could I risk—"

"How did my father die?"

"What? Danny, what's wrong with you tonight?"

"Tell me!" he yells.

Lot looks over her shoulder at Alex. His eyes are open, watching everything. She presses her lips tightly together and shifts her attention back to Danny.

"Your father had ALS. It was tragic. I promised him before he passed I would care for you as though you were my own son, you know this. You haven't spoken about him in years, now, tell me what this is all about."

Danny grinds his teeth. Memories of his father scorch him. *She's a liar!* "You took away his wheelchair! You took everything away from him, including his son! You wouldn't let me see him! You locked him away and let him die, alone!"

Lot's face lights up as though she suddenly understands. "Danny, come here, sit." She motions to a chair next to her, but he ignores her request. "We can talk about this. I can see the death of this boy's guardian is weighing heavily on you. It's bringing up memories and emotions from when you lost your father, things you've never dealt with."

Danny looms over her, arms crossed and a scowl on his face. He's not buying it.

"Your father could no longer use his wheelchair and we, together—him and I, *we* thought it best to spare you the indignities of his final days. He didn't want his little boy to watch him slowly suffocate to death."

"Really? Is that *really* what happened? Why would my father trust you to raise me? We only knew you for a few months!"

"Danny—"

"Do you plan to raise the boy? Just like you did me? Is that what you'll do? *Exactly,* like me?"

"Please Danny, you're obviously over-tired and emotional. When is the last time you slept? Or washed up? You're a mess." Lot flicks her wrist at him. It's something she's always done, as long as he can remember, a gesture he's seen so many times before it's almost comforting.

One moment in particular grabs at Danny just now: when she brought him to Paris for his tenth birthday. He wanted to know if he dropped a penny from the Eiffel Tower if it would really slice through someone's head. They sat in a classy French bistro, eating cheese like every good tourist, and she flicked her wrist at him, closing the subject.

He remembers it so well because right after, she let him drink wine for the first time. It was sweet and warmed his stomach. She allowed him to have a glass then, and a few back in the hotel room, as a birthday present. He'd enjoyed his evening with her that night, very much.

Danny's cheeks burn, and he feels dirty. "How could I be so naive? I can't believe I never saw it before! How could I be so dumb? It's so obvious, everything you did to me—"

Lot slaps him across the face, her fingers matching the slap from Casey's earlier. He didn't even see her stand and it shocks him, stems the tide of anger. She's never struck him before, not once.

"Stop it. You stop it right now! I don't know what you're accusing me of, but I won't have it. I only ever did what was good for you! I did what *you* wanted and I loved you. I cared for you when no one else would. When no one else wanted your pathetic self, *I* protected you from the world! Even when The Plague descended upon us, I made sure you were untouched and safe.

"I've risked everything for you, done everything for you, given you everything a boy could possibly need; could possibly want—and this is how you repay me? By coming in here like a crazed lunatic in the middle of the night? Jealous of a child? Shame on you! It's horrifying how delusional you are! How you twist things for attention! All I ever did was love you, and you throw that back in my face, you ungrateful brat."

The venom spilling from Lot stings more than the slap. It's enough to quash every morsel of rebellion Danny had been fostering. Is it true? Had Lot only done what he wanted? Because she loved him so much? Is he really just jealous? Twisting things? Wasn't it him that wanted her affection? Hadn't he begged for it so many times after she turned him away. Wouldn't he gladly accept her affection now, in any form? Isn't that really what he wants?

Danny staggers back, ashamed, humiliated, he thinks he might vomit. He is disgusted with himself. His world spins as he stands dumbly in the middle of Lot's bedroom staring down at his feet, paralyzed, once again a browbeaten and powerless child.

"I—I'm sorry," he doesn't know what else to say.

Lot stalks across the room and tears open the door. She points crisply into the hallway. "Get out."

Lot slams the door behind him and locks it. Once he's gone, she leans against it and closes her eyes for a moment. Her jaw locks hard as she thinks about the brazen intrusion. She's no stranger to conflict, but this is new territory. After a few moments, she opens her eyes and breathes. Well, she thinks, the beast has successfully been forced back into his cage, for now.

Lot turns away from the door. In her bed lies Alex, perfectly still, his eyes wide and alert. Lot hopes she's right, that he understands very little of what's happening around him.

"Close your eyes, honey," she soothes Alex. Things will be different with this one; she'll make sure of it. "Go back to sleep."

**

The solemn rite of funeral begins. It's one of those things that has taken on an even more sacred meaning as the world crumbles. So many people never have the chance to say goodbye to their loved ones. So many people never have closure; never know if their family and friends have survived. So many parents see a child for the last time as that child lumbers forward dangerously, like a deranged dancing bear, spreading disease forth with every step.

It doesn't matter to anyone that lighting a funeral pyre will draw monstrosities from the unforgiving depths of the forest beyond. That ghastly, ulcerated bodies will drag themselves across the field in search of flesh to consume. All that matters is that those who have passed will receive their last rights, that they will be honored, remembered, and that their bodies are gone, never to join the ranks of The Risen. It's a duty and a privilege to attend such an event.

Reverence, however, does not pull the wool over the eyes of

those left behind. A hardness has built up around the hearts of those still living, a realism. Regardless of ritual, the protection of the community comes first and foremost.

Heavily armed guards surround a rickety cart being drawn toward the exit. Two bodies wrapped in death shrouds adorn it. No chances will be taken today. Although each body has a head wound, one can never be too careful. If a kill shot is slightly off, there is the slim possibility a corpse could reanimate. Precautions are always taken.

The cart is pushed through the small door at the front of the hotel. Grim faces squint against the blinding light of day. It's still early, not quite noon yet, but the sun is unrelenting. The armed convoy makes its way to the pyre, built a good distance from the hotel. It will burn for hours while the community watches from inside.

Lot understands just how much the people love their ritual.

More armed guards wait at the pyre, supervised by the ever-present Opie. He's Lot's eyes and ears at all times. They've been building since dawn, and although there are many watchful eyes, nervous looks are still tossed toward the forest from time to time. Most of the creatures from the previous night's terrors have been destroyed, but this is still dangerous work. It's never possible to tell when, or how many, will show up.

Some days, it seems as though killing one of The Risen only creates two more; like the heads of the Hydra, they just keep sprouting. Other days it feels like The Plague is lulling. For a long time, out here in the backwoods it had been safe, less of The Risen were around. Now, the population seems to be growing, as though they've reached a tipping point and will soon consume the earth itself.

The cart stops before the pyre and the practiced ritual of protection begins. Those with weapons stand guard, forming a circle around those who heave bodies under the baking sun. Pitchforks, knives, bows and arrows, all face outward, ready to take on any intruder. Danny scans the field with the muzzle of his rifle, but his mind is elsewhere.

Lost in his own morose thoughts, a tap to the shoulder jolts him from his reverie. He turns his heavy gaze, and it comes to rest on Opie's pinched face and beady eyes. Opie draws Danny's attention to a form slowly crossing the field. A group of noisy crows circle above it, attracted by the cadaverous smell, but spooked by the semi-life that miraculously keeps its grip. A few guards murmur concern. "More will follow."

A large-nosed man that stands next to Danny wipes trickles of sweat from his brow. "It's possible it doesn't even notice us."

Danny wrinkles his face. "Unlikely." He thrusts his gun toward Opie, motioning to trade it for Opie's well-sharpened machete. Opie takes the gun from him, but he's reluctant to hand over the knife. Danny snaps his fingers impatiently.

Opie raises his eyebrows. Rudeness toward him is a new thing. It doesn't matter though; it won't have time to mature. Early that morning, he sat down with Lot. She was on edge, something even Opie rarely sees. "It's time for Danny to go," she told him. "Silently and without fuss." Questions will be asked, but they can't afford to keep him around anymore.

Opie was surprised. He can't count how many times he advised Lot be finished with Danny, but she was stubborn. She felt she could control him, and seemed to enjoy the challenge of doing so. She was like a puppeteer with a marionette, but now it appears she is no longer enjoying the show.

He isn't sure exactly what brought on this sudden change of heart, and he knew enough not to ask, but he has a feeling it has something to do with the boy, Alex. It will be difficult to make Danny disappear, it needs to be handled delicately, but his marching orders were well received.

He should be relieved, happy their dysfunctional cycle will soon be at an end. The damaged man-child before him will no longer be Opie's problem and that should have put a smile on his face. Instead, guilt's gnawing teeth bite ever sharper. After tonight, he will no longer be able to tell himself things have worked out for the best for this particular blond hair blue eyed boy, and Opie isn't sure he can shoulder the same burden twice.

He's no longer a young man. Perhaps, he thinks, a time will come where he doesn't have to clean up other people's messes.

He hands his machete to Danny. At least he doesn't have a gun anymore, Opie thinks.

The grotesque figure staggers across the field. It's slow and labors to move, but it has a definite sense of purpose. Danny strides away from the pyre. Behind him, one of the guards scrunches his face in annoyance. The creature lumbers forward, a teenage boy, or girl, probably, but who really knows? Grey, mildewed skin clings desperately to muscle. One arm is missing, the end of its shiny clavicle protrudes out as though picked clean by the circling murder overhead.

The corpse hasn't a shred of clothing; the chest is an open wound, and its rotted entrails drag in the dirt, tangled with sticks and other brush. It probably ate until it burst, just like all the rest. Lips, hair, and nose have been lost, but the eyes still remain, lidless and bulging, corneal rips bleeding black, congealed ooze. It sees Danny.

He stops, knife dangling at his side; the corpse is about ten feet away. He waits as it pulls its rot-ridden limbs through the knee-high grass, grinding the remains of its menacing teeth. *Is this all that's left?* People like him, and Lot, and that mute kid, and this—*thing?* The entire world has gone to shit. What is everyone fighting so hard for when it's obvious God despises his own children?

SIX FEET.

FIVE FEET.

Danny stands tiredly, feeling as though he's been alive for centuries. He thought he wanted a battle, a release for his anger, but now melancholy rolls over him like an unrelenting tidal bore. After last night's failed confrontation, he spent another night staring at the ceiling blankly until someone came to fetch him.

He joined the pyre building late, and no one said a word, afraid of being dressed down by his, often cruel, temper. He took his place in the guard line, still wearing his wrinkled, bloodstained clothes from yesterday, Casey's blood. He's sure Opie will have something to say about that later.

Danny doesn't even know why he cares if that Casey chick died. He barely knew her. He's lost count of the number of people who have died around him, why is she any different? Why can't he just continue on like he had before he met her? And, what does it matter what Lot wants to do with that stupid kid, at least he's not out here.

FOUR FEET.

THREE FEET.

TWO.

The creature reaches up its remaining, almost skeletal arm. It opens its maw, its tongue chewed and gone long ago. Its face is so close Danny can count its ruined teeth.

ONE.

It grasps Danny's arm with its fingers and leans in for the kill.

SLICE!

Danny hacks the thing's neck with the machete. His blade unexpectedly lodges in the vertebrae, leaving the creature to writhe at the end of the long knife, trying desperately to find purchase for its greedy teeth.

Danny almost loses his grip on the machete's handle as he pulls it away from the reeking flesh. He steps back wildly, just in time. The corpse's jaws wisp by as it lurches forward hungrily. Danny swings his knife. This time the head easily separates from the body, toppling backward. The body collapses, still twitching as its head hits the ground and bounces once. Its jaws gnash and its lidless eyes roll wildly. What's left of its neck wags like some sort of putrid prehensile tail.

Danny holds the head steady with his boot and slowly pushes the tip of his machete into the creature's eye. The blade pierces pupil and slides through brain. Black ooze covers it as he drags it back out of the rotten face. Sweating in the oppressive heat, Danny turns to face the funeral pyre. People still work at loading the bodies. Opie is walking sternly toward him, clearly unimpressed with Danny, as always.

Opie sees it now, what Lot spoke of, Danny is unhinged. While it's easy to chalk this up to the cocky and aggressive, loner behavior Danny is well known for, he's also known for never taking unnecessary risks. It's one of the reasons he always comes back, no matter how dangerous a mission Lot selects him for.

He'd always hoped Danny would just turn out all right and Lot would forget about him. Now it's obvious that's never going to happen. Somewhere deep inside, the irritating nip of guilt bares its needle teeth yet again as he storms up to Danny. If Opie doesn't do something about this behavior, people will be angry, and angry people ask questions.

The only blessing is that shows like this one will make explaining Danny's sudden disappearance a lot easier—Danny always needed to show off, ran off without backup. You just never know how these things will react. You might think one is slow and find out it was an Olympic runner in a past life, or that it has seventeen friends crawling around at its feet. Dumb kid got himself killed, tragedy really.

Opie finally reaches Danny. "What the hell are you doing? Do you think you're funny playing around like that?"

Danny lazily swings the large knife. He toes the dead creature's skull with his boot and then smiles charmingly. "How long have you known Lot?"

"I hope to God you're not bitten, you idiot." Sold to the right people, a strong, healthy male like Danny will earn quite a bit. Opie knows Lot expects Danny dead, but the dime-sized weak spot he has for the boy thinks he deserves better than a mound of dirt. Danny is resourceful, and Opie is sure in time he can forge a new life for himself, assuming he isn't labored to death before he has the chance. Of course, there will be no chance, and no profit, if Danny gets himself killed beforehand.

Danny continues to smile pleasantly, his fatigued eyes crinkling with humor.

Great, he's totally off his rocker.

Without warning, Danny's smile drops away, leaving behind the true stone façade beneath. Opie finds the point of the ooze-blackened blade pointed suddenly at his throat. Instantaneously, members of the pyre group begin running toward the couple, weapons raised.

"Do you think if I were to scratch you with this blade I just sunk into the brain of one of those creatures, you would be infected?" Danny asks.

Opie swallows nervously. He's afraid to move, to even step back, because Danny might snap and kindly remove his head, as he did the dead thing on the ground. "What do you want?"

"I'm just curious to know what you know."

"What do I know?"

"How did my father die?"

Opie's mouth drops open, he can't hide his surprise. This isn't the question of a man who's lost his mind; it's the concern of a man finally lucid after years of floating in the abyss. The situation is more dangerous than he originally thought.

Opie holds up one hand apprehensively, staying those running to help. He's more worried about what they might hear than what Danny might do.

"Danny, you should speak with Lot."

"I want to speak to you."

"I don't know."

"You know something. You've been her closest advisor for years. You helped her run The Center before The Plague. You're the only person besides Lot in this entire place that knew my father!"

Danny presses the tip of the knife harder against Opie's throat. Opie is sure it will break the skin any second. "Danny, I swear I don't know how your father died."

Danny scowls. He's not hearing what he wants to hear. Opie stammers nervously.

"All I know is Lot gets what she wants."

"And what did she want, Opie?"

Anxious spittle gathers on Opie's lips as his mouth runs dry. It's hard for him to form an answer, but he pushes one out. "You."

The glistening of well-hidden tears shine behind Danny's blue eyes for just a moment, and then they're gone. He drops the knife away from Opie's throat and flips it over, his fingers sliding through the black ooze coating the blade. He hands the machete, handle first, to Opie.

Opie's hand shakes as the knife comes safely back into his possession. Blood pumps so powerfully through his veins it feels as though they might explode. He barely hears the words as they pass his lips, but Danny's icy glare tells him they've found purchase. It's the guilt speaking.

"I'm sorry."

Danny slaps his hand on Opie's chest and wipes it across the weasel's shirt, leaving a black trail of oozy brain matter. He storms away, toward the concerned group surrounding the pyre, awaiting Opie's signal to pounce.

Sheep.

The signal never comes, and Danny rejoins the group to finish their grim task. He can practically hear their thoughts rattling around in their empty heads, their judgmental eyes crawling over him. In their desperate need to feel as though society still has a chance, they kiss the feet of a monster even greater than those they face outside.

10

Disinfecting rays of sunlight pierce the smoky air. The lobby's fireplaces and oil lamps add to the sweltering heat. Their toxic vapors spew toward the heavens, only to be captured by thick wooden walls and heavy ceilings.

The entire community has come together in mourning. Some hang on each other crying; most stand stoically, watching. A window at the front has its barricades pulled back. Thick bars and chicken wire line the opening, providing peace of mind against the growing horde outside.

Most of the creatures that drag themselves across the field are slow, shambling messes. They are a confusion of missing limbs and rotten meat, each one individually able to be outrun, but like fire ants, they are deadly as a swarm. The viewing window will soon need to be closed as The Risen realize a buffet awaits inside, just beyond their reach.

Flames from the funeral pyre arc skyward. They have so far only attracted a few of the loathsome ghouls, but it's just the start. The creatures don't notice as their weak flesh quickly carbonizes, incapable of registering pain. Guards stand to either side of the window with makeshift bayonets, waiting for when the thing's attentions turn.

Save for a few moans of grief, everyone is quiet.

Lot's eulogy is beautiful, moving, and as always, Danny thinks, self-serving. Every word out of her mouth is thoughtfully designed to increase her stranglehold on the hearts and minds of her subjects. It's almost unnecessary; this herd is domesticated, but he can't blame them—can he? It's only now, after years of servitude, that he's beginning to break free of the mold she poured him into. Can he expect more from others than he does of himself?

Lot sits in the front, surrounded by her most loyal and adoring devotees. Standing next to her is Alex. He looks so different than when he came in. His hair is trimmed and he's as clean as a whistle, dressed in clothes that fit. Jeans, comfortable shoes, and a plain blue t-shirt. He's like a brand-new boy. Except for the ratty old black backpack he has his arms coiled around.

Lot's slender fingers slip gently through the child's blond mane. A powerful wave of disgust punches up the hairs on the back of Danny's neck. Although he can't see it, because someone blocks his view, he knows she also plays with her damn necklace.

As though Opie feels the deep brooding, he throws a watchful look over his shoulder from where he stands near Lot. Danny stands far in the back of the crowd. His arms are crossed tightly over his chest and dark bags hang under his eyes as he glowers, fixated on Lot.

It isn't long before The Risen gather at the pyre in earnest. Their guttural growls and inhuman noises break through the crackling of the flames. Soon after, the barricade is replaced, thwarting the comforting rays of the sun.

***

Funeral or no funeral, the maintenance of all weapons is needed to ensure everyone can be protected. Usually glad for the distraction from his thoughts, Danny now finds himself unable to concentrate on the work. He sits in the cordoned off part of the lobby known as The Armory. To his right is Penny, a horse-faced woman who's nice enough and next to her, the big-nosed guard from the funeral pyre, Dino.

A paralyzing anxiety crushes Danny. It holds his head under water, drowning him in a black lake of guilt. It's hard to breathe, his lungs just can't bring in enough air, and he feels like his shirt is strangling him. He wants to claw at his throat but can't move.

Every muscle is rigid, as heavy as a rock, and he sinks, struggling for air, falling to the bottom of the lake while Penny and Dino prattle on.

"I think I might volunteer for the run to Agatha County," muses Dino.

"Me too!" replies Penny. "But, I hear it's a two-day trip just to get there, minimum, and the last time the mission was attacked non-stop—and not just by The Risen, they ran into a group from Whitebridge."

"I'm going stir-crazy here. I need to get out, to do something, meet some new people, maybe some women?"

"Yeah, okay. I should have guessed."

"Oh, come on. It's really an altruistic gesture, you know, broadening the gene pool."

"Altruistic, my foot."

The pair giggle like schoolgirls.

"You should come too. I hear they've got a lot of single men."

"Nah, I've got my eye on you know who…if I can get Lot to approve…"

"All the more reason to get on her good side."

"We'll see." Penny glances over at Danny, who is staring grimly into space. He's a total mess, and has been wiping the gun in his hand in the same exact place for minutes on end.

"Are you cleaning that gun or making love to it?"

Dino wags a finger at Danny. "Yeah, man, at that rate we'll never be done. Maybe you should just go get some sleep, you know, and change your clothes?"

Danny slides his eyes over the large pile of weapons the other two have already cleaned. He feels like he's operating his body from a great distance, like some sort of rudimentary video game. His breath slowly returns to him.

"You alright, Dan?" Penny waves her hand attempting to get his attention.

Danny's eyes snap to meet hers. They are spiteful, full of choler.

"Why don't you mind your own fucking business?"

Penny and Dino stare at Danny a moment then break out laughing. Dino slaps his own knee jovially. Danny's the same old grouch he always is, and the two shrug at each other, then pick back up their idle chatter. Danny places the clean gun on the table before him and stands to grab another, his mind sinking back into the beckoning fog that surrounds the lake, until his eyes land on white ash.

Casey's bat.

It leans against the wall, forgotten amongst numerous other makeshift weapons.

Danny reverently lifts it, stares down at it. The logo, paint, and what he thinks might have been a signature have all but worn off. The bat is imbrued with blood, dried and brown, darkest at the tip of the barrel where the stain is the thickest. The hair that was once caught in the flaking, splintered wood has been cleaned away.

Something about the bat makes him feel as though Casey is standing right there with him. As though he's able to channel her by running his hands along the grain and her light guides him away from the dangerous banks of self-destruction. He strokes the cool, worn wood. If someone had asked him in that moment what he was thinking, he couldn't have said. It's almost as though he has no thought at all, just a reptilian brain driving him forward.

He clamps his hands around the neck of the bat and storms past his surprised companions.

***

Opie grins at Odette. He thought it would be nice to stop in and see her. She smiles back and brings her cleaver down, separating a chicken's plucked leg from the rest of its bare body. She winks at him and curls her finger, luring him close.

She whispers in his ear that she's ready to test her batch of homemade wine and wants to know if he'll be kind enough to join her tonight. Opie smiles, seeing an opportunity to bring things to the next level, but it'll need to be a late night. There are urgent matters to be attended to this evening.

After leaving Odette, he is walking on clouds. Even the troublesome task of dealing with Danny cannot sour his mood. He will meet with his two head guards and set them straight on the wolf in their midst. He chuckles, what is it Lot calls them behind their backs? Oh yes, Thick Marge and Arnold.

A quick bend of the ear and twist of the truth will be all he needs. After that, they'll be falling over themselves to help ensure Lot's safety. It always amazes Opie how easily people swallow lies.

He holds his candle up to illuminate the room before him as he steps through the door. Thick Marge and Arnold wait inside. They know this must be something important. Their boss only meets with them like this when big things are about to happen. Opie closes the door behind him. "Thanks for coming. We have a serious situation on our hands that must be dealt with tonight."

***

Danny pounds his fist on Lot's door. He can see her eye in the peephole and holds Casey's bat low, trying not to look menacing and play his hand too early. The door pops open, revealing Lot, annoyed and wearing nothing but a bathrobe. "What do you want now, Danny?"

Danny shoves the door in as hard as he can. Lot jumps out of the way as he blasts by her. Tunnel vision blocks out everything but Alex, the boy is curled up in a corner of the bed, naked, and gripping the sheet to himself.

Danny storms toward the bed, Casey's bat in one hand, the other stretched out to grab Alex. The child shrinks back against the wall in fear.

"What are you doing?" Lot yells.

"What are *you* doing? *That's* the real question."

Danny grabs at the frightened child. Alex tries to dodge him, but he's too fast. Danny pulls Alex out of the bed by his arm and snatches a neatly folded pile of clothing. He tosses it at the boy. "Put your clothes on, kid."

Lot stutters, and Danny feels a glimmer of happiness. She never expected this out of him, she thought she had him in his place, but she was wrong. Oh, so wrong. Seeing the shock in her eyes is momentarily exhilarating.

"Danny, you're making a big mistake."

Danny turns on Lot, veins bulging in his forehead. "My mistake was letting you live in my head for so long, letting you control me!" he yells. "I couldn't face it then, but now I can. I refuse to turn a blind eye and let you ruin this kid's life like you have mine!"

Lot takes a step toward Danny, her gray eyes countering him with a domineering stare. *How dare he.* Danny violently shoves her onto the bed behind them and she nearly bounces back off from the shear force. Alex watches everything silently, trembling, his head jerking slightly, arrhythmically, his clothes held limply in one hand. Danny looks over at the boy, his voice rising in urgency and frustration. "I said get dressed!" he booms.

Cajoled by fear, Alex stuffs himself into his clothing. Lot sees her opportunity to gain the upper hand quickly diminishing and steps away from the bed, her eyes on the boy. She stops short as Danny raises the bat. He has her cornered and a flicker of uncertainty creases her face. She can feel the cold tendrils of death sliding across her skin.

"You would never…"

Danny wrestles with himself. This woman, despite everything she has done, and will do, raised him. She made him breakfast every morning, taught him how to speak French, how to do long division, and even how to sew. She applied Band-Aids, soothed tears, and read bedtime stories. She also demanded his innocence and complete obedience in return.

Danny lines up the bat with Lot's head. He draws it back, ready to strike, and hesitates. The yoke Lot has strapped around his neck is tightening. A vulnerable flash of worry plays across on her lined face and the yoke squeezes, strangling him. His heart pounds furiously.

Lot reads his flaccid effort before he even knows it himself and seizes the opportunity. She goes for Alex.

It's that reptilian brain again. The brain that isn't caught up in emotion—set adrift in the past. The brain that is freed of the superego's stranglehold. He can't control it any more than a wolf can prevent itself from killing a sheep.

Danny swings the bat through the air with the full force of his muscles. At the last second, he curves the shot and connects with Lot's bicep instead of her head. Lot screams. The impact slams her to the floor.

Danny swoops in and grabs Alex. He drags the kid behind him by the hand, desperate to escape the room before others come running. As they pass into the hallway, Alex reaches out for his knapsack, sitting by the door. His fingers catch around one strap and it bounces behind them.

Danny tows the boy into the hallway and pauses to lift the resistant Alex from his feet, slinging him over his shoulder. Alex struggles against his abductor, his bag dangling from one hand, but Danny tightens his grasp and runs as fast as he can into the darkness.

***

He reaches the lobby of the hotel in short order. People bustle about in the fire-lit dimness, and Danny suddenly becomes conscious of the fact this isn't a well-thought-out plan. In fact, he doesn't actually have a plan at all. He slows, trying to look as though he's going about normal business, but Alex continues to struggle. It's a woman who notices them first. "Hey! What are you doing?" she asks loudly, almost a shout.

Danny pushes by her, beelining toward the exit as others take notice. He swerves around several people at breakneck speed. An older man grabs out, trying to stop him, but Danny eludes his grip.

A large man steps out directly in front of him, blocking his path. Danny skids to a stop, panic pooling in the back of his head.

"Put the kid down, Danny."

Danny doubts he could survive a fight with this bull of a man. The man crosses his arms, and a brave young woman grabs Alex's arm. She tries pulling the boy from Danny's grasp, but Danny holds tight. He and the woman each pull Alex in different directions.

Danny feels his grip slipping. Another person joins the woman's effort. "No!" he shouts.

Alex is ripped away, and Danny's left standing in the middle of an angry mob. He frantically scans for the boy, who's in arms of the woman, fighting her now, trying to escape.

Danny readies his bat to strike as Jamal, with two other armed guards, breaks through the crowd.

Any second, someone will run in with word of what Danny's done to Lot. This is his one and only chance to escape. He has to think fast.

Jamal peers suspiciously at Danny. "What the hell is going on over here?"

"What's going on?" spits Danny. "What the fuck does it look like, Jamal? I've been swarmed by mindless peons!"

The woman protecting Alex pipes up. She's having difficulty maintaining her grip on the struggling boy. "There's something going on here!"

Danny scoffs at the woman, as though she were the stupidest person in existence. "What do you think I'm doing? Stealing the child? Are you kidding me? What would I do with a kid?" She blushes, and Danny feels the slightest prickle of hope. The large man blocking his way gives Danny a dirty look. "What *are* you doing with him?"

Danny turns to face the man, bluffing a quiet, angry stare.

"Tell me why I should have to explain myself to you, or anyone else. I have my orders from Lot and that should be good enough. If you don't like what's going on, I advise you to march yourself over to her room and tell her yourself!" Danny sweeps the rest of the crowd with a rock-hard gaze. "That goes for all of you! Now give me the kid and back the fuck off."

People in the crowd look away, worried they might be recognized and the guards lower their weapons. Danny hides the nerve-wracked shake in his hands as he raises the uncooperative Alex over his shoulder once again.

11

Danny barrels into the blinding afternoon sunlight. He feels the guard's eyes behind him, uncertain but afraid to stop him. It won't be long before Lot is found, if she hasn't been found already. When that happens, the entire community will be chomping at the bit to take revenge, but there's no time to think about that now.

Alex struggles violently, slung across Danny's shoulder like a rag doll. He kicks and punches, yet somehow maintains a grip on the knapsack that flops in his hand. Danny wonders why the kid can't see he's being saved.

The ghouls spot them, and the horde of ravenous flesh-eaters, attracted by the still burning funeral pyre, scatter across the field. All eyes are on Danny and Alex, living and dead alike, as they hurtle toward the dark tree line across the overgrown field.

The recently deceased, hampered by rigor mortis and the rotten ones, who probably crawled from ancient graves, are slow. They lumber, dragging limbs as Danny darts around them. It's the more intact and agile ones that pose the real danger right now. Not only are they fast, but they never get tired, and they're right on his heels.

He sprints, Casey's bat in hand and a tight grip on Alex. The child may not realize it yet, but it's better to take their chances out here, where they can at least defend themselves. Inside, man and boy alike are defenseless.

Danny breaks through the thick brush at the edge of the forest, his adrenaline surge carrying them quickly into its shadowy depths. Afraid to look back, he barrels ahead, clearing fallen logs and dried creek beds. His lungs burn and his uncooperative captive takes an exacting toll. Pushing harder than he ever has in his life, Danny runs until he thinks his body will give out. The creatures from the field are left far behind, unable to keep tabs on his rabbit-like weaving.

He runs until he can't anymore, then ready to collapse, he finally stops. He drops Alex to the ground but keeps a firm grip on the boy as he bends over, gasping. With one hand holding the kid's arm, he coughs and gulps in air.

Alex is scared: and he kicks Danny in the ribs as hard as he can. The kick drives Danny to his knees, winding him even further, but he doesn't lose his grip. Weary-eyed and breathless, he dodges another attack. The boy's teeth click shut as a bite misses its mark.

"Listen—" Danny's pushes Alex out to arm's length. He blocks another vicious kick. This kid is no slouch, scrawny maybe, but all power. "Stop it. Listen to me."

Alex throws a punch. Danny blocks.

"QUIT IT!"

That was dumb. He didn't mean to shout, but frustration and exhaustion are taking over. Danny peers anxiously into the woods. He's not sure he can run again so soon.

He grabs Alex by the shoulders, trying to regain calm. They won't make it like this, he needs the boy's cooperation. Alex's head jerks slightly. He looks everywhere but Danny's face.

"I know you're mad at me. I'm sorry, okay? I'm not going to hurt you, I promise. Alex, please listen, I just couldn't see you—see you go through the same thing I did..." Danny's throat catches.

It isn't like him to be swept up in emotion. *What's going on?*

Alex kicks Danny again, hard, and almost gets away.

Danny angrily shakes the boy, his emotions veering all over the place. "Damn it, kid! You think Lot's so great? Huh? You wanna go back there? You think I don't know what she was doing? You think that's normal?"

Alex stops struggling. Maybe Danny struck a nerve or maybe

he's just scared of the emotional and intense man shaking him and yelling in his face. Either way, the boy just stares, and keeps jerking his head.

A twinge of shame creeps up on Danny. He's acting like a lunatic.

"You need to understand something. It may seem safer back there, with Lot. She may make you feel special right now, but it won't last. Sooner or later you'll be a slave to her every impulse, and you won't even know it. She'll destroy everything you are."

The kid continues to stare. Danny sighs heavily; nothing is getting through. "Alex, please. Do you really want to go back to the same lady that had Casey killed?"

Alex's entire body jolts, as though he's been shot. His knees give out and Danny fumbles, trying to keep the boy on his feet. So, the kid *is* listening!

Slowly, Alex regains his footing.

"Do you understand? I'm trying to help you. What Lot was doing to you, or making you do—it was wrong. I'm trying to save you from all that. I would have saved Casey if I could have. *I'm the good guy here.*"

There's a loud crash and a creature lunges through the bushes. With no time to run, Danny shoves Alex toward the nearest tree.

"CLIMB!"

Alex streaks from Danny's arms and is up the thin tree, knapsack and all, in a flash.

Danny whips around to face his assailant. Casey's bat lays on the ground nearby, and he dives for it.

He swings at the creature. Wood strikes skull, sending a zing through Danny's shoulders. The thing stumbles and then lurches forward, undeterred. Danny wails on the creature's head again, driving it into the soft pine-needle bed underfoot.

Danny whacks the thing again as it tries to regain its footing. There's no letting up, only when its head is demolished does the creature finally stop moving.

Still trying to catch his breath, Danny looks up at Alex, who sits like a monkey boy on a branch. As he does, another creature breaks through the bush. *Shit.* Danny charges the creature, and two more appear.

Danny rips away half of a ghoul's decomposing face with the bat. Its head splits like a boiled peanut casing, exposing a black, gummied brain. The creature turns to chase Danny.

Without its protective skull, the thing's brain droops halfway out of its head, tethered only by a flimsy brainstem. Danny brings the bat down on the dark, jellied blob, closing his eyes against the explosion of chunky black bits. The creature's body falls to the ground mid-step.

The remaining two creatures attack in unison. Danny dodges them, almost backing up into yet another as it appears. The thing is huge, taller than Danny, and it wears a pair of bloodstained coveralls. Danny feels like a gladiator, fighting a losing battle against a pride of angry lions. All that's missing is the crowd chanting wildly for his death.

Danny nails one of the three creatures with Casey's bat and it drops to the ground, just for a second. He swivels himself away as the next attacks and kicks it in the face, the thing's teeth coming too close to his arm—so close Danny can see the flesh caked between them.

The third creature lunges and misses, its feet tangling in its own intestines, which hang from its burst stomach, slowing it for a minute.

Danny's stamina is quickly evaporating. Sleepless nights and a hundred meter dash while carrying a fighting sack of potatoes doesn't exactly make for a battle plan. He has to turn this fight around, *now,* or it will be all for naught.

He spies a nearby tree with its lowest branch long ago snapped to a dangerous point. It's a Hail Mary. Holding the bat horizontally between his hands Danny uses it as a ram, shoving the nearest of the creatures with all his might into the tree. The broken branch stabs through the back of the ghoul's skull and erupts out the front, exploding forehead and black ooze. It struggles a moment more, then stops moving.

Danny turns to face the other two creatures as they attack.

He sidesteps one and wallops the other in the face with the bat. Teeth and bone smash away as he sheers off the thing's bottom jaw, sending it flying into the bushes. The creature's sore-laden tongue unfurls, hanging down its neck like a fucked-up bolo tie, swinging with every movement.

The coverall-wearing creature attacks from behind and knocks Danny off his feet, sending Casey's bat flying from his hand. The thing is strong and unwavering in its determination to consume Danny alive. His exhausted muscles burn as he wrestles with the creature's massive frame.

The ghoul with the missing jaw charges them. Danny kicks at it, and it grabs his foot, dragging him several feet through the dirt, trying doggedly to tear meat from his leg. The coverall-wearing creature is relentless. Its huge bloated stomach presses into Danny, crushing him under its weight, and it battles to shred flesh with its deadly teeth. It's like wrestling a great white shark and Danny uses all his energy to fend it off.

Pain shoots through his knee. He feels like the smaller creature is trying to dislocate his leg. His arms shake with the exertion of keeping the big one from ripping off his face. Skin from the thing's face slides under Danny's hands. It's nearly impossible to stop it from biting him. He wrenches his own face away from teeth. He can't get away.

SLAM!

Coveralls lurches to the side.

SLAM!

Danny can't understand what he's seeing: knapsack-wearing Alex wails on the larger creature's head with Casey's baseball bat. The thing stumbles, trying to get to its feet, and Alex bashes it again… and again… and again…

Danny jerks with a sudden flourish of panic, pulling his leg away from the smaller creature. Blood and black ooze saturate his pant leg. He kicks the creature square in what remains of its face and it tumbles backward. With all the force he has left, he springs on it and begins to stomp its face. Bone splits beneath the treads of his boot, and he keeps stomping and kicking.

Next to him, Alex continues to smash larger creature's head with the bat, bits of skin, skull, and teeth flying like confetti. A rotten eye is forced from its socket, landing with a little cloud of dirt.

Together, the two blonds smash and bash, until both creatures stop moving.

Danny looks over at Alex. The boy's chest heaves, and specks of flesh and blood spot him from head to toe. He has a death grip on the blood-stained bat and his eyes are wild and angry.

Trying to catch his breath, Danny walks over to Alex and crouches down. He gently pries Casey's bat from the boy's hands. A number of things are flowing through Danny's head at this very moment, but at the forefront is the thought that this seemingly dumb, mute kid has a lot more going on than he's given credit for.

This kid, this *kid* just saved Danny's life by bashing the brains out of a flesh-eating monster that used to be human. No matter how long he lives in this world, he will never get used to these kinds of facts. Danny pats Alex's head awkwardly.

Suddenly, Danny remembers his leg. He frantically pulls up his pants to reveal bruised, but unbroken skin. Nearby lays the severed bottom jaw. It would only take one tooth, maybe just one scratch—it's not an experiment Danny's willing to perform.

More creatures are likely to follow their annihilated friends and they must move soon, but first, Danny feels like he's swallowed a desert. He hopes Alex is hiding a bottle of water in his prized pack. He points at it. "Got any water in that thing?"

Alex stares at Danny blankly.

Of course, no response. If Danny hadn't witnessed with his own eyes what just happened, he wouldn't believe it. "Mind if I have a look?"

Another blank stare. It makes Danny feel like he's speaking some sort of archaic dead language. He rolls his eyes at the speechless boy.

"Avez vous de l'eau, s'il vous plait?"

Nothing. *Oh well.* He spins the boy around and unzips his

bag. The name "Alex G." is written in permanent marker on the inside flap. Is Alex actually the kid's name, Danny wonders, or did Casey just start calling him that because it's written here?

He rummages through the bag. Inside, he finds a copy of *Robinson Crusoe*, a book of matches with a single match, an old threadbare t-shirt, a bag of marbles, a can opener, and half a bottle of aftershave. No water, dammit. Bemused Danny removes the bottle of aftershave. "A little young for this, aren't you?"

Alex spins around and swipes the bottle from Danny's hand, shooting him a dirty look. He shoves it huffily back into his knapsack and zips the entire thing up. Despite his exhaustion, Danny smiles. This kid is pretty funny, and at least he's not trying to get away anymore. It only took a near death experience to prove he wasn't the enemy. Danny holds up his hands in surrender. "Okay, okay. I'm sorry."

Alex stares at him blankly and Danny suddenly feels like he's looking into a mirror, if that mirror reflected the past.

Breaking branches cut short their little moment. Danny groans inwardly and jumps to his feet. A slow, lumbering creature breaks through the bushes, its body barely holding itself together.

Danny grabs Alex's hand, and they run.

***

Thick Marge and Arnold are solemn. Lot sits before them, frail and shaking; her wounded arm wrapped up in a homemade sling. Even through the fabric they can see the swelling. She is weak and unsteady, lifting a teacup with her trembling good arm. Opie, like the ever-present lap dog he is, stands grimly at her side.

"I understand Opie spoke with you both earlier in the day about the problem we were experiencing." Two heads bob up and down, their eyes begging to please.

Lot presses her lips together thoughtfully. "Then you can see how I would be disappointed by what's happened. Every person in this room was made aware of Danny's fragile state—that he was suffering a mental breakdown. How is it then, he was allowed to lash out, violently attack me, and kidnap a child?"

Thick Marge opens her mouth to say something, but Opie shakes his head imposingly and it quiets her.

"The fact is, this was a terrible lapse in security. Everyone underestimated him."

The guards nod in docile agreement, fear bubbling just below the surface. Lot softens her face and breathes out, cool and calculated. "Everyone, including me."

Silence hangs in the room. Thick Marge and Arnold are unsure what to say. The military man absently scratches at his USMC tattoo. "Do you have any idea why he would do something like this?" he asks.

Lot searches the bottom of her cup. She nods wanly and bats misty eyes. "Unfortunately, yes, and I suppose the cat's out of the bag now."

The guards lean in a little closer and Lot's voice wavers.

"I love Danny so much. I thought if I could just keep him under control… I didn't think he was truly capable of something like this… I just couldn't face what he is, didn't want to believe it, and now he has taken that poor, innocent little boy… Who knows what he plans on doing? I tried hiding his deviant ways. I thought I could help him, cure him."

The guards hang on Lot's every word, like babes suckling at her bosom, but Opie can't hide his surprise. He's seen Lot put on many faces in his day, and this is by far one of the most disturbing.

"Cure him from what?" asks Thick Marge.

"His appalling disease of the mind. He—he has a predilection for children."

Arnold and Thick Marge gasp, overwrought with outrage.

Thick Marge looks as if she might spit on the floor.

"I always knew there was something wrong with him. I'm sorry, Lot, but I always felt he was a bit *off*. It's not your fault, and we're going to find the boy and bring him home safely. I can't promise the same for Danny."

Arnold agrees. "Don't blame yourself, Lot, please. Whatever Danny's done, and plans to do, it's on his shoulders alone. You tried to help him, to stop him. I only wish we'd known about this before. Maybe we could've helped. You loved him like a son, and you're only guilty of doing what any mother would do."

Lot wipes her eyes. "No, I've operated selfishly. I couldn't bear to see harm befall my son and now a child is paying the consequences. I *have* to do what's right from now on. When you find Danny, he must be treated like any other citizen of this community and he must be brought back to pay for his crimes."

"You don't have to go through that," says Thick Marge. "We can…take care of him, immediately after we find him."

Arnold shakes his head in disagreement. "No, Marge, she's right. He must face the consequences of his actions, like anyone else. An example needs to be set."

Lot sits back in her chair. "I can no longer protect him, Marge. Justice must be served."

12

Thick Marge peaks out the foyer peephole, peering across the field at the forest. Creatures aggravated by Danny's little jaunt form deadly clusters, on the lookout for fresh meat. This is taking too long; Danny already has a head start and it'll be hard enough to track him as it is. Every minute they wait further reduces their chances of finding him.

She closes the eyelet and joins a group of men near the entrance. They murmur about tactics as she sits and begins bouncing a leg, unable to hold still. If they hustle, they should be able to outrun most of The Risen outside and catch up with Danny, wherever he is. She always knew he was a creep, she could just tell, and the boy he's stolen needs to be saved.

Marge doesn't have children of her own, never did, but she once had a kid brother. There was a fifteen-year difference between the two of them, so he felt almost like a son, and they'd been close. When The Plague struck, he'd been torn away from her.

It was the most miserable day of her life. Some lunatic charged her SUV as she drove her brother from school. She usually picked him up on Fridays when she wasn't on base, trying to get a little extra time with him. It was getting harder to see him as he got older. He wanted to be with his friends, playing video games, not with big sis.

She remembers how the crazy woman attacked their vehicle when they stopped at an intersection. If she'd known then what she knows now, she would have accelerated through the stop sign and never looked back. Or maybe she would have just shot the bitch right there with the military issue handgun stowed in the glove compartment. Instead, she tried to keep her cool.

Her little brother didn't feel the same reservation. He rolled down the window and yelled at the lady to get out of the way. Marge's memory gets blurry from there. The woman looked like she'd jumped from the pages of a textbook showing horribly advanced syphilis. Somehow that disgusting creature bit her brother's arm. Marge floored the gas, driving right over the nutter, who then got up and attacked the SUV again like nothing had happened. It was unbelievable.

A call to 911 brought the police. They Tasered and shot the lunatic with no success; she just kept attacking. More people were bitten before she was finally cuffed and detained. Marge's brother was taken to the emergency room, and then...well, the story wrote itself.

The hospital was bedlam, crazy people coming out of the woodwork and ending up in the ER. Her brother's condition deteriorated as a speedy and hard-hitting infection spread through him. He flatlined and the doctors pronounced him dead—then he recovered. It was a miracle, they said, but it was anything but.

The last time she saw her little brother, he was strapped to a hospital bed, writhing as though possessed and trying desperately to attack and bite the doctors surrounding him. They were trying to get some sort of vital readings from the boy.

Although that was three years ago, Thick Marge is still stuck there, remembering the events as though they happened yesterday. She often wonders if that sweet boy is still strapped to that bed in an eternal hell, never able to release himself, never able to escape.

Of course, the situation is different now, much different, but she nevertheless feels compelled to rescue the towheaded Alex. She's prepared to do what she has to to save the child, even if it means laying down her own life.

Thick Marge continues to bounce her leg anxiously. Arnold, whose real name is Javier, walks up to her. "Any change?"

"Not really."

He nods grimly, shifting the supply sack on his shoulder into a more comfortable position. He knows what some call him behind his back, but he doesn't care. What point are names in a world filled with death? Everyone dies, and everyone's name is eventually forgotten. He doesn't care what they call him, as long as they do their job and help him find their target.

Arnold has fought next to Danny enough times to respect his capabilities and knows this won't be an easy mission. Their route to find him isn't established, the sun's setting, and not only are there cannibalistic cadavers to contend with, but also a smart and dangerous man. The deck is stacked heavily against them. He thinks they'll be lucky if they get the boy Alex back alive.

At least he has a good idea of where Danny will be heading, and it's their only hope in hell to find him. Arnold has some tracking skills, being trained for it in the Marines, but he's by no means a professional. If he'd known every corner of the world would succumb to utter devastation, he would've brushed up on his training before it all happened.

It felt like the world had fallen apart before his very eyes, town after town, city after city, and country after country. He'd always worried about a nuclear winter, but this? Never this.

Hospitals were the first hotspots. People didn't know what they were dealing with. Well-meaning family members rushed the sick and "infected" into ERs. Police stations and jails quickly filled up too. It wasn't long before the majority of first responders were either dead or infected, leaving the army as the nation's only line of defense.

Their orders were simple: destroy areas that were overrun by the dead—there would be civilian casualties, but desperate times called for desperate measures. They tried to cleanse towns and cities of the spreading disease, but it was a losing battle. There were always more living corpses spewing from the mouth of hell.

Weeks passed without any sign of relief as Arnold's squadron hunkered down and followed orders. They didn't know it at the time, but The Plague was only just beginning. Then came the call to hit a school full of families seeking refuge. The situation had become so critical that if there was even one suspected infection, annihilation was the only order.

The commands were sent via satellite phone from politicians in bunkers, fat-cats far away from any action or possibility of infection, making decisions based on data collected from the ground. It was easy for them, sitting back in their leather chairs with their unscathed children playing at their feet. They just pointed their pudgy fingers at targets on maps, like it was a game board. Pass the crackers, please.

It was difficult for Arnold to leave the safety and security of the military he had known for a decade. It was even harder to disobey the direct orders given to him by a superior officer, but it helped that there were fifteen of them that deserted.

Soon after, he was separated from the group. It's possible they're all still alive and well, and he prays every night for them.

Years of tough training serve Arnold well now. Not only did it build character, but it also built stamina and grit, all of which he will need to barrel headlong into a dark forest after a deranged man holding a child hostage. It's men like Danny that brought The Plague to humanity's doorstep, but it's men like Arnold that will stop it.

He and Thick Marge look over their small group. There are five men: Rob, Brody, Habib, Dennis, and Jamal. Three of them had volunteered for the now defunct solar panel mission, and they are all hard, experienced fighters.

Thick Marge unlocks the foyer cage. "Alright, boys. Let's do this."

***

Alex follows Danny as they push their way through the thick underbrush. In here, trudging through the woods, there's no way to know where danger hides. The sun is setting, nearly gone, but the road isn't an option. It would be safer, but they would be too vulnerable to discovery.

Somewhere around here is an old deer trail. If they keep going Danny knows they'll find it. Get to that, and it will lead them through, to the other side of this nightmare. It'll be a few days-worth of walking, but if they can survive, Whitebridge is only another few hours from the edge of the forest, and a possible place of refuge.

Lot has been feuding with Whitebridge for a long time. She claims they are Godless heathens. A community bent on inbreeding and immoral behavior. It doesn't help Whitebridge's reputation that they routinely send raiding parties to stake out routes and kill Lot's people.

Of course, many of Lot's missions were once raiding parties too, not a few of them headed by Danny, but that was until she established trade with some of the surrounding communities. Now, raids were a thing of the past. Danny never really understood where the problem emerged with Whitebridge, but there's bad blood there. Maybe they know something he doesn't.

Lot's influence grows by the day because of her trade routes. Most of the surrounding communities would happily turn anyone over to Lot if they hear she was looking for them. Whitebridge has somehow resisted Lot's charm and Danny's gambling they'll accept a defector.

He tries to focus on the matter at hand, survival, but can't. His mind spins at an unstoppable pace, unburdened by the rational thought of well-rested judgment. The meticulously built walls he spent years constructing now lay as rubble, scattered at his feet. His thoughts skip and bounce with little rhyme or reason as connections he shut himself off to long ago, show themselves. Despite the fact he's sleep deprived and terrified, Danny feels like he's finding pieces of a missing puzzle and, for the first time in his life, a full picture is forming. He finally understands how Lot is building her empire. He finally sees the rotten system built by a rotten leader.

A comment here, a lie there, Danny's putting it all together and wonders how many other people know exactly what's happening. He wonders if they care and he wonders why he never saw it before. It's funny how tiny things tell a big story when you're not afraid to look.

Danny's stomach flips. Had anyone realized what was happening to him? What Lot was doing to him? Looking back, he knows the answer is yes, someone had to have known. Someone could have stopped it, someone could have saved him, but no one did, and he couldn't save himself.

Lot was all Danny knew for years. After his father's death, she kept him on a short leash, always by her side, and eventually she infiltrated his mind so thoroughly he no longer had any sense of self. There was no sense of being without her, she made his decisions, she controlled his actions, and she controlled his thoughts.

He was so completely under her spell that he tried everything he could to keep their connection as he aged. He even went as far as to stop eating. By severely limiting his diet, he delayed puberty by at least a year. Now, with unclouded eyes, he realizes it was a thought she put into his head. That was what she did—what she does best.

When Lot finally severed their relationship, it was cruel. She was done with Danny, cut and dry. He wallowed, unable to come to terms with the fact he'd been evicted from her bed, and he blamed himself. She let him. All he had left was emptiness and anger, he didn't know how to function. Lot had so completely eviscerated his identity that without her, he was nobody and nothing. Even now, running from her with Alex in tow, a small part of him hopes he can return to her one day. He hates himself for it.

Danny's stomach tightens, nauseous with guilt. He can't stop thinking about her, about how he's betraying the only person in the world that loves him. Her hooks drag through him as he pulls away, taking chunks of his very being with them. He knows he will never truly be free of her. She's an entrenched obsession, cultured from years of abuse.

Danny staggers.

Abuse, he never thought of it that way before, but it's

impossible to hide from it now; no matter how much he wants to. The floodgates are open, and he's drowning.

"Lost?" a man's voice startles Danny, and he realizes he's stopped walking. He can't remember getting here. He's been on autopilot, lost in a maze of violent emotion. Alex stands next to him, peering into the dark.

"Who are you?" Danny asks.

"My name is Sal."

"What do you want? We have nothing."

"Oh? On the contrary, I see you're both wearing clothes, and you have a nice set of boots on your feet…"

"Don't come any closer."

Danny grabs Alex's arm, shoving the boy behind him, and then raises Casey's bat.

Sal steps forward, unafraid, his face still hidden by shadows.

"I don't want your stuff. I was just proving a point."

"Which was?"

"That you're an appealing target to those who would harm you, and you seem woefully unprepared to protect that child of yours with just a bat to defend yourself."

"What *do* you want then?"

"Well, I'll tell you what I *don't* want. What I don't want is to see some poor bastard and his kid get mauled out here because they've been walking around in circles. I have a safe place you can spend the night."

"We haven't been walking around in circles, I know exactly where I'm going."

"You could've fooled me."

"Why should I trust you?"

"You don't have to. It's your choice."

Sal turns and walks away with a deep limp. Danny watches as the man's form is quickly eaten by the shadows. He peers into the dark as a coyote yips far in the distance. The bat is heavy in his arms and his eyes burn with exhaustion. It's been ages since he's slept, and he knows he can't go much further.

***

Most of the low hanging clouds have dissipated with the summer night's breeze. Thin tendrils of moonlight strain in their battle against the dark forest. Everything is quiet and still, but Thick Marge and her cohorts know it's a ruse, because littered throughout the branches and fallen leaves are unspeakable evils.

They step quietly, trying not to attract attention. No torches or flashlight, no GPS or satellite radar to guide their way. They rely solely on Arnold, the Marine, to navigate them through this house of horrors.

Arnold thinks Danny will head to Whitebridge, where they are rumored to have taken in a traitor once. He'll probably stay off the road, to avoid discovery. It's a shot in the dark, but it's their best bet.

Rob catches up with Dennis and they whisper, falling slightly behind the others.

"This is messed up, huh?" Rob asks. "I can't believe Danny did something like this, and now we're out here looking for him and that kid instead of securing solar panels. It's crazy"

"I know! You know what? I caught him staring at the kid before we brought him back."

"You're shitting me!"

"Yeah, I mean, I thought he was into that chick that was killed. I thought he was looking at her, I mean, but man, was I wrong."

"The 'I'm not bitten lady'?"

"Yeah, her." Dennis ducks under low branches.

"Jesus. This whole thing is fucked up."

"Yup."

Rob grunts, stepping over a mossy rock. "That was a bad night; if I ever got bit I'd kill myself, right there and then. Save everyone the drama of doing it for me."

"I hear ya, brother."

The two fall into silence as the group slows, approaching a clearing. Rotting bodies lie motionless in the dirt, their skulls obliterated. Nearby, a creature dangles from a dying tree, a sharp branch skewering its skull, pinning it like a dead butterfly to a collector's bulletin board.

Arnold quietly assesses the scene.

Thick Marge bats away a cloud of mosquitoes. "What do you think? Was it Danny?" she asks.

"There's no way to tell for sure Marge, but it's obvious there was a struggle here. I think it's our best bet and our only lead."

Jamal wrinkles his nose as he toes a headless coverall-wearing corpse. "I'd bet it was Danny."

Arnold nods. "Think he could do all this himself?"

"Jeez, you know, it's hard to say." Jamal rubs the back of his sweaty neck. "This is a lot of carnage, but Danny's a strong guy, and he knows what he's doing. If you're asking, do I think one person could have done this? I think yeah, it's possible."

Thick Marge scans the surrounding forest. "Okay. If we're betting this is Danny, then which way did he go?

Arnold holds a broken twig up in the moonlight. "It's hard to be certain. Trails from The Risen can look just like a regular person's, so I can't be sure if any one trail was left by Danny or something else—"

"Super."

"But, I think he's headed this way." Arnold points into the forest.

Habib, who was content to stand by and listen until now, finally speaks up. "What makes ya say that, Javier?"

"See these footprints here?" Arnold points at the ground and everyone nods, engrossed in the explanation.

"The Risen are generally missing shoes, or dragging legs, and they don't necessarily travel side-by-side. In that soft spot over there I see two pair of footprints, a man's, I'd say about Danny's size, and a child's next to them. Danny probably got tired of carrying the boy and has got him by the arm now."

Thick Marge purses her lips. "Done showing off?"

Arnold smiles widely. "Yes."

"Good. This is the best evidence I've seen that says he's making a run for Whitebridge, like you thought. If we keep in that direction, we'll eventually hit a deer path and it should lead us through the forest. If we're lucky, that's the way Danny's headed. Let's go."

The group murmurs agreement. The longer they stand here, the more vulnerable to attack they are, and the farther away Danny gets with that poor boy. Arnold takes up the head of the search party, followed by Thick Marge and the rest. They push through the undergrowth, hoping Arnold's tracking skills from the Corps aren't too rusty.

13

Danny and Alex stand with Sal at the base of a very wide tree. Moonlight filters through the dense canopy above, showing scars where low lying branches have been hacked from the trunk.

Sal fishes down a rope ladder with a stick. Danny looks up, and if he weren't so bone-weary, he would be surprised. Built into thick upper branches is a well-fortified treehouse. Sal climbs the ladder, motioning for Alex and Danny to follow.

Once inside, the mysterious man pulls the ladder up and shuts the door tightly, then crosses the surprisingly large room and lights a candle. The flare of the match burns Danny's eyes, leaving a reddish blob dancing through his vision for several minutes after.

As the candlelight grows stronger, Danny can finally see who Sal is. The man is probably in his mid-fifties, with a heavily lined face and shortly cropped salt-and-pepper hair. He's slightly hunched but still tall, about Danny's height, maybe taller if he were to stand straight.

Danny looks around the room. The walls are made of just about everything, scrap metal, fencing, boards, and even the dismembered seats of old wooden chairs, although two survive, sitting at a makeshift table. There's a wood burning cook stove with a jerry-rigged vent in the corner and even a cage of game birds pecking seed from a tray. "Quite the setup you've got here."

Sal says nothing. He motions for his guests to sit at the table and pushes a homemade chess set to the side. Danny thumps into a chair, noticing the man's left hand is lined with old surgical scars and doesn't work well. Alex pokes his finger at the caged birds, oblivious to anything else.

Sal takes the seat across the table. He is as gruff and guarded as Danny. "So, what should I call you two boys?"

"Danny. That's Alex."

"Father and son against the world?"

"Not exactly."

"Brothers?"

"Just guy and kid."

"I see," Sal studies Danny. "What brings you to my neck of the woods?"

"Just passing through."

"Oh, I see. Out for an evening stroll, see the sights, get eaten alive? That kind of thing, right?"

"Yeah. I guess."

"Okay then," Sal sits back in his chair, making hard eye contact. Danny coldly returns the stare, tired but still cocky enough not to back down.

"So, Danny, you'll be off in the morning, I assume."

"Yeah." Danny feels a tug on his shirt and looks down at Alex. "What?"

The boy stands there, looking at him and tugs on his shirt again. An instant of overwhelming frustration bubbles up, choking Danny for a split second before he pushes it down.

"What do you want, Alex?"

More tugging.

Sal raises an eyebrow. "Kid doesn't talk?"

"Can't."

Alex's tugs continue relentlessly until Danny awkwardly pats Alex on the head as if the child were a dog. Sal smiles, amused, briefly showing he was once a handsome man. "When's the last time the two of you ate anything?"

Alex's eyes light up. Death and monsters mean nothing when a kid's got to eat.

***

Alex wolfs down a meal of eggs, dried meat, and fresh berries served on cracked plates. Danny's food sits before him, untouched. He grinds his teeth and fidgets with the leather strap of his father's watch, feeling like he might vomit. Just the sight of the food on the plate before him is almost enough to make him heave. He looks away from the food and puts a chipped mug to his lips, drawing in a mouthful of water and forcing himself to swallow. His stomach lurches, but he keeps it down. He needs to stay hydrated if he's going to survive a run for Whitebridge.

Sal eyes Danny's plate. "Not used to survival food?"

"Just not hungry."

Alex picks berries off Danny's plate. Danny absently shoves it toward him, and the gaunt child begins picking up food by the handful, stuffing his face with a second meal.

"If you're not related to the boy," Sal says, "do you mind if I ask how exactly you came across him?"

"What if I do mind you asking?"

Sal crosses his arms over his chest and sits back in his chair, the younger man's attitude a clear source of annoyance. They sit in silence, staring at each other, Sal boring a hole through Danny with his eyes.

When Danny can't stand it anymore, he looks away. He just wants to sleep—needs to sleep. "Why do you live way out here, all alone?"

"I'm not a people person."

"Then why help us, bring us here, feed us?"

"Just because I'd rather be alone doesn't mean I want to see other people dead."

"Fair enough." It doesn't really matter because Danny and Alex will be leaving come daybreak.

**

The rescue party quietly trudges through the forest. Finally, thick brush gives way to a deer trail. There is no sign of Danny, or the kid, not a single footprint.

Arnold fears they've missed something. The lower the moon falls, the more difficult it'll be to find any sign of direction, and what if Danny isn't going to Whitebridge? What if he backtracked to the road knowing anyone following him would be in the forest? Assuming he could avoid the search party, that would be a smart move.

"I think we should stop," he whispers over to Thick Marge.

"Okay," she responds. This is what she was afraid of, what they're all afraid of. That they are out here, in the dark, infested forest, with no hope of locating their target.

They've successfully avoided the few creatures they've come across so far, but they're running around out here blind. If they stumble across a herd they don't stand a very good chance, not like this. Marge wonders if Danny can even survive out here with a struggling child. There's a very real possibility she and the group should be looking for remains, or that those remains are looking for them.

As they stop, Thick Marge motions for a perimeter around her and Arnold. Dennis, Brody, Jamal, Habib, and Rob circle around, guns raised. Marge digs through her knapsack and pulls out a candle and lighter. She doesn't use it often—one day soon the lighter will run dry—but for now it's a blessing.

She lights the candle and crouches, searching the ground with Arnold while the others stand watch. She hopes they find something, anything that tells them Danny passed through here with the boy.

***

Lot watches the glow of dying embers as she sits before her fireplace, deep in thought. There's nothing she would love better than to personally place them scorching onto Danny's open eyes, and feed him the burning coals, shoveling spoonful after spoonful into his betraying mouth. She would watch until they burned so deeply they fell from his throat through a melted hole of skin and tissue.

Lot taps her fingers angrily on the arm of her chair. One of the burdens of leadership is sacrifice, and she'll be unable to smite Danny with her own two hands. A situation like this must be handled with care, people will be watching. At least, she thinks, she can take solace in the fact that an outraged community will eagerly dish out any punishment she can devise, in the name of justice. In fact, they will demand it. They will require a public execution, and she will gratify them.

***

Danny peeks out the window of Sal's treehouse. The moon shines dimly through clouds that blot the sky. His eyes burn, and he needs sleep, but his body refuses to cooperate. He lies back down on the floor and dozes for a few minutes, then his troubled mind churns, and he wakes again.

He peers through the dark at Alex. The boy is peaceful, lying on a cot Sal uses for a bed. At least *he's* getting some sleep, Danny thinks. It was nice enough of their host to let Alex have the bed and he's probably a nice guy, but who the hell really knows? People are never what they seem. Danny almost prefers the creatures outside to the living humans he's met.

He sits up and looks around the room. Nearby, Sal sleeps on the floor, his head resting on a pile of animal skins. Danny can't help but think that earlier today the man was right: he is woefully unprepared to protect a kid out here by himself. This guy is well set up and won't miss a few things.

In the corner, Danny remembers seeing some old bags hanging on a nail. He stands quietly and creeps across the room. The floorboards of the treehouse squeak under his shifting weight. He stops and listens. The deep breathing of uninterrupted sleep reassures him and he shuffles on, trying to avoid more noise.

A plastic bag crinkles as he pulls it gently from the nail and Danny curses under his breath.

In Sal's pantry, there are eggs sitting in a basket, dried meat slices piled in a jar, a small bowl of berries and root vegetables, cans of spaghetti sauce, cocktail wieners, gas station fruit pies, even pudding cups. Danny grabs the dried meat and drops it into the bottom of his sack.

The sound of a gun cocking behind his head jettisons the blood from his heart. He drops the sack on the floor, and swallowing hard, raises his hands slowly into the air.

Sal angrily shoves him toward a chair. "Sit!"

In a split second, a world of thought cascades over Danny. He can't allow Sal to get the upper hand. If he does, there's no telling where this will go or what Sal will do to the guy robbing him.

Adrenaline jumpstarts his movements. Danny whips around and grabs the gun. Sal is surprised, but not easily over-powered and he doesn't release the weapon.

The two men struggle, slamming into walls and furniture. Alex bolts upright in bed. A shadowy jumble of arms and legs rolls past him through the dark, the grunting of life and death exertion rumbling the walls of the treehouse.

BAM!

Danny staggers back a few steps, the moonlight strobing his movements, then falls to his knees, grabbing at his left side. Sal stands over him, gun in hand.

***

Thick Marge and Arnold continue to scrutinize the ground around them. Nothing, not a single footprint, it doesn't look like this path has been walked all summer. If Danny trekked through here, there would be something, at the very least rummaged leaves, but the trail is pristine, abandoned. The team feels the frustration of a goose chase mounting as they begin to think Danny has outsmarted them.

Pop!

It's faint, but distinctive. Arnold holds his hand up for silence before anyone has a chance to speak. He listens, straining his ears, but there's no other sound.

"Gunshot?"

"Yep."

"Could be Danny."

"Could be anyone."

"It's all we have to go on," Thick Marge interjects. "Javier, can you tell what direction it came from?"

Arnold thinks. "Maybe it came from the Northeast, but I can't be sure. Could be a quarter of a mile away, maybe closer, probably closer."

Brody peers into the dark. "If we heard it, so did every damn creature in this forest. If we go in that direction now, we'll be massacred. We don't even know if it was Danny."

The group nods.

"Okay," Thick Marge replies. "You all knew the risks when you volunteered. This doesn't change anything. If that's how you feel Brody, then turn back now. I'm pressing forward." She shoulders her bag and leaves the group behind.

Two seconds later, they are following.

***

Danny is slumped against a wall. The gunshot wound in his side doesn't hurt as much as he thought it would, unless he moves, and right now Alex has a death grip on his arm and is shaking him. With each jolt, a searing pain wraps around Danny's abdomen, but it's hard for him to understand it. Shock muddies everything. He's never been shot before.

Danny looks down at his hands. They are covered in dark red blood. It's thick, sticky, and hot as it oozes steadily from his left side. His shirt is soaked with it. He feels like he's looking at Alex from the bottom of a mineshaft as the kid keeps pulling on his arm. The kid's eyes are wide, petrified, and he tries to lift Danny to his feet. Danny groans in pain and rolls his eyes toward the man who shot him.

Sal stands unapologetically over him, still pointing his handgun at Danny.

Danny's face shrivels in anger. "Fuck you."

"Fuck me? Fuck you, you little prick. I try to help you out and you try to rip me off?"

"I just needed a few days' worth of supplies. That's all! You shot me!"

"Which never would have happened if you didn't grab the gun in the first place."

Danny can see Alex is starting to lose it. He still pulls on Danny's arm, jerking his head with that weird tick and breathing so hard he might hyperventilate. Then Danny hears it, the first horrifying croaks and gurgles as they drift up from the forest floor—The Risen, attracted by the gunshot. It won't be long before there are too many to fight off. There will be a seething ocean of spoiled flesh and menacing teeth right below them.

This is it, Danny thinks. There's no getting the kid to safety now. This has all been for nothing.

He tries to hug Alex, to calm him, but the boy doesn't want to be calmed. He shoves Danny off and tries desperately to drag the wounded man to his feet.

Thick tears begin to blur Danny's vision. They spill from his eyes and streak down his face. Every last element of his carefully crafted façade washes downstream with them and he breaks down, sobbing uncontrollably.

Danny's tears don't last long, stopping from utter burnout. He just doesn't have the energy to spare anymore. Alex kneels next to him as he leans his head back against the wall. "What's wrong with me? I knew, of course, I knew. I'm so sorry, Alex," Danny mumbles. "I brought you to her like some sort of sacrificial lamb. I thought she'd be so happy she'd be falling over herself to thank me. I knew, deep down, what she would do and I led you straight to her, but I couldn't face it. I couldn't let it happen again."

Danny's voice chokes in his throat and he tries unsuccessfully to swallow his emotions. The pain in his side is getting worse and he shifts his weight, groaning with the effort, and tries to see Alex better. "I'm so sorry. Jesus Christ, if it weren't for me, none of this would have happened. If it weren't for me, Casey'd still be alive and you'd still be with her."

Alex strokes Danny's arm as though he saw someone else do it once.

Sal waves his gun at them.

"Who was Casey, your wife?"

Danny laughs bitterly. "I barely knew her. She was Alex's surrogate mother—until Lot had her killed."

"Love triangle?"

Again, the bitter, frayed laughter, this time with manic edges. "Lot, my mother, my lover, my idol, my entire world. She had Casey killed."

"I see."

"No, no you don't see."

Alex wipes tears from Danny's face and the tenderness is almost too much to bear. It's such a kind, lucid gesture it nearly sends Danny plummeting over the edge of the bottomless pit he's standing on. "I'm so fucked up in the head," he confesses.

"We all have our demons, kid." Sal's gaze drifts toward an old photocopy of an ultrasound picture tacked to the wall.

Danny follows his eyes. "You take him."

Sal's attention snaps to Alex. "No way."

"I'm in no condition to protect a child, I probably won't even survive. You used to have a kid, right?" Danny points at the photocopy. "You want one? Take him. You can take care of him, I can't."

He knows he'll be lucky to survive a gunshot wound like this, even on a good day, let alone with no medical attention. The wounded man pleads with his eyes and watches as a downpour of darkness instantly distorts Sal's face. There is no rescuing him. "No. No kids. No family. Nothing! If you mention it again, I'll throw you to the ground to be eaten alive. Do you understand me?"

Danny nods silently at the half-crazed man.

Sal steps across the room and, keeping his gun on Danny,

rummages through supplies. He pulls out a white box with a red cross on the front—a first-aid kit—and tosses the box at Danny. It clatters at his feet.

"Fix yourself up. You're gone come first light."

They have no choice. Once again, man and boy must take their chances in a forest besieged by demons and ghouls. He tried, Danny thinks, he really did, but this will be their last stand.

14

Danny's side throbs and his entire body is in torment. It's too bad Sal doesn't have any painkillers in his rinky-dink first aid kit, and the bandage he found in it isn't doing much for the bleeding. The only thing Danny has going for him is that the bullet passed through. He's no physician, not by a long shot, but he thinks that's probably a good thing. That, and the fact he isn't dead yet, means maybe he has a chance. Maybe.

He winces, peering down the side of the tree. Many of the creatures that gathered after the gunshot have wandered away, but there's still a good number left. He wonders how they're going to get past them, but Sal seems prepared for everything. Attached to a long line that snakes far out into the forest is an actual tambourine, along with a pots and pans. A few yanks and the corpses blunder toward the noise.

Danny and Alex leave without sound or ceremony.

Sal releases the rope ladder and points out the door. Danny climbs down, slowly, each step searing through him. Alex follows. Sal drops Casey's bat to the ground, sweeps up the ladder, shuts the door, and that's that.

Alex lifts the bat from the dirt and brushes it off. Danny isn't sure which way to go. For a good minute, he stands there, paralyzed with indecision, his side slowly dripping blood onto the dirt. The forest is full of danger, and he doesn't even know where they are anymore.

Alex reaches out his hand and tugs on Danny's, ready to go. If they continue to stand here stupidly, there will be no more decisions to make. It's only a matter of moments before one of The Risen gathered under the tambourine senses living flesh.

Danny looks up at the sky; it's dark and cloudy and looks like it might rain. He can't see the rising sun, his only compass, so he decides to go straight, just straight.

There's no path to follow and the forest grasps and pulls with fingers nearly as dangerous as those of the wandering dead. Danny hunches, holding his bleeding side, the pain deepening with every step. He can't believe he's still alive, let alone walking.

Alex tightly grips Casey's bat, as though it's a magical broadsword. He walks just behind his guardian as they navigate fallen branches and walls of vine. Danny stops and holds back a wicked-looking pricker bush, motioning for Alex to go first. It begins to drizzle rain and Danny thinks things probably can't get much worse.

***

The search party bundles up against the rain. Even during the summer, a good storm can chill a person to the bone. Thick, wet undergrowth drags at their clothing, soaking them as they slog along, making the trek through the dark forest slow and painful. It's taken much longer than anyone thought just to get this far, and the sky is lightening just now.

Good thing I brought a dry pair of socks with me, Arnold thinks. As the sky grows steadily brighter, he worries their only lead is lost. There's no sign of Danny, and no way to know if it was truly him who fired the shot. Even if it was Danny, he must be long gone by now.

Arnold almost walks into Brody as the other man stops cold in his tracks. Just ahead is a mob of The Risen, dumbly circling the same spot. A small breeze shakes the trees and a tone-deaf orchestra of pots and pans serenades them. Thick Marge notices there is also a tambourine hanging with the cookware. She holds up her hand for the group to halt and counts ten creatures.

She silently commands the men around her. With nervous

precision, they sneak through the forest and surround the enemy. Thick Marge gives the signal to attack and, not waiting to see if they follow her order, she charges the creature closest to her. It turns, hearing her, or smelling her, or however the fuck they notice things, but it doesn't matter, because it gets a face full of hunting knife.

She plunges the knife deep into the creature's eye as it thrusts itself forward on her blade. Its rotten face reeks and it is missing teeth. The thing's tongue is a blackened lump of coal in its mouth and if it had breath, Thick Marge would have been able to smell it a mile away.

She twists the hunting knife and the creature jolts. It snaps its teeth twice more and as it slumps toward her, she shoves it away and whips around. Behind her, Rob struggles with two creatures. He dodges an attack.

Thick Marge leaps onto one of the things and sinks her knife into the soft spot at the back of its head, just under the skull. Her hair, wet from the rain, streams behind her as it flails and spins. She rides it like a bucking bronco and stabs the thing in the back of the head again. It collapses to its knees, growling, trying to reach her, and then it falls over, dead.

Rob gives Thick Marge a hand up, and she looks around. All the creatures are dead, and the entire group is alive. She nods at them. "Job well done."

After a moment of well-deserved, quiet celebration, they follow the long rope that holds the pots and pans. It leads through thick foliage to a patchwork treehouse perched high above the ground.

The soil under the treehouse is too hard and rocky to find any footprints, but there is blood. There are wet patches of dark maroon dirt marking where the earth has greedily absorbed it, and drying drops speckle protruding rocks. Thick Marge grins. The tree's wide umbrella protects the evidence from the rain.

Arnold picks up a stone and hurls it at the side of the treehouse. It hits with a hollow thud and falls back to the ground. He picks it back up and throws it again. Sal opens his door, pops his head out, and looks down at the search party.

"Go away."

Arnold smiles up at him. "We took care of your pest problem for you."

"Go away."

Habib cocks his gun and points it up at Sal.

Arnold spreads his hands in a show of trustworthiness. "We just want to talk to you. We can even do it from here if you tell us everything we need to know."

"Eat shit."

Sal slams the door of his treehouse, shutting out the world. Arnold grunts unhappily. He shouts up at the man in the treehouse. "Did you hear a gunshot?"

No answer.

Rob picks up the stone again, but Arnold shakes his head. "No point. There's blood. That's all we need."

***

The light drizzle slowly turns to a heavy, cold rain. Big, wet drops cling to Danny's skin, soaking him, freezing him. His feet feel like they're encased in concrete as he drags them through the mud. The boy trots in front of him, water-logged but undiscouraged.

"Alex."

Alex spins around with Casey's baseball bat raised high, ready for a fight.

Danny slumps against the trunk of a tree. He's sweating profusely but shivers against the rain, breathing hard. Pain eats away at him, yet from somewhere deep within, he musters a smile for Alex.

Alex runs to him.

"I've gotta take a break, buddy, just for a few minutes."

Worry creeps across the child's usually deadpan face and he nods. Danny raises his eyebrows in surprise then smiles again, this time genuinely. At least he's getting through to the boy and that feels good. It lifts his spirits just enough to keep him going.

Alex leans Casey's bat against the tree and kneels in the mud next to Danny. He pokes a finger at the gunshot wound. Danny's yellow shirt is now mostly brown with rings of blood that mix with rain. It stains everything, dripping down his leg, darkening his pants. He shakes his head. "It's not that bad, don't worry. I just need a quick rest, okay?"

They sit quietly together in the mud. Alex holds his knapsack over his head, shielding himself slightly from the increasing downpour. The forest is quiet, except for the noise of water bouncing off leaves. Danny closes his eyes and time slips away for a while.

CRASH!

Danny jolts his feet before he even knows what's happening. With a grimace, he leans over his knees, breathing hard as searing pain rips through his side. A deer flits to the other side of the clearing, kicking its heels and flashing its white tail.

There's noise from deeper in the forest. It must be what spooked the deer. Danny tenses his entire body. He and Alex stare through the dense trees, afraid. "Run, Alex. Find a tree far away and climb it. Don't come down until I call you, no matter what."

Alex stares at Danny, unresponsive.

"Go, goddammit!"

The boy bolts away, disappearing into the thick forest with his knapsack bouncing on his back. Danny lifts Casey's bat, his ears buzzing with maddening pain. He's pretty sure he won't survive this fight and hopes the boy's smart enough to go it alone, to get somewhere safe.

Branches crackle beneath nearing footsteps. Danny puffs air from his mouth, trying to psych himself up. Just because he's going to die doesn't mean he should go down without a fight. He plans on taking out as many freaks as he can before his body gives out and they tear him to pieces.

Habib steps into the clearing. "Danny?" He can't hide his astonishment.

Danny, once intimidating, can barely stand on his own two feet. He's as pale as a ghost, covered in blood and muck with thick, dark bags hanging under his eyes. He holds up a bat shakily, trying to look threatening.

Seconds later, the entire search party is there, and they surround him. Habib brazenly steps forward, backed up by Jamal. Hand out, he demands the bat.

"Careful, man, he's dangerous," Jamal warns.

Habib looks back. "I think he might be bitten."

WHAM!

Danny's knees nearly buckle as he cracks the side of Habib's head with the bat. Habib falls to the ground with an unsettling groan. Gasps of collective disbelief ripple through the search party as Danny tries to stay steady on his feet, raising his weapon for another attack.

Thick Marge hurls herself at him, dodging as Danny swings again. He crashes to the ground with her, yelping as pain blossoms in his side like a horrid flower. The bat tumbles from his grip.

Arnold, Dennis, and Brody rush to Habib's assistance. The injured man lies in the mud, staring up at the sky, blood leaking from his ears and nose.

Danny stretches through the muck, reaching for Casey's bat. Thick Marge swings her foot in and kicks it away then jams her knee into his spine, grinding it cruelly into his back. Danny fights for breath, spitting mud as she wrenches his arms behind him.

Jamal and Rob jump in and take over for Thick Marge, allowing her to step back. She snags her supply pack, opens it, and pulls out a zip-tie restraint.

Danny bucks, trying desperately to shake Jamal and Rob off. They punch and kick him, pushing and pulling, seemingly lustful in their enjoyment the struggle. Wretched pain tears through his side and his vision blurs as one of them grates his face into the rocky forest floor.

The bat is just inches away and Danny reaches for it again, but Thick Marge pins his wrist under her heel with her heavy boot, grinding his bones into the ground and breaking his watchstrap. He thrashes like a wild boar in a fight that's taken one too many spears, bellowing hoarsely.

The twisting brawl slips forward and back as Danny crawls through sludge, trying to gain his feet. Jamal is on top, pummeling downward with his fists. Rob runs around kicking wherever he spies an opening until he joins Rob again, holding Danny down and punching. Heavy bodies cling to him, drive him into the ground. Wet, muddy skin slides against him, presses in on him, rubbing against him through hot and heavy breathing. The men crush Danny beneath their bodies, trample him beneath their boots. They are jubilant.

Weapon and target, hunter and prey, master and slave.

Thick Marge cinches the zip-tie around Danny's wrists as tightly as she can, binding them. The hard plastic bites his skin as he writhes in the muck, arms behind his back, groaning, choking on pain and mud. There is no escape.

Rob and Jamal fall away, exhausted, panting and satisfied, proud of themselves. Jamal, who once loosely considered himself friends with Danny, now gleefully shouts in his captive's face. "We got you, you sick fuck!"

The hunters scoop their trophy up under the arms, dragging it to its feet.

With his last vestige of strength, Danny sinks his teeth into Rob's bare arm.

Rob screams and Danny lets a vicious growl rip from his throat. A fist slams into the side of his head and his legs give out. The men tumble to the ground in a frenzy of confusion. Danny bites again.

Jamal stomps his face and Danny's nose explodes in a shower of blood, broken.

Rob yanks his arm away from the madman. Deep teeth marks leak blood. His eyes turn to saucers and his mind suddenly derails.

"He bit me. He bit me! Oh my God. He's infected! The virus! He infected me!"

Thick Marge places a calming hand on Rob's shoulder. "Calm down. Let's have a look."

"HE'S INFECTED!" Rob screams.

Jamal steps back from Danny. Infected?

Rob jerks Jamal's gun from his friend's belt. Dirty metal clicks against his teeth as he fills his mouth with the muzzle, weeping like a child.

"Wait!"

"Oh my God!"

BLAM.

Rob drops to the ground, the gun falling from his hand. His body shudders.

At first, there is only silence as the shot's echo fades, then a rising squall fills their ears, terribly human and absolutely disturbing. It grows louder with each passing second—a noise that can't be unheard, Rob's rasping, inarticulate, faceless sobs. The wail of life. The wail of regret.

No one moves; it's an awful scene. Two men down, one with a traumatic skull fracture, and the other, victim of a botched suicide attempt.

Arnold shakes off the shock. He rushes from Habib to Rob's side. Thick Marge joins him and takes Rob's hand. "We're here for you."

"Be careful," Jamal mummers from the sidelines, wringing his hands. "He's been bitten. At least he won't last long, small mercies."

"Now, just wait a minute," Arnold stands and stomps over to Danny.

Danny tries to sit up. He rolls his eyes and gnashes his teeth through the blood pouring from his broken nose. Jamal finally gathers his senses about him and helps Arnold lift the bound man to his feet, nervously holding him at bay. He flinches as Danny snaps his teeth at him.

Arnold lifts the prisoner's shirt and peers underneath at a

hastily applied bandage. The dressing, saturated with blood and rain, rips off easily. Arnold considers the wound for a moment, then jabs his index finger into it. Danny screams, falling to his knees. He's nearly sick.

Arnold wipes his hand on his pants. "He's been shot. I don't see any other wounds."

"Are you sure?" asks Jamal.

"Well, I'm not stripping him to find out."

Danny tries to bite Arnold. The Marine belts him across the face, knocking him from his knees to the ground. "Stop that."

He stoops down, grabs Danny by the hair and wrenches his captive's face around to witness the carnage that surrounds them. "Look at what you've caused."

Brody, Dennis, and Thick Marge care for the two critically injured men. Danny feels ill beyond the pain. He knows both of the wounded, knows everyone here, in fact. They may have come to zealously hunt him down, but he doesn't feel happy as he smiles a big shit-eating grin up at Arnold. "Good," he says.

Arnold's eyes turn to slits. He motions for Jamal to sit Danny up and crouches down to be at eye-level with him.

"Where's Alex?"

"Murdering kidnapper," Jamal spits on the ground.

"Where's the kid?" Arnold asks again.

"What do you think murdering kidnappers do to little boys they've kidnapped?" Danny smiles again, wishing this were over.

Brody, caring for Habib, shakes his head. "We're too late."

"Disgusting deviant," Dennis hisses at Danny. "I always knew there was something wrong with you. I saw the way you were looking at that kid after we found him."

"What?" Danny drops the fake smile, trying to understand.

Dennis points a finger at Danny. "You're the worst kind of person. Lot told us everything about you, you pig, you child molester."

Danny's muscles begin to cramp, his whole body becoming a solid, immobile mass. What the hell did Lot tell them?

It takes all his effort just to open his mouth. "What are you talking about?"

"Not so cocky now, are you?" asks Dennis. "You know exactly what I'm talking about, you sack of shit. You're a cancer to our community, a disease."

"No, I would never. I-I…" Danny stutters, devastated.

"You're a beast."

For years, Danny had worked side-by-side with every person here, yet not a single one of them can fathom precious, almighty Lot doing anything that isn't rimmed with gold. No one believes she's capable of heinous acts, but Danny though, Danny… how ready they are to believe.

He feels like crying; feels like curling into a ball and giving up.

If that's what they want him to be, if that's what they need, that's what they'll get, he thinks. As long as it keeps Lot away from Alex.

He grinds his teeth and smiles crazily up at the group one more time. Arnold again connects his palm violently with Danny's cheek. "Cut the shit, just stop the foolishness. Where's the child? Is he alive?"

"No."

"Why?" Thick Marge asks. "Why kill an innocent child, Danny?"

"He slowed me down. Do you have any idea how hard it is to control a kid with The Risen dogging you?"

"Why not just let him go? Why kill him?" Arnold clenches a fist, looking like he desperately wants to punch Danny's teeth out, but he controls himself.

Danny bites back the urge to vomit, the urge to scream at the top of his lungs, the urge to tell everyone everything—not that they'd believe a word of it. "If I couldn't have my mother's attention, I sure as hell wasn't gonna let that kid have it." He wants to rip his own tongue out.

"Where? How?"

"A while back. Choked him. No noise. Wasn't hard."

"You'll show me," Arnold demands.

"With pleasure."

Disgusted, Arnold stands and faces Thick Marge. "I'm not fully convinced," he says.

She shakes her head, "We've gotta go, Javier. We're already pressing our luck. That gunshot was like a dinner bell."

15

Judy's mind might have been swirling if it wasn't for the incessant itching of the damnable uniform against her skin. Rub, rub, rub. It was crazy making. Her skin felt raw and swollen, but she supposed it was a blessing. If the scratching, pulling, pinpricking of the fabric wasn't there, she'd have nothing else to focus on. It kept her grounded.

She gently played with the blue-spiraled triangle at her throat. It was brand new and beautiful. She felt high. Maybe she was, on the revving cocktail of endorphins. Scratch, scratch, scratch—it was so bad it almost felt good and she was intoxicated on those good feelings, so much so she probably could have pounded a nail through her palm and it would've felt amazing.

She quietly surveys the sleeping boys before her. Two rows of young children, not a single one over the age of thirteen. Angelic faces, eyes closed, dreaming of snippets and snails and puppy dog tails. Their blankets tucked under their chins, not a single soul awake.

Now, on her first shift at the Saint Nicolas Institute for Troubled Boys, she felt vindicated. She deserved this—had worked so hard to get here, triumphed against all odds. It was all worth it to be close to them. Every sleepless night spent studying, every meal missed because she couldn't afford groceries after paying for textbooks and tuition. Every person who goaded her about finding a man and settling down, who looked at her cockeyed for wanting to be a "career woman". No one would care for these boys as she would.

Judy quietly stepped down the middle of the isle, surveying her sleeping wards. One little face above all the others caught her eye, a thin boy with blond hair. This one had a splash of freckles that highlighted his cheekbones in such a handsome way. He was so peaceful it was hard to imagine he had done anything worthy of landing him a spot in this place.

Judy made a mental note to read over the child's file. Hector, Hector Griffin. These boys only ended up here as a last resort. Not a single one was as angelic as he looked.

Little Hector, what have you done?

When she interviewed for the position, the head administrator had listed off some of the horrible crimes the children had committed. Murder, rape, sodomy…at such a young age. One had even shot, gutted, and skinned the neighbor's dog because its owner let it shit on his mother's lawn one too many times.

Judy was undeterred. "They just need someone to love them," she responded.

The administrator wanted order above all else. He didn't want trouble, and he didn't want waves. "When they're fourteen, they're not our problem anymore, Judy. They can be released back to their families, or put into the state prison system, depending on what you recommend. I've seen a lot of people come through here with lofty goals. They think they can rehabilitate every boy in here."

Judy smiled sweetly at him. "I have no such illusions and I know the difference I can make is only a small one, but I'm willing to be happy with that. I don't think I can save these boys, I only want to improve the time they spend with us."

"I've stopped counting the number of people I've hired for this position. We can't have someone in here that's a soft touch. These boys will eat you alive if you can't follow through with discipline."

Judy folded her hands into her lap and considered the man before her. He was short, slightly balding, and a sickly grayish color. Maybe he had once held that same lofty hope to rehabilitate the boys, but true to form, they had, indeed, eaten him alive. She smiled reassuringly at the pallid imp across the desk.

"I assure you, sir, I am no stranger to using a firm hand when necessary."

She was hired on the spot.

***

They were nearly ready to beat down the door after the incident with Danny. It wasn't quite a mob, but it certainly wasn't a calm and orderly gathering. Was Lot okay? Was the search party going to kill Danny? What did he want with the child? Who exactly is Alex anyway?

Lot let the pot simmer, hiding away and refusing to answer questions. Now, as she stands at the end of a large conference room jammed with citizens, it's time to bring it to a boil.

Despite the shocking circumstances that have everyone riled up, there is an electricity in the air that can only be described as festive. The anger-fueled excitement is palpable, the unfolding drama a break from the monotony of people's dreary existences. Men, women, and children all stretch their necks to catch a glimpse of their beloved leader.

A hush surges through the crowd as Lot holds up a hand for silence, wincing at the pain in her battered arm. Those close to her murmur in concern.

Once the room is quiet, Lot speaks, her heavyhearted voice carrying over the heads of her loyal subjects. "Please, everyone. I know you all have questions."

A few random people shout displeasure. "What's going on?"

"You should have called this meeting yesterday!"

There is shushing.

"No, no. It's okay. They are valid questions. The truth is, it's taken me so long to gather you all here because I didn't know what to say. I've never dealt with anything like this, and I am also embarrassed, so deeply ashamed to have to share with you my darkest days."

Murmurs ripple through the crowd. Opie waves his hand impatiently to calm people down.

"Tell us, Lot."

"What's going on?"

"I consider you all family, you know this, my brothers and sisters, but there's only one person I ever considered to be my son: Danny."

The room filled with hissing and jeering. *Good.* Lot looks down at the ground, fending off tears for the benefit of the group. A few voices rise, telling others to quiet down, to shut up. Lot composes herself and continues, her voice wavering with emotion.

"I have been weak…Danny is a predator…I did my best to contain him, and his urges. I thought I could shelter you all from him, that I had him under control, but I was blinded by my own selfish need to have my son by my side."

Her words sit on the room, suffocating it; no one knows what to say or how to react. Lot stands hunched before the crowd, a fragile mother, beaten down by the reality of what her son has done. She wobbles on her feet and reaches out a hand for Opie, who stabilizes her. A few tears escape, sliding down her cheek.

"I never thought he would do this, that it could come to this. I knew he was…deviant…but I thought I could help him, change him. Now he's taken the boy Alex, for his own uses. A search party has gone after him with the slim hope of saving the child."

Silence. The crowd is breathless, but it only takes one person to burst the levee. Hannah, Jamal's mother, the defense lawyer turned mortician, breaks free of the crowd and steps forward.

She kneels before Lot and takes her leader's hand. "We can't begin to repay you for everything you've done for us," Hannah looks over her shoulder, challenging the leering crowd. "You've done something for every single one of us here. You've given us food when we were hungry, antibiotics when we were sick, and shelter when we were cold. You've provided us training and taught us skills to survive. You've been a shoulder to cry on when we thought we had nothing. You've always kept order fairly and selflessly and I'll never turn my back on you. You are mother to us all."

Almost instantly, consoling hands surround Lot. They pat her and hug her. Lips on her cheeks, hands on her arm. Fingers reach out and brush her hair, touch her blouse, and the skirt she now wears. They want to feel her. The crowd churns with worshipers desperate to see, to be seen, to comfort, to encourage.

They press in, swarming like ants, the entire room a living mass with Lot as its head.

***

Opie holds the door to the hallway, allowing a frail and overwhelmed Lot through. The people are still trying to reach her, some are even crying. It's been going on like this for about an hour, and Opie has never seen anything like it. This is the kind of fervor he imagines enshrouded the followers of Elvis Presley or Mahatma Gandhi…or Adolf Hitler.

He closes the door, shutting out the crushing force of the crowd, and holds up a candle against the dark. They are alone and can finally breathe.

The mass religious experience Opie just witnessed is a side note to the metamorphosis taking place before him, right now. He's seen behind Lot's mask innumerable times, but this stuns even his jaded eyes. The penanced camouflage of a crestfallen leader slides easily from her face, leaving cold control and manipulation in its place.

Lot wipes her face free of tears, fake, every single one, and smiles at Opie. "That went well, don't you think?"

Opie nods just once. Up. Down. Never in his life has he been so grateful to be on Lot's good side. He had warned Danny not to poke a stick at the lion and had been ignored. If the fugitive isn't dead already, Lot will surely make him wish he was, and those clowns in the other room will pat themselves on the back for a job well done.

***

Lot stands at a window, staring out. Thick vines grow at her feet and cling to window glass. She's on the top floor of the hotel, her performance in the boardroom hours past. This is the only place without fortified windows, the only area that has any natural light.

Many of the southern-facing rooms have been converted to crop growing space. As the colony grows, so does its food needs, and while the outdoor courtyard in the middle of the hotel produces plenty of fruits and vegetables, it just isn't an adequate supply to feed all the hungry mouths. For now, the indoor farm helps, and is a temporary measure until a safe outdoor area can be constructed.

On the north side, where the least sun shines, they keep chickens and even a few goats. Eggs and milk are a staple of the community's diet. Without them, protein would be much harder to come by.

Lot finds it relaxing to be up here. This is the only place she can find true escape. It's easy to imagine she's in an atrium, in some exotic location. One of the only things she misses about the Old World is being able to travel and to see the sights at will.

She has been to Paris once and had always planned to go back. It isn't a dream she's prepared to give up. There still has to be functioning jetliners out there in the world somewhere, and the pilots to fly them.

Lot thinks in a few years, when she has solidified her hold on the surrounding communities, she can round up former electricians and engineers. People that might know a thing or two about maintaining infrastructure. She envisions a time when she commands authority over large swaths of countryside.

There is a power plant about sixty miles northeast. With the proper people and TLC, maybe it can be brought back online. From there, it's only a skip and a hop to modern niceties such as travel.

The world would come back to life under her guiding hand.

No more politicians, no more pretend democracy. Only what Lot, and others like her, created. Like many things in life, the destruction of civilization is just a blessing in disguise.

Before The Plague, "The Center" was under investigation for tax fraud. It was a desperate move by law enforcement to find something, anything, that could be used against her.

They were scared of her growing influence.

It started after the suicide of a church member, who also happened to be the son of a politician. All hell had rained down. First the FBI, then the IRS. There were raids and interrogations, but not a single person broke. Her people always remained loyal, they loved her more than their own children. She made sure of it.

The authorities discovered nothing. The ruse to investigate her found every "t" crossed and "i" dotted. Even the donated life savings of every member of her group had been claimed as income, but that hadn't stopped the harassment.

When the world disintegrated, it took with it the e-mail hacking, the wire-tapping, the nonstop phone calls and pointless raids. It took with it the greedy lawyers, obsessed prosecutors, and disgruntled family members. Lot was able to spin The Plague as evidence of divine intervention to her followers and cinch her position of power even in the face of death.

Of course, very few of those faithful, original followers were spared—just Opie, Danny, and a handful of others. Only two of those people know her true face, and that number is about to fall by one. Should have fallen years ago, Opie had been right all along.

Anger burns inside of Lot like a hot coal. She just can't let Danny's betrayal go. How *dare* he, the one thought that runs on a loop. How dare he try to turn those that love her against her? How dare he take what is hers? How dare he think he can leave her? She owns him.

Lot watches the forest. The land is still. Not a single creature to be seen, no movement, nothing. It is deceptively stagnant outside. If she could make the search team appear with sheer force of will, she would.

They had better locate Danny.

As much as she wants to see his head on a pike, she wants to see him suffer more. She wants to look into his eyes and see defeat. She wants him to know he never had a chance, not against her. She wants to break his spirit and his body. She wants to see him beg, and when he begs, not for mercy, but for death, she will draw out his torture. She wants him to know she can't be beaten, that he is nothing. She wants to consume his soul.

Lost in obsession, Lot continues to stare out the window, longing for the search party to bring Danny back alive. Big plans have already been set into motion and everything will be ready when they drag him back, kicking and screaming. God, she hopes he screams.

16

They've only been walking for a short while and Danny's side throbs unceasingly. Each step allows the gods of the underworld to strum their fiery fingers across every nerve bundle in his body. He stares ahead, his arms bound behind his back, his head swimming in a thick fog of shock. Deer flies bite through his shirt, sucking what blood he has left. A rough prod from behind keeps his feet moving.

Shadows stutter through the trees. It's hard for Danny to focus; they might not be real. Black whispers. No one else notices; they have their hands full with two gravely injured men. A valiant effort is being made to bring everyone home alive.

Habib drags between Jamal and Thick Marge, barely conscious. He's the lucky one. Brody and Dennis toil under Rob's weight, trying to guide him forward as quickly as possible. He whimpers and moans unceasingly. Noises gargle from the hole where his mouth and face used to be. Hamburger. There was discussion of putting Rob out of his misery, but no one was willing to do it. He has to be given a fighting chance.

More shadows. Danny's sure he sees them now and stops. Thick ropes of pain constrict around him, deforming his face as Arnold jams the muzzle of his gun between his ribs. "Get going," his captor gripes, while looking down at his compass.

Danny feels like a horse leading a cart in a demented sideshow. "This is the place."

Arnold's head shoots up and he halts the group.

"Where's the body?"

"Over there."

Danny nods toward a bunch of low-lying bushes.

"Where?" Arnold isn't easily fooled. A creeping anxiety trickles through Danny's subconscious. He swallows hard, mouth dry, heart pounding, oozing precious blood onto his already saturated shirt. He shivers.

"I'd point for you but you've got me tied up. If you'd be kind enough to cut the zip-tie—"

"Shut up." Arnold approaches the bushes uneasily and peers through the branches, trying to catch a glimpse of the boy's body through the twigs and thicket.

He cautiously leans closer. A bird shoots out toward the sky with a loud rustle and he jumps back, heart pounding. He glances back at Danny, who's unsteady on his feet and barely reacts. Arnold shakes his head, thinking they'll be lucky to get him back to Lot alive. He turns back to the bush.

Someone screams—the high-pitch of pure fear. With a hand on his knife, Arnold spins around to see a ghoul clawing at Brody's leg. Teeth rip through thigh muscle, blood geysers through the air. Skeletal fingers pry deep, scraping bone and Brody collapses, shrieking in terror and pain.

Dennis drops his hold on Rob-hamburger-face and fumbles for his weapon. It slips from his fingers into the mud and he backs away from the ghoul that tears Brody to shreds.

Left alone, Rob panics, running in blind zigzags.

More creatures pour in from the surrounding forest. They lurch for Thick Marge and she whips out her machete. Next to her, Jamal lets go of Habib and the semi-conscious man slumps to the ground.

A creature barrels for Arnold. It's fast, but he sidesteps it. It spins on a dime and goes for him again. He jumps out of the way, tries to get behind it, but where he turns, it turns.

He buries his blade in its decayed sinuses and uses the knife as a handle to control the ghoul's head, keeping its teeth away. It swings its arms tirelessly, grasping for its prey.

Rob hits Arnold from behind.

The impact sends them both plunging to the ground, the

creature going down with them, a tangle of arms and legs. Arnold loses his grip on his knife. Snapping teeth whisper by.

Arnold revolts. He kicks Rob to the side and shoves the creature's repulsive face and menacing teeth away with his hands. The skin on the ghoul's face splits and peels like an over-ripe tomato, uncovering decayed muscle. Arnold is left with handfuls of rotten meat.

The creature sinks its teeth deeply into his arm.

Terror sweeps through the group. Creatures grapple mercilessly with the living, never slowing, never tiring, never-ending. Danny stands untouched as chaos swirls around him. He backs slowly away from the madness.

The sharp stick of a large-bladed hunting knife pokes him in the back. The point presses almost hard enough to pierce the skin. He stiffens.

"Over my dead body," Thick Marge growls in his ear and shoves him to his knees. A decayed carcass slams down right in front of Danny, a knife in its eye. Arnold kicks it once, for good measure, and turns to put down another.

Thick Marge plunges her knife through the skull of another ghoul that crawls on the ground. It's missing a leg, lost somewhere in the skirmish.

Arnold knifes the last creature. He wheezes, trying to catch his breath, trying to subdue panic. Dead bodies litter the surrounding area. All that's left of Habib and Rob are stains on the ground. They've been completely torn to shreds.

Brody isn't so lucky. He reaches out, begging weakly for help. Great lengths of intestine pool around his body. Half the skin on his scalp and face are missing. The lower half of his body is hanging by threads. There's no good reason the poor man should still be alive.

Arnold closes his eyes and takes a deep breath. When he opens them, Dennis is standing over Brody.

Brody looks up at Dennis, eyes wide, not understanding. "Help me stand up, would you, please?"

Dennis frowns and looks back at Arnold. Arnold nods—it has

to be done. Dennis squats and fishes his lost knife out of the mud. Brody reaches up. "Just help me get to my feet man, would ya?"

Dennis holds his friend's head gently in his lap and draws his knife across Brody's neck. It's quick and merciful. Brody's hand falls to the ground and he is still.

Arnold turns his eyes to his arm. It hurts like a bitch. A huge chunk of flesh is missing. Half of the USMC tattoo on his forearm is gone, the eagle missing its head and half its body. Dismembered wings bleed hot and sticky down the side of the earth still clasped in its talons.

Arnold calmly walks to Thick Marge, stepping around the kneeling Danny, and puts a hand on her shoulder.

"I'm bit, Marge." The statement falls flatly from his mouth. He can hear his own words, but they don't sound real. Thick Marge glances at Arnold's bleeding arm while keeping Danny in her crosshairs. "How long?"

"An hour, maybe two if I'm lucky. Then I'll turn. Could be less, much less. I doubt longer."

She nods.

"Jesus," Jamal chokes.

Arnold feels like something suddenly kick-starts. He crash lands back into his own body, ready to live, ready to fight. His heart races. "I could be immune you know. I've heard of that. They say the dead rise because hell is full, but I'm not going to hell. I'm a good man. I could have a chance."

Thick Marge closes her eyes for just a second and shakes her head. "Javier…"

"No!" he shouts, pounds on his chest. "I have a chance! I am a God-fearing man!"

Jamal crosses his arms, hugging himself. "You're done for, man. You know that. God has nothing to do with this. Terrorists engineered this bacteria—"

Arnold spins around to face Jamal. He usually tries to keep his emotions in check, to always be level headed, but now he hollers at the other man.

"Shut up. You have no clue what you're talking about!" Spittle flies from his lips. "There were no terrorists, this—"

"Shouting won't solve anything," Dennis inserts himself between the two men and pushes them apart. "All it'll do is bring more of The Risen straight to us."

Arnold turns to face Marge. They've worked together for almost two years, but she looks away. "Javier, you know how this has to go."

Jamal hugs himself a little tighter. "Oh God."

Desperation claws at Arnold's bowels. "Cut off my arm!"

"What?" cries Thick Marge. They stare at each other.

"Won't work," Danny's cuts in.

Dennis places a foot on Danny's shoulder and shoves, tipping him back into the mud. "Who the fuck asked ya? Shit-bag."

"Hurry up. Let's do it. Cut off my arm." Arnold frantically rolls up his shirt sleeve. A fine network of red, ultra-thin spider veins already stem from the deep ring of teeth marks. He rips his rope belt off. Loops it around his arm and tightens it with his teeth.

"Okay. Let's do this," agrees Thick Marge.

Jamal and Dennis share a surprised glance. Thick Marge grabs her machete and checks the sharpness of the blade. It will do. She points at Dennis. "Watch the prisoner." Dennis obeys. Danny lies in the muck, too battered to rise.

"Javier...lie down," Thick Marge says to Arnold. Arnold drops to the ground, feeling as though his chest will explode any second.

"Jamal," Thick Marge says, "sit on Javier's chest."

Jamal sits on top of Arnold, straddling his chest as instructed.

Thick Marge breathes evenly. She painstakingly lines up her blade with his arm. Down slowly. Up slowly. In a straight line, practicing the blow. She raises it high into the air, ready.

"Wait!" Arnold looks up at Jamal. "You better have a cigarette ready for me when this is over, you always seem to have them, don't hold out on me now."

Jamal pulls a gold and green pack of Jack Hatter's from his breast pocket and shakes it. The three remaining cigarettes in it rattle around. Arnold smiles. "You'll have to let me in on your secret after this." Arnold hasn't smoked in six years, but this is as good of an excuse as any to start again. He reaches out and grabs a stick, bites down on it. His muffled words push around the wood. "Okay. Do it." He turns his scared, sweating face away.

Thick Marge adjusts her grip on the large knife and takes one more deep breath. With all her might, she brings the blade down. Skin splits and bone crunches as it slices through Arnold's throat, going halfway through his neck. Jamal fires up from his friend's chest, shocked. "Holy shit!"

Arnold blinks once. Thick Marge brings the blade down again, this time finishing the job. The knife sinks into the wet ground as blood pours from an empty neck. The severed head rolls a few inches away.

Dirt and blood clot Thick Marge's blade. Complete silence follows her every move as she wipes it clean on the fabric of her pants. Even Danny is shocked. She turns to face her two remaining teammates, prepared for their accusing eyes, but there's no time for judgment.

Another creature crashes through the brush, gunning for Jamal. Dennis lunges for it, wielding his knife, just as Jamal dodges, unwittingly putting himself in the path of the blade. He stares down at the knife as it penetrates his chest. His eyes are so wide they look as though they could fall from their sockets. Dennis stutters stupidly, his hand falling away from the handle.

Thick Marge plunges her machete through the ghoul's eye and out the back of its skull. The creature falls to the ground. Jamal falls too, his hands fluttering toward the protruding knife. He tries to speak but can't.

There is surprisingly little blood.

***

Alex waited patiently for hours. He fought off sleep, fought off the ache and burning in his thin muscles, fought through alternating waves of anxiety and boredom. The rain stopped some time ago, but his clothes are still damp and now he strains his ears, listening for Danny's voice. For the all-clear, but there is nothing.

He extends his sap covered finger and lightly touches it to an ant. Godlike, he lifts his finger from the bark of the tree, ripping the ant away from everything it knows. Alex turns his finger over and examines the tiny insect. Coffee colored and shiny, six legs kicking vigorously, two pinchers opening wide, ready to clamp. He pops his finger in his mouth, covering the bug with saliva, and sucks it into his stomach. Food is food, and this comes with a nice pine flavor.

Finally, he has no choice. Alex works himself down the small pine that has been his safe-haven, knapsack and all, and stands at the bottom of the tree. Beams of sun filter down. They are bright and hazy with pollen floating lazily through them. Birds chirp. They are loud. Almost too loud, and Danny isn't here.

Alex's heart skips a beat as he realizes he's alone.

Alone.

Alone.

Alone.

He turns, takes a step forward, then moves back to his original spot. Left looks the same as right. He can hear the valves of his own heart opening and closing, and tears burn hotly behind his eyes, hysteria hiding just behind the veil.

Alex jerks his head and spins in place. It all looks the same. A stick snaps under his foot and he jumps, almost leaving his skin behind.

Relieved the noise was nothing other than himself, he stares at the ground where he was just standing, noticing faint indentations in the mud. He drops to his knees and narrows his vision. The tracks are his footsteps from earlier, not quite washed out from the rain. His face brightens. He knows which way to go now, he's not alone, Danny will be waiting for him and things will be okay.

***

Alex trots along his newfound path for a while, every now and then stopping to inspect for signs he's still going the right way. His world is alive with the sounds of birds and insects, but he's locked on the feeble trail.

Leaves shuffle and branches break, sending cold fear to crush his heart. He scans the area. The filmy trees that loom overhead, their wavy branches far out of reach. The forest floor is gray and shadows smother the ground, where only moss survives. There's no place to hide.

Far in the distance, a figure with a pronounced limp drags aimlessly closer. Alex dodges behind a tree, flattening himself against it, his breath catching in his chest. The only thing separating him from the creature is the trunk.

He digs his fingers into the bark behind him, his head jerking nervously. The creature nears slowly, dragging its bad leg. It was a woman at one time, once pretty, now grotesque. Its long hair is matted with dried blood and forest junk and its scalp is peeled back in two places, revealing white skull beneath. Tarnished gold jingles on one arm and a diamond wedding ring still sparkles from a finger that is half bone. One mud-caked, black designer pump with a red sole remains attached to a foot, it makes the creature's limp worse.

It turns its rotted face in Alex's direction. He presses himself flatter against the tree and doesn't breathe. The thing's eyes bulge. Black pus oozes from ripped corneas and drizzles down cheekbones, where it pools above an exposed jawbone. It looks as though the creature-woman is weeping as she passes by, just inches away.

It's nearly ten minutes before Alex feels safe to move again. The ghoul is gone, but there could be others, there are always others. Alex reminds himself Danny will be waiting for him.

***

It isn't long before Alex reaches the clearing where he last saw

Danny. Trotting triumphantly in, he's sure he'll see the tall blond man waiting for his return, grumpy and annoyed, but his hopes are dashed.

Alone.

The muddy ground is torn up.

Alone.

Thick blood mixes with pools of rain.

Alone.

The cawing, cheeping, chittering, buzzing, roaring, screeching, of the birds overhead drive thin shards of glass through Alex's brain. He cups his hands over his ears, trying to block them out. His head jerks. The world is too bright, too loud. Sunlight scalds his eyes, glinting off glass. There is something, partially hidden in the leaves.

Danny's watch.

Alex stoops over and scoops it up. He stares at it lying limply in his hand, its face cracked, no longer ticking, and panic begins to well in his breast.

Alone.

His head jerks again. He clamps his hand around the broken timepiece and wanders in the clearing, walking in circles, disconnected, staring, as if Danny will materialize before his eyes if he looks hard enough. He tugs anxiously at his hair with sap covered fingers.

Alone.

Alex trips over something.

Laying in the mud, forgotten and lonely, is that shining talisman of life, Casey's bat. Old and splintered, stained with dirt and blood, it nearly glows against the gray of the world.

Alex lifts the bat from the ground, enraptured, shock slowly receding from his face. He imagines he can feel Casey standing nearby, lending her strength, and Danny nodding his approval, beckoning him to follow the new path beaten through the forest.

Alex wraps his fingers powerfully around the neck of the bat and lets it rest against his shoulder, feeling its weight. He looks small holding it, malnourished, sodden with dirt and mud, but his jaw is set hard, determined, and his mind focuses sharply with a new directive.

FIND DANNY.

***

Lot still stands among the plants in her poor man's atrium, the late afternoon sun speckling her face. Next to her, Opie drones on about some trade route they've been trying to establish. He's like a dog with a bone. Can't he just close his mouth for a few minutes?

Lot's arm aches frightfully, but the pain is only secondary to the utter frustration building inside of her. The team she sent out after Danny should have been back by now and the thought of that traitor getting away is intolerable. He must pay for his crimes.

Darkness clouds out Opie's words. What if Danny does get away? He'll have gotten the best of her. She imagines his smug face laughing at her. Oh, how she would love to rip out his tongue and then feed it to him, piece by bloody piece. She wonders if she could get away with such an obviously cruel punishment.

No, probably not. The peons in this community need to think everything is their idea, they are weak. Lot has to maintain decorum, especially in matters like this, or risk losing her hold. Still, the idea of jamming a pair of rusty pliers into Danny's screaming mouth and tearing his tongue out from the root is pleasurable. Very pleasurable.

"Lot," Opie's annoying voice demands attention. "Look."

He hands her a pair of binoculars. Lot follows Opie's outstretched finger. Several stories below, the survivors of the search party are dragging themselves from the forest's edge.

Supported by Dennis, Jamal slowly stumbles, a knife protruding from his chest, blood leaking ominously from his mouth. More importantly, Thick Marge trudges grimly ahead and in front of her, prodded forward at knifepoint, staggers Danny.

Lot smiles, gripping the binoculars tightly. "Grand." Excitement courses through her veins. She watches Danny stagger forward, his swollen, colorless face bobbing in and out of view. His dark, bruised eyes and blood-covered hair are stains in the sun-bleached field. Her hand trembles, jubilation taking hold.

Lot swings the binoculars over the rest of the group, searching for the boy. Her heart beats heavily, anger mixing with triumph as she realizes he's not there. Danny will indeed suffer for this. She lowers the binoculars and turns to Opie.

"Leave me."

Opie licks his lizard lips and scurries out, the door banging shut behind him. She is alone and lifts the binoculars to her eyes again. Guards from inside the hotel are running to join the search party, defending them from the creatures that again wander the field.

Her eyes fall on Danny once more. He looks like death, miserable and downcast, and it's delicious. Lot breathes heavily, the blood in her veins burning. An overwhelming need dizzies her mind. She drops the binoculars to the floor and falls against a wall. Her good hand touches her cheeks then paws at her breasts lightly before falling to trace her wanton thighs. She hikes her skirt up in the front and touches her blazing skin, panting as her fondling fingers find their mark.

Her mind turns to Danny in his wretched condition, her plans for him pushing her further into ecstasy. She thinks of him screaming, begging, and it fills the very fiber of her being. She moans softly and closes her eyes, giving herself to the uncontrolled waves of bliss that wash over her.

17

There's little point in considering the risks. Being alone in the woods is dangerous even without the threat of man-eating creatures. The only thing that matters right now is the need to repair order. With Casey gone and Danny missing, chaos will reign.

It's this single-minded need for things to be as they were that drives Alex forward. Without a place to safely moor his ship, he'll soon find himself adrift, lost at sea, unable to reach the world around him. Danny is supposed to be that pier to which Alex can tether his boat, just like Casey before him.

But none of this penetrates Alex's upper-mind as he weaves and dodges through the forest. All he knows is he feels a connection with Danny, much as he did with Casey. It's a connection he can't allow to be severed, even if it means his life. Not after he lost Casey—not after what Lot did to her.

Alex quickly follows the path left by the search party, easily seeing their footprints on the muddy forest floor. He slows his pace as he approaches an area where he can see bodies through the trees. Their smell is quick to assault his nose and he hears insects gathered for a late afternoon meal as he cautiously steps closer.

Wading through the carnage, Alex sees bodies everywhere, fresh and rotten alike, left unmolested in their death struggle. Blood coats the ground and chunks of flesh and innards, seething with flies, litter the earth.

He's unphased. If the bodies aren't moving, they're no threat. He steps over a corpse, his bright blue eyes scanning.

Danny?

His heart pounds.

Danny?

He searches. Nearby, a squirrel gnaws on an acorn. Gnaw. Gnaw. Gnaw. It grinds into Alex's brain as he scrutinizes faces on bodies. Only an unraveling string holds back the dark curtain of aloneness that threatens to smother him.

Danny isn't here. With that in mind, Alex's anxiety is temporarily mollified.

A high-pitched squealing startles him from his thoughts. He twists around, Casey's bat at the ready, but there is nothing. No cadaverous ghoul pitching itself at him, no danger.

The only thing out of the ordinary is the squirrel. It writhes in place on the ground, screaming, as if possessed by a fit of religious fervor, speaking in tongues.

Alex moves closer to the gray mass of convulsing fur, fascinated. It tumbles slightly out of the weeds revealing a creature's head, its teeth set into the squirrel's side. A tiny, clawed foot rips valiantly at the head's swollen eyes and the rodent clamps its teeth time and again on the soft tissue of the creature's unflinching face. The squirrel wails, but the head is unforgiving.

Bits of acorn speck the small animal's lips as a death shudder overtakes it. Finally, it goes limp and Alex steps a little closer. The head whips its eyes toward him, releasing the mangled body of the squirrel and snaps its jaws at the boy.

Alex sneaks a little closer, recognizing the face. Its teeth click like a windup chatterbox. Yes, this man was there when Casey was killed. "Executed," Danny's word reverberates in his mind. The head had been standing right there. Had watched the whole thing. Had done nothing.

Alex toes the head with his shoe and it rolls away, teeth still snapping. He kneels down in the mud, placing the bat next to him, but within easy reach, and pulls off his knapsack. He sets it before him and with a heavy air of ritual, he unzips the bag, peering inside.

Alex lightly caresses each object inside his knapsack with his fingers. The bag of marbles had been a birthday present. Not the last one before the dead rose from their graves, but just an old favorite. The glossy balls with streaks of colored glass inside them are easy to get lost in. He can stare at them for hours, imagining each marble as a tiny world; the entire sack a pocket-sized universe.

His parents had always encouraged him to remove the marbles from the bag. To take them outside; to play with them. They'd hoped a toy like this would help Alex to socialize with the other kids in the neighborhood, but they never did understand. Besides, the neighbor kids were into video games.

Alex slides his fingers over a matchbook with one match. His mother's. She had smoked, but quit when she was pregnant, they said. Still, she went back soon after each of her sons were born. She tried to hide it from the kids, but Alex knew because she always smelled liked cigarettes. Her clothes, her hair, her skin—perfume and cigarettes. Alex grew accustomed to that smell and had looked forward to its predictableness.

Late one night, while claiming his prize from the trash, Alex heard his parents talking about him, concerned. They didn't know what to do, or who to talk to. The doctors were of no help (they never were). She'd been crying.

When his mother came out of his parent's bedroom, she spotted him but didn't know he'd been listening. She smiled at him and he wondered why she would smile if she were "overwhelmed" and "scared"? She rubbed his head and poured him a glass of water to take back to bed.

Now, every time he holds the matchbook, it comforts him. Reminds him his mother smiled for him, even when she had no reason to.

The pages of *Robinson Crusoe* bend under his palm. His older brother's book. Lyle would read it to him, for hours sometimes. It was what they did together, every night, like clockwork, until Alex allowed him to stop. They had finished the book seven times.

He fondles the cold glass of the aftershave bottle. His father's.

His mother gave it to his father on Alex's behalf as a Father's Day gift. Even though he knew Alex hadn't actually picked it, his father wore it proudly.

The family had been without running water or electricity for almost a week when the newscaster on the crank radio announced emergency centers where the community could go. They urged people to be aware and to only travel during the day.

The next morning, they packed and left the house. Alex had grabbed the bottle of aftershave because he was sure his father would need to shave at their destination.

The bottle reminds him to always try a little harder. It was something his father asked of him regularly. "Try a little harder to pay attention, Alex. Try a little harder to think of other people, Alex. Try a little harder."

Finally, Alex clenches his hand around the old, threadbare t-shirt lying rumpled at the bottom of his knapsack. He'd been wearing this shirt when Casey found him. She could have left him where he was, two other people did, but they weren't like her.

She had always wondered out loud how he had survived, set adrift with no connection to reality. She never imagined it was her that brought him back to shore. She fed him, bathed him, clothed him. She protected him and sacrificed for him. His own mother would have been proud to know Casey was there with her boy.

Alex pulls the t-shirt from his knapsack and then hesitates. He looks at the Arnold-head, its lips drawn back, its teeth exposing an infectious sneer. He needs the t-shirt, but he needs Danny more. Without Danny, Casey will disappear.

Try a little harder.

Alex wads the t-shirt into a ball and grabs a stick from the dirt. He positions the head with his feet, holding it like a snake filled soccer ball. The head's jaws open and close, snapping viciously. Open. Close. Open. Close. Open—

Alex drops the wadded shirt into Arnold's mouth and uses the stick to jam it back as far as it will go. He crams it in until the head's jaws are locked open with fabric.

Proud of himself, Alex lifts the head by its hair. It hangs limply, eyes rolling comically and jaw muscles trying ineffectually to work out the t-shirt. Bite marks and deep scratches from the squirrel scathe the head's darkly tanned cheeks. Alex smiles widely into its face.

***

Screams drift down the dark corridor leading to the makeshift infirmary-morgue. Inside, Jamal tries to sit up, Julie shoves him back down. "Stop moving!" She pulls a lantern closer. Dennis' knife is buried up to its hilt in Jamal's chest.

Her steady hand slices away shirt with scissors. There is very little blood. Hannah, the undertaker, stands next to the nurse, hovering over her only son, beside herself with fear.

"Mom! I don't want to die!" Jamal thrashes on the table. "Please, Mom!" His words gurgle in this throat and bubbles of blood burst over his lips.

"Stop talking," Julie snaps. Blood is filling Jamal's lungs and the more he moves, the more he talks, the more quickly he will drown. Hannah holds her son's hand and cries.

Julie scrutinizes her medical supplies. A pile of bandages, a few shiny instruments, nothing that will save this kid from dying. He needs a hospital, he needs a surgeon. He tries to sit up again.

"Stop moving. You're making it worse, Jamal!"

"Oh my God! I don't want to die. Please! Don't let me die!"

"Stop yelling!" Julie shouts.

Hannah's face is misshapen with grief as she looks at Julie. "Do something! Please! You have to help him!"

***

Darius, a young guard with a unibrow, nervously pops open the padlock that secures a walk-in cooler. He's seen Lot, spoken to her a few times even, but he's never been alone with her. Although she's much smaller than him, he feels like she takes up the entire room. His hand shakes nervously as he lays the key in her outstretched palm.

"Leave me now," she says.

His eyes search Lot's face. How can he leave *her* alone with such a dangerous criminal? Lot places her hand lightly on his arm, and he tries not to tremble.

"It's okay, Darius. I'll be fine."

The calmness and confidence in her voice are enough to ease his worries. Who is he to second-guess her? He nods in a way he hopes suggests strength, and then leaves his leader standing alone in the chrome-plated hotel kitchen.

The light from Lot's candle glints off of every surface not covered in dust and the hinges on the cooler door squeal as she pulls it open. She holds her candle up high, illuminating the small space within. Slumped against the back wall, arms still tightly bound behind his back, is Danny. His shirt, saturated with blood, clings to him.

He squints against the flickering light and blinks slowly, face drawn thin with pain. Dark black circles ring his eyes, standing out against anemic skin. Lot has seen this death mask before. She is simultaneously delighted and worried by how terrible he looks. She can't allow him to die before he can be punished.

"I'm sorry for the accommodations, but we're not really set up for inmates, as you know."

Danny stares into the void, as if he can't hear. Lot steps nearer, favoring her slinged arm, and crouches down beside to him. She places her candle nearby. He rolls his dulled eyes toward her and she can taste the defeat dripping off him. "I've been told you were shot, Danny. What happened to you?"

A thick storm of fury crosses his face and excitement jolts through Lot. It's the spark she's looking for. She wants him to go down fighting.

"You happened to me," he spits.

"Oh God," Lot flicks her wrist. "You're so dramatic, you always have been. I gave you my best years, I took care of you when no one else wanted you."

"I had someone. You killed him."

"This conversation is tiresome. Do you want to know the truth? Do you Daniel? Your father took his own life."

"Liar!" Danny hisses.

Lot's heart flutters in her chest with titillation.

"It's true. He was weak, scared of suffering."

"No! He would never leave me!"

"He did. Do you want to know how he did it?"

"NO!"

Lot's face flushes. Seeing Danny squirm helplessly is such a thrill. It's so easy to grind salt into ancient, festering wounds, instant gratification. Shooting fish in a barrel, she thinks, is underrated.

"If he were alive today how do you think he'd feel about what you've done? Murdered a child in a jealous rage. You just couldn't help yourself, could you? You had to destroy such a sweet, innocent life to get back at me."

Lot slides in a little closer to Danny. He glares at her, shaking with a bitter rage so consuming it nears madness.

"You just couldn't handle my affections turned to someone else, could you?" Lot reaches out a hand and lightly strokes his hair away from his forehead. It's filthy with forest muck and blood. She glides her fingers across his skin, and he overpowers the need to shudder, refusing to show weakness.

"You obsessed about me day and night, Danny. You seduced me, bent me to your will, and ultimately murdered a little boy because of your sickness, because of your disease."

"I was only seven," Danny's voice cracks. It's barely a whisper. The anger is still there, but there is something evil lurking in the crevices: guilt.

Lot touches his cheek and he closes his eyes, stomach turning, head spinning. Lot's smooth, measured voice overrides his thoughts. "I only ever did what you wanted, my boy. I never did anything you didn't like."

"I was only seven."

"Yes, to begin with. And as you grew older you wanted even more."

"No," Danny screws his eyes shut, trying to block her out.

"I only tried to make you happy, to give you what you asked for."

"You're twisting it."

"Am I?" Lot brings her face close to his. He shrinks back into the corner, tears escaping his closed eyes. She strokes her hand gently across his chest and he turns his face away, but has nowhere to hide. He is tiny and powerless, a frightened child once again, victim to Lot's whims.

Her hand drops to his inner thigh and his skin crawls under her caress, yet still he wants her. It makes him want to rip her touch from his body and burn the flesh. He presses his back against the wall, trapped and unable to escape.

Lot pushes in closer. She could dine on the heady mixture of anger, fear, and self-loathing coming from Danny. Blood swirls through her body and the giddy feeling of total control, total power, wraps her spine in warmth.

She tenderly puts her lips to his ear. "You've been a bad boy, Danny. I'm very upset you took my new toy away from me."

Danny can't fight the black hole of emotion that swallows him, feasts on his thoughts, devours his body, engulfs his entire soul. He slams the back of his head into the wall of the cooler, sending bright flashes of light careening through his vision. "SHUT UP! SHUT UP! SHUT UP! SHUT YOUR FUCKING MOUTH! I CAN'T LISTEN TO YOU ANYMORE!"

Lot forces herself to stand. She wants to stay and play some more, but it's too dangerous a game. This is just an amuse-bouche, she'll have to wait for the main course.

Darius bolts into the kitchen, as expected after Danny's outburst, and he's brought friends. They are at her side in seconds. Danny continues to holler.

"Are you alright?" Darius looks ill with fright.

"Yes. Thank you."

A guard slams the cooler door shut, cutting off Danny's voice. He throws the padlock on. "Are you sure you're alright?" The concerned faces of guards surround her. "Did he touch you? Did he hurt you?"

"I'm fine, really, I promise. He's manic. Psychotic. I shouldn't have come down here, it's too much of a strain on me." Lot leans against Darius for support. "Please help me back to my room."

"Yes, ma'am."

"And please have Julie see to the prisoner, he needs medical attention."

All the guards nod.

Darius supports Lot through the kitchen. Just as they are about to leave, she looks back over her shoulder at the remaining guards. "Tonight, he'll be standing judgment for his crimes. Please see to it he's well gagged when the proceedings begin so no one else has to endure his hysterical abuse."

"With pleasure."

"Thank you. And please, try to be gentle."

When she's gone the guards share a look. They'll be gentle all right, as gentle as kittens.

18

A twig whips across Alex's cheek, leaving a thin red mark. He forces his legs to pump as fast as they can, his beat-up shoes snagging traction wherever possible, his knapsack bouncing on his back with each step. Alex keeps Casey's bat clenched hard in one small fist.

Two once identical creatures lope behind him, their matching tennis outfits dirty and torn. The twins, now starved hounds determined to catch a fox, are still together in undeath, by miracle or mayhem. One is missing half an arm, the other his once precious nose.

Alex careens through the forest. He hurdles over a large rock, landing hard in a bramble bush and wincing as its thorns drag across his skin, opening long ragged wounds. Blood leaps to the surface, spiraling to the ground from the shallow gashes. The thorns grip his clothes, impeding his escape.

Behind him the twins' strength is unwavering. They never slow to catch their breath, to nurse a wound, or to consider another plan of action. They pursue. No thought, no consciousness. They have only the drive to kill. To eat. To destroy.

Alarm bells sing in Alex's head, clanging so loudly it's hard to think. The bush's pointed fingers hold fast to his knapsack and his muscles twitch with fear-induced adrenaline. His head jerks, his lungs burn, and he rips his bag away, tumbling to the ground as the thorns mercifully release.

The twins crash through the brush with ferocity. They don't feel the thick thorn laden branches bite into their rotten flesh. They don't notice the soggy chunks of skin they leave behind.

They growl and snap at Alex as he scrambles back, jumps to his feet and runs, just ahead of the monsters.

***

Opie sits in a chair centered in the middle of a well-stocked and immaculate hotel room. It's large, with framed art hanging on the walls and curtains hiding the protective scrap metal over the windows. A mahogany desk boasts a large stack of classic books and even a handful of working ballpoint pens. Several lanterns gutter softly, hanging from an appropriated hat rack.

Lying on the ground before him are Odette's boy and girl. They press brand-new crayons onto coloring book pages, smiling and chattering, even the teen.

Opie worked hard to procure the books and crayons, and it makes him happy to see them enjoyed. It's a new feeling; he doesn't think he's ever before felt happiness because of someone else's happiness.

Odette floats into the room with a steaming teapot and cups on a tray. To Opie, it almost feels as though nothing else exists outside of this room, but it's more than a feeling, it's a wish. He wishes he could stay with Odette and the kids, just like this, forever, and forget about the raging plague outside. Forget about the nonsense with Danny and Lot.

Odette pours coffee from the tea spout, filling two cups, then sits in the chair next to him. The concerned look on her face bursts Opie's blissful bubble.

"I can't believe they brought that animal back here. After what he did to that poor boy? It's crazy, don't you think?" she asks.

Opie lifts his steaming cup off the table. It's lined with real gold, the pot an antique. It doesn't matter to him that the teacup holds coffee, which he prefers over tea. It's good to have the nicer things in life, regardless of what shape the world is in now.

"Odette," Opie pats her knee reassuringly, "Danny must face justice for his crimes, stand as an example. It's the only true way to protect the people, and your children—our children." Toe the line, he thinks.

Odette smiles. This is the first time he's ever referred to the children as "his". He smiles back, his weaselly face no longer used to the muscle operation required to curve his mouth upward instead of down.

She has no clue, he thinks, wants no clue really, no one does. Everyone wants to live their lives as though things can somehow go back to the way they used to be. As though there's still a line drawn in the sand between good and evil.

The fact of the matter is the line was blurred even when the police were a phone call away and you could buy your food in the local supermarket. Now, that hazy line is completely obliterated, but people delude themselves into believing it's still there. They have to, or they'll see their world has completely fallen apart.

Without Lot, without himself, and without the few others who are able to face reality, this entire community would be in shambles. These people, Odette and the kids, they need him, and those like him, to get ahead in this new world.

Opie sits back, content to allow Odette to bathe in ignorance and naivety. It's a luxury she doesn't even know he's giving her. In more ways than one, he considers himself a hero, and the self-reassurance tamps down the demons for yet another day.

Odette sips from her cup. "I hope they make him pay for what he's done. Lot can't protect him any longer."

Opie reaches over, taking her hand comfortingly. "Don't' worry. I'm sure Danny will get everything he deserves."

***

It's so unfair. After everything they've been through. The world came tumbling down around them, but they managed to survive with pure grit and determination. They were survivors. They. Survived. What does it all mean if he's gone now?

Deep sobs wrack Hannah's body. She's covered in blood. The floor is covered in blood. Jamal, her dead son, is covered in blood.

It's everywhere, so much of it. Spilled from his chest, pooling on the table beneath him, its metallic odor filling the air. She wishes she could siphon it up and pour it back into his body.

She and Julie did everything they possibly could. Jamal had cried and begged for life with his very last ounce of strength. He knew he was going to die, but he didn't want to go, wasn't ready, and she wasn't ready to let him go. His pleading voice, begging her not to let him die, is carved into her soul.

Hannah grips her son's lifeless body, shaking him. "No, no, no, no, NO! NO! NO!"

Behind her, Julie stands somberly.

Everyone alive today knows his or her fair share of tragedy and death, but it never gets easier. As the unofficial mortician, Hannah has seen even more than most. Julie rests a gentle hand on the grieving mother's shoulder.

"Hannah, we need to be sure he stays with God."

Hannah lifts her head, tears streaming from her eyes and glares at Julie. "Don't you think I know that?"

Julie nods, sympathetically. She can't imagine the pain of losing one of her own three children. Somehow, by some miracle, she's been able to spare her teenaged sons, but it's been a long road, seeking shelter in the company of the men that would have her, just to be sure her boys were always protected.

Opie was nothing short of a savior when they first met, a bright light in an otherwise murky existence. He never laid a hand on her, never asked for what most men took. For bringing her and her boys under Lot's sheltering wing, he only requested compliance, medical advice, and a closed mouth. For such a pittance, her boys were able to be boys once more, never again to see their mother submitting on her back for gun-toting men.

She owes Opie everything.

Julie watches Hannah as she crosses the room and opens a drawer. Inside are a hammer and a railroad spike. Hannah lifts them, her bloodstained hands shaking. Her heart aches more than tears can ever show.

Hannah's heavy feet carry her back to Jamal's side. He's so still now, so quiet, and yet it's hard for her to believe he's really gone.

"Julie, can you leave us please, I'd like to be alone with my son."

"You don't have to do this. I can—"

"No. He's the only one I had left in the world, the only person that mattered. Go be with your three treasures and leave me. The last thing I can do for my son now is to prepare his body for final rights."

Julie nods, unable to say anything helpful. Hannah's grief-worn eyes stare back at her.

"I need to be alone with him now," she says.

The door clicks shut behind Julie. Hannah lifts the railroad spike and hovers the point above her son's forehead. Her hand quakes, unable to touch the rusty point to Jamal's ashen skin.

***

Alex doesn't think he can run much longer. It feels like he's been running forever, and the twins are still in staunch pursuit. Ahead, a large log lies in his path. He leaps, his drained body making its best effort, but it isn't good enough. His foot tangles in the undergrowth and he sprawls to his hands and knees, his palms scraping rocks. Six feet ahead is a jagged ledge with a steep drop.

The twin with one arm clears the log without effort, landing directly behind Alex. The second creature gets its leg jammed between branches.

The one-armed creature hooks its fingers around Alex's knapsack and drags him backward. Alex twists, tries to hit the thing with Casey's bat. Teeth whisper by his ear, and he smacks the ghoul's face away just in time, then swivels out of his knapsack, leaving One-Arm with its cotton and rayon prize.

There's no other place left to go but back. Alex rolls between the first creature's legs, bat still in hand, and comes face to face with No-Nose, trapped by the log.

He rams the butt of the bat into the thing's face. Its head snaps back, giving Alex the split second he needs to scramble to his feet and leap away, back over the log.

He soars above No-Nose and the creature snags his ankle. Alex crashes to the ground, his teeth rattling in his head. He flips gymnastically around, wrenches his leg away, and clambers backward.

One-Arm, no longer suckered by the knapsack, rockets over the other creature and dives for Alex. Alex grunts, slamming both of his feet into the thing's face. Lips split and teeth cascade from the front of the ghoul's mouth, the blow sending it flying back into its brother.

Alex races to his feet and sprints away, running blindly. Another steep drop unfolds before him. At the bottom is a rocky streambed, muddied by the rain and as bereft of life as the two corpses hot on his heels.

Alex slides in the gravelly loam beneath his feet, the worn treads of his shoes unable to grip. One-Arm hits with the weight of a freight truck and they slam forward, skidding over rocks and branches, sliding to a stop just before plunging over the side of the drop. Chunks of dirt and rock spray downward, landing twenty feet below.

Alex shoves at the creature on top of him, snorting with the effort, and using Casey's bat to hold it at bay, he's able to swing himself on top of the ghoul. The thing struggles relentlessly, its jaws opening and closing around the ash wood separating it from a late afternoon meal.

The second twin, at last free from the log, tackles. Alex is sandwiched between rotten flesh. The force of the impact is so great it knocks the wind out of him and the ground beneath the three gives way. Casey's bat flies down the slope, along with One-Arm. The creature spins and bounces, hitting rocks that break bones as it smashes to the bottom.

Alex plummets over the side of the ledge, directly toward One-Arm. He flails, grasping at loose dirt and mud. A rock strikes his ribcage, nearly bruising his lungs and he gasps, involuntarily trying to regain his breath as soil and dust clog his airway. His fingers drag across hard, wet earth, unable to find purchase.

As he plunges toward certain death, Alex wraps a hand around a tree root and grips it with all his strength. His descent abruptly comes to an end, almost tearing his arm from its socket. He dangles from the root halfway down the slope. The thing below frantically tries to climb, its rotten smile welcoming Alex into hell.

Above him, No-Nose, somehow avoiding the fall, hungrily dances back and forth.

Alex pants, his bruised ribs are a nuisance. His feet dangle like tasty meat pies, just out of One-Arm's reach, as he clings to the side trying to regain his breath.

Slowly, he pulls himself up the slope, seeking out roots and rocks, dragging himself up hand over hand. The muddy slope is slippery and threatens to throw him into the gullet of the ghoul below.

No-Nose trots back and forth waiting impatiently for its food to crest. The creature almost looks as though it's smiling with glee—there's nothing quite like delivery. Alex carefully nears the top, stopping just out of the thing's reach. He eyes it, clear, alert, and focused. *Try a little harder, Alex.*

With bleeding fingers gripped firmly around a protruding rock, he waves a hand, antagonizing the creature above him. The creature throws itself to the ground, its long, nearly unscathed arms stretch down.

Alex dodges a dirty hand. As No-Nose bellows with displeasure, he grabs one of the creature's wrists and, with a grunt, pulls with all his strength. The monster's grotesque, twisted face passes a hair's width from the boy as it spills over the side.

As it thrashes by, the creature snags Alex's foot. It hangs by one hand, unconcerned with staying its fall, but trying desperately to latch onto its meal. The weight of the creature is that of a full-grown man and it stretches Alex to the point where he feels like he's ripping in half. The rock he holds on to wobbles in the dirt.

Alex kicks at the creature frantically with his free foot. It claws at him, trying to climb his leg, its teeth close on his shoe, but it gets nothing but a mouthful of worn canvas. The shoe slides away from Alex's foot and No-Nose tumbles down the slope to join its brother.

Sweating and over-exerted, Alex lugs himself the rest of the way up the embankment. Safe at the top, he falls to the dirt, gasping for air, grimacing with each breath, his bruised ribs paining him.

For a few minutes, he can't move. He lies on his back, shielding his eyes from the rays of sunlight that push through the trees. They grow so bright he has to look away. Finally, he peeks his face back over the ledge. Far below, the twins paw at the sides of the creek bed, too stupid to know how to climb. They turn their ugly, gnarled faces toward Alex and groan inhumanly, hungry for his flesh.

Just over the side, Alex notices Casey's bat caught up in some weeds. He's able to grasp the handle and pull the weapon up. Now, all he needs is his knapsack.

***

Lot gazes over the sea of people, squashed together like sardines. There are so many that proceedings had to be moved from the meeting room to the hotel's modest banquet area.

Children lean in on tiptoes for a better look. After her last performance, word traveled on horseback, rumor on wings, and almost every single person in the community is here, waiting with bated breath.

Over the past few hours, heated debates and arguments swirled. Unanswered questions allowed conjecture and assumption to reign supreme. How can something like this happen here? What kind of monster would hurt a defenseless child? *What if it had been my child instead of that boy?*

Anger rolls through the crowd like an oily soap bubble, coating everything it touches, ready to burst at any moment. It's a distraction from the horror of the world beyond their refuge. The horror of loved ones that rise from the grave with empty stomachs and a taste for flesh.

But even in this world, people crave justice—especially in this world. They need that clear-cut sense of right and wrong, something to latch onto, something to make them believe they have a chance. The people need this.

Opie extends his hand, stabilizing Lot as she climbs a homemade pulpit. As she looks down on her subjects, it feels like coming home. It's been years now since she addressed a crowd from a stage. Back then it came so naturally. Lonely, lost people flocked to her guiding hand in droves. The hand that would mold them, that would shape them into the person they thought they should be. This will be no different.

Lot slowly caresses the crowd with her gaze. A fire is already raging here, and she barely needs to add fuel. In fact, if she were to throw Danny into the crowd at this very moment they would probably tear him limb from limb.

She can see it now, the mass of people closing in on him as he lies helplessly in the middle, their greedy hands outstretched, eager to deliver punishment. Their eyes so clouded with fear and anger and hate they can see nothing else. Slow and coddled minds would rest easily with the knowledge they are doing the right thing.

The Mass would kick and grab and pull and bite. They would sink fingers into Danny's writhing body and pull up huge bleeding, lumpy ribbons of flesh. They would tear at each other's clothes, drunk on justice, bare skin rubbing on bare skin and The Mass would throb. Bloodlust would take over and Danny would be devoured as she stood on her pulpit, watching, filled with the light of pleasure.

Lot's thoughts swing back into reality and her flight of fancy falls away, leaving an aching hole in its place. The angry, sweaty face of The Mass is turned up at her and a grumbling chant rides a building wave.

"Slay the brute. Spill his blood. Crush his skull. Do him in. Slay the brute. Spill his blood. Crush his skull. Do him in."

19

Lot thrusts her powerful voice upon The Mass, her tone faltering beneath impassioned chanting. "Slay the brute. Spill his blood. Crush his skull. Do him in." But, little by little The Mass submits, allowing Lot's words to embrace it, and it responds, quivering, awaiting command.

Lot grips the pulpit with her good hand. Her other hand is clenched, hidden in the homemade sling strapped around her shoulders. The muscles where Danny hit her with the bat are swollen and purple, crushed and wailing. Her fist brings tears that shimmer in her eyes and are reflected in kind by the light of many lanterns and candles. Hands emerge from The Mass, they stretch out, fingers gently whisper at the hem of her skirt and she smiles, so giving, so loving.

The hum slowly dies down and the silence left in the room is deafening. Lot wipes her eyes and stares out across the glut of faces.

"I have failed you. I have misused your trust for my own selfish reasons."

Pockets of noise erupt, but quiet down quickly. She clears her throat. "Stepping up here to admit to you my failings is one of the hardest things I have had to do in my entire life. I covered up, I manipulated, I turned a blind eye. I allowed a disease to grow among us—to masquerade as one of us. Danny—"

The Mass screams. Pure rage shakes the walls, echoing in on itself. Lot raises a hand and it quiets, obeying its master. "*My* Danny, my little boy, my son. I am guilty of putting my love for him above all else, and now Alex, an innocent child, has been murdered by one of the most shameful predators in existence.

"Alex came to us for help, for safety, and instead fell into the clutches of The Beast. We will never know the indignities poor little Alex suffered at his hands, but we know he did suffer, and he shouldn't have."

Whispering filters toward Lot as The Mass croons like a well-tuned violin in her skilled hands.

"It may be Danny who physically committed such hateful acts, but I should be punished alongside him. If I hadn't been too afraid to acknowledge his true nature, none of this would have come to pass, and so I stand here, ready and willing to receive your judgment and my punishment."

A legion of eyes grips Lot as she steps down from the pulpit. With head hung low, she presses against The Mass, penetrating it. Hands, faces, bodies reach out to touch her, grasping, embracing, feeling, welcoming her in. She falls to her knees, sacrificing herself to the will of the many.

The Mass envelops Lot. Sporadic chanting dribbles through the air, its sound slowly and powerfully building. Inside, hot breath and bodies drape her in a living robe and she is cocooned in the flesh of her followers. The Mass lifts her lovingly to her feet, crushing around her, every touch, every word a symbol of forgiveness, which strips her of all sin and forges something new.

With a groan of effort, The Mass pushes out The Leader and she humbly takes her given place: the pulpit. She places her hand over her heart as a symbol of servitude, once again able to face her public.

The Mass cheers for its newly resurrected deity. Tears flow and hands pound against each other. A wave of chanting slowly becomes clear as voices synchronize. "Slay The Beast. Spill its blood. Crush its skull. Do it in. Slay The Beast. Spill its blood. Crush its skull. Do it in."

As the chant thunders under the spackled ceiling, Lot looks down at Opie. He stands just off to the side, a dazed spectator, unsure of what he's actually witnessing. He catches the flash of a covert smile. As the only one in the room not enchanted by Lot's spell, and the knowledge of her true power makes him uneasy.

***

The courtyard was once well manicured for the pleasure of high paying guests that frequented the hotel. Now, it's a wild, luscious garden filled with blooming plants and supported by an ingenious irrigation system where rows of nearly ripe tomatoes cling to dark green vines. Thick shadows, accentuated by the moon, are cast across row after row of fresh fruits and vegetables.

The garden is like a slice of Eden. It's the only outside area that's safe. The fruits and vegetables that push and struggle on the top floor aren't nearly as healthy as what grows here. Only a select few have the privilege of eating from this bounty.

All of this is lost on Hannah as she kneels in freshly turned earth. Streaks cut by tears shine through the mud on her face. Her hands and clothing are filthy with dirt. Three inches below the surface, Jamal festers in the ground.

Hannah doesn't know how or why the dead come back from the grave, she only knows everyone eventually does. There's no telling how long, minutes or days, but she knows she'll be here when her son comes back to her.

***

Alex slows his pace. It's dark and the moonlight filtering through only serves to make the shadows swim around him. It was hard enough to navigate by himself during the day, avoiding hungry monstrosities and certain death, but now everything looks the same, and it has for a while.

FIND DANNY.

FIND DANNY.

Where am I?

Alex isn't sure if he's going in the right direction anymore. It's as though the forest has morphed into a maze of smoke and mirrors with the fading sun. Dread slowly begins to circulate through his veins and with each step the awful poison grows stronger. He stops, his breath choked by the slithering of doubt.

Alone.

Alone.

Alone.

Should he stop? Should he turn back? Turn back…to where? Casey is gone. Danny is gone. Everyone is gone. Alex takes an uncertain step forward, the habit of walking driving him. He stops. He starts. His head jerks. Fear eats away at his brain.

He pushes through a wall of brush and stumbles as the forest spits him out into empty space. A long stretch of summer-baked grass, blinding white in the moon's light, stretches out before him. Dotted across the landscape, dark figures drift aimlessly, their rotten eyes scanning for prey. Far in the distance stands the silhouetted hotel.

***

Candles illuminate the long corridor and the light from their dancing flames pierce Danny's eyes. His head is pounding. Every noise, every smell, and especially the light, drills a hole straight into his skull. The greasy taste of the rag stuffed into his mouth turns his stomach. The rope tying it in place bites his cheeks and peels the skin from his lips.

Even worse than his head is the pain in his side. Under heavy guard, Julie patched it up, enough to make sure he didn't die in that cooler anyway, but she hadn't spared him any painkillers. Every push and pull on his body sends strikes of agony through his very core, making his legs so weak he can barely keep steady on them. The herd of stone-faced guards surrounding him prods their inmate forward. He can read it in their faces: it's time for this monster to face the music.

Odd thoughts swirl through Danny's pain-addled mind. This is all there is, this moment. This is what has always been and what will be forever. Lot wins. Danny loses. Lot wins. Danny dies. Lot wins. Mentally, he is already lying in a grave and all he can do is watch as he shovels dirt over his own body.

The voice of The Mass grows louder as they approach the hotel's banquet hall. How many weddings had been held here? How many corporate retreats and snake oil seminars, carefully designed to part the public from their money? The people that stand in there now, had they once attended such events? Do they feel that twinge of familiarity as they stamp their feet and chant?

"Slay The Beast. Spill its blood. Crush its skull. Do it in."

The thunderous voice of The Mass disgorges itself from the room as Danny's captors open a door. Booing, hissing and chanting churn the hot air as he's dragged forward. A tomato launches from The Mass, exploding over Danny's face, its rotten funk sticking in thick chunks to his skin and hair.

Moon-eyed, Danny stares at the wall of faces that's distorted in anger and disgust. He recognizes them all as they jeer and chant. Danny's brain buzzes with fear and death. He can feel it, the yoke he's worn for so many years is back, and tighter than ever. This is where he has always been, this room—for as long as he can remember. This is *his* house.

The Leader, standing at her pulpit, makes a grandiose gesture, playing for the amusement of The Mass. She signals for two sets of guards to pull a hastily constructed platform forward. Cheering erupts. The Mass is hungry for entertainment.

Standing in the center of the platform is something that looks like a stunted cross nailed together from splintered planks of wood. Boards jut from the cross' back, forming a stabilizer that allows the device to angle back slightly.

Danny turns death-murky eyes up toward the platform. The sight of the cross freezes his heart and perfect fear floods his very being as he's dragged forward. The chant of The Mass grows to an even more fevered pitch.

Danny is pushed onto the platform. There is no struggle. Like a stunned beast to the slaughter, he stumbles toward his own death. Rough hands yank him to his knees in front of the cross. They bind him, pitilessly stretching his arms, up and over the "t" shaped boards and trussing them behind his back. They pull on the pulsing, infected muscle of his wounded side. Agony coils deep inside of him, but he only stares out, unblinking in the face of their loyalty, their mockery of civilization.

The guards step back to admire their handy work. The Beast is gagged, immobile, on its knees leaning awkwardly back. Its chest is forced out, leaving it unprotected and vulnerable. Its arms are stretched behind to their limit. Its legs bound in place.

"Slay The Beast. Spill its blood. Crush its skull. Do it in. Slay The Beast. Spill its blood. Crush its skull. Do it in."

Tears leak from The Beast's eyes. Its chest heaves, it shakes, and finally it screams in terror against the gag, its vocal cords nearly tearing with the effort. The Mass roars back in approval.

It is a good night for an execution.

***

The overgrown field rustles with each step Alex takes, echoing in his ears. His breathing quickens as he passes closely to a group of creatures devouring an unfortunate deer. The poor animal, nursing an arrow wound from a botched hunting attempt days ago, never stood a chance.

The ghouls gorge, overloading themselves with warm meat. The stomach of one is so bloated the skin looks ready to burst. It stuffs another dripping handful of venison down its gluttonous throat and its stomach pushes out more, stretching until it rips wide open, spilling its contents to the ground. The creature greedily claws at its own innards and packs its mouth once again with the felled flesh.

Alex tiptoes by, grass swishing at his knees.

Cankerous faces and bulging eyes turn hungrily toward him.

***

The Leader stands on the platform facing The Mass. Behind

her, The Beast writhes against its bonds. The Mass howls. She holds up her hands for silence and an eerie quiet takes hold.

"Who among you will take reparation for the murdered boy, Alex, and for our own flesh and blood? Who among you will volunteer to become a vessel of justice?" she asks.

The Mass murmurs thoughtfully. Hands rise, and bodies eject toward the platform like tentacles from the core. The Leader approves. She gestures theatrically and a squeaky-wheeled cart full of weapons is rolled forward.

"Tonight, I am here to serve you. This Beast," she points at the struggling form on the cross, "is the personification of disease from which we must be cleansed.

"Habib, Jamal, Javier, Rob, Brody, and Alex. These are the names of the fallen, taken from us by this confessed child murderer, this pedophile. This evil that walks among us. If we allow this disease to continue unchecked, the innocence will be ripped from our children and the lives from our brethren.

"I ask you to bear witness and not to shy away from what is about to happen. I ask you to carry this story with you into your daily lives as a warning to those who would seek to sow chaos. Carry tonight's proceedings with you as a vaccine against this disease, this ultimate form of evil, because if we allow it, The Beast will destroy our children in the very beds in which they sleep."

The Mass erupts forcefully, its screaming chant drowning out cheers of agreement. "Slay The Beast. Spill its blood. Crush its skull. Do it in. Slay The Beast. Spill its blood. Crush its skull. Do it in."

The Leader's cheeks flush with delectation, each word melting over her, tenderly touching every part of her body. She turns to face The Beast. Crimson drips from its newly bandaged side, slowly pooling on the ground. Its shirt is plastered to its body with a mixture of sweat and blood and she can see its heart vibrating beneath the fabric.

She crosses the platform to stand before it. The thing looks up at her, black ringed, bloodshot eyes pleading with her to stop. She reaches her hands behind its head and loosens the gag. The rope falls around its neck and it spits the rag out onto the platform.

"Lot—" The Beast's mouth has trouble forming words. "Please."

She leans in closely, listening, hoping it will scream, needing to hear it scream. Her cheeks are on fire and her skin tingling with pleasure as its voice wavers with dread. "Finish this quickly."

The Leader's eyes smile, and her breath delicately falls in The Beast's ear, only for it. "You never should have crossed me, little boy."

She lovingly grazes its cheek with her lips. There is something about the finality of the kiss, about the way The Leader turns so crisply and walks away, which ignites The Mass. The thirst for blood blazes hotly.

The Beast screams. It screams in hatred of The Leader. In contempt of the universe. In repulsion of The Mass. In utter terror. It screams, but its voice is carried away by the ugly mantra that fills the room. "Slay The Beast. Spill its blood. Crush its skull. Do it in. Slay The Beast. Spill its blood. Crush its skull. Do it in."

The Leader steps down from the platform and presses through The Mass on a surge of euphoria. Hands reach out and stroke her as she passes. She struggles to keep her composure, to dampen her merriment just a bit, she can't let them see her smile.

Tonight, Lot will watch Danny burn.

20

Rochelle, a waif-like woman, peers up at the stars through a small gap in the window coverings. She misses being able to walk freely outside. Being continuously stuck indoors is soul crushing, and boredom can easily get the best of anyone.

She remembers a time when she visited the zoo as a child and saw a tiger, in all its majestic glory, its thick glossy fur rippling with every step it took. She watched, fascinated as it paced the length of its large enclosure, back and forth, over and over, never stopping, never looking anywhere but straight ahead.

Eventually, she moved on to another exhibit, elephants, gorillas, wildebeest, giraffe, they all had the same look in their eyes. She didn't recognize it then, but later in life, she heard the word for it: zoochosis. Rochelle supposes it's only a matter of time before the entire human race has that same look.

At least she can see the stars tonight, no clouds, and it's quiet in here for once, with everyone attending the trial—a rare thing indeed. At least there are some perks to getting the short end of the stick.

She peeks over at Nick, a middle-aged man sitting beside her. He has his feet propped up on a stool as he snacks on some dried jerky. Rochelle thinks the dried meat is okay, but sometimes it seems like life has become the stopgap between jerky. These days, she only eats what she absolutely has to. What she'd really like is pizza, even a shitty pizza from some shitty chain would be amazing.

"Did you ever picnic under the stars? Before everything changed?" she asks Nick.

"Nope," Nick responds through noisy chews. "But I did picnic with the kids at the park once."

"Sounds nice."

"It was a total disaster. I stepped in dog shit, there were yellow jackets dive-bombing our food, and the oldest had hay fever." He tears into his jerky once more and chews on the piece in silence for a moment, thinking. "Know what, though? I'd give anything to be able to do it again."

Rochelle nods empathetically, her eyes still on the stars. She knows Nick's last surviving child died the winter before of a lung infection.

A dark shadow moving across the field draws her attention away and she squints for a better view.

"I think I see someone."

"Probably just one of those damned things."

"No…I'm pretty sure someone's running this way. It's hard to tell."

"Oh yeah?" replied Nick. He stands and eases himself in next to Rochelle to share her peephole. Far in the distance, a black blob appears and disappears, bouncing across the field.

"Holy shit!"

***

Alex tries not to take his eyes off the hotel. He tries not to imagine the creatures behind him as his legs carry him as speedily as they can go, but the fastest ghoul isn't far behind. He can hear its muscles popping over un-lubricated joints as it runs.

All around, cumbersome creatures shuffle toward him, blocking his way and closing him in. One reaches out its thin arms, its old decayed skin sloughing off easily with the breeze. The moon highlights its ruined face. Split lips hang down the thing's chin on moldering threads and only a single bulging eye is left. The other is just an empty socket filled with sticks and debris.

Alex swerves and almost slams into another walking corpse. Its cold hands grip his shoulders, fingers digging into his skin. He shoves the lumbering monster back with Casey's bat and dodges another, barely slowing.

He deflects another attack and sidesteps the fast one as it lunges, only one step behind. The creature loses him for a moment, caught up in the onslaught of slower bodies.

Alex skids left and right, weaving and ducking. For every one thing he escapes, it seems like three more take its place. Spoiled hands grab at his body and decaying faces push forward with lethal teeth.

He spins, looking for an opening, and smashes a creature with Casey's bat, but the blow isn't strong enough to kill. All around, pushing in, are others just like it, just as deadly, just as hungry.

BAM!

A creature drops to the ground. Another shot, another felled creature. A third, a fourth. There is an opening.

"RUN!" A woman's voice shouts.

Alex doesn't need convincing. He leaps over the bodies that lie in the grass before him and sprints for the hotel at breakneck speed. Halfway between him and safety, he sees a man and a woman. They are armed to the teeth and cover him as he runs.

Alex doesn't slow his pace as he nears his saviors and they pass in a blur. He can see the small opening in the front of the hotel that means protection, candlelight spilling from it with a utopian glow.

The opening grows larger until it becomes a door, and then suddenly, he's through it. Alex slams into the back of the caged foyer, bounces, and is thrown to the floor. He lies there, panting, silent tears pouring from his eyes.

Seconds later, Nick and Rochelle barrel in, slamming the door shut behind them and locking it tightly. They lean against it, catching their breaths. On the floor in front of them lies a wet-faced child with one shoe, holding up a bat against them like a cross against vampires.

Rochelle crouches down next to him as Nick unlocks the back

door of the cage. She reaches out a hand to Alex, "It's okay, you're safe here."

Alex lowers the bat, trying desperately to breathe. His ribs ache as he presses his cheek into cold marble. Its bloodstains fill his vision, tinging everything. Casey's blood. Huge wordless sobs rip open his chest and hot, burning tears flow in rivers down his face.

"Isn't this the kid Danny supposedly killed?" asks Rochelle.

***

"Slay The Beast. Spill its blood. Crush its skull. Do it in. Slay The Beast. Spill its blood. Crush its skull. Do it in."

Opie stands on the platform in front of Danny. The churning acid in his stomach is almost comforting in this new territory. He has seen many things in his life, but he has never seen anything like what's happening tonight.

Lot stands off to the side, surrounded by admirers, her eyes shining expectantly. Tonight she not only solidified herself as the omnipotent leader of the community, but birthed herself into God-ship right before his very eyes. Her manipulation of the crowd can be described as nothing less than artistic.

Opie's eyes fall on Danny. The once strong and sullen, blond-haired man is now just a broken sheep, ready for sacrifice. Opie almost feels sorry for him. Danny had always been a pawn, a plaything for Lot's appetites.

He sighs inwardly. Danny will pay the ultimate price for crossing Lot and there's nothing to be done about it. This world, Opie tells himself, has always been every man for himself, something Danny never fully understood.

He turns to face the small group gathered in front of him, ready, as usual, to do the dirty work for Lot. The crowd behind the small group is electrified by the theatrical proceedings. He holds up his fist where the tops of sticks poke out. The only way to be fair is to draw straws determining who will strike the first blow.

Thick Marge draws first. Her face drops when she sees it's a long stick, and Opie proceeds down the line. Seven sticks for seven people. It's Davis, a large, red-faced man, who draws the shortest. He'd been close with Arnold, but Opie doesn't really care. He just wants to get this over with, the chanting and cheering are giving him a headache.

This whole thing is too much drama for his tastes, why not just simply kill Danny and be done with it? But he knows better. Aside from little boys, Lot has a growing penchant for grisly executions. This public forum was the next logical step for her.

Davis steps up to the cart of weapons. He looks thoughtfully over the neatly laid rows. There are knives, a hacksaw, a hammer, a manual hand drill, an awl, a meat hook, a steel police baton, and a jar filled with liquid, next to it a book of precious matches.

He lifts the jar from the cart and sniffs its contents, gasoline. He puts it back down—that will come later. He hovers his hand over the hammer a moment and then it draws away. The eyes of The Mass are on him and he wants to take his time, to pick correctly. Finally, after much debate, Davis comes back to the hammer and lifts it over his head in triumph. The Mass cheers.

"Slay The Beast. Spill its blood. Crush its skull. Do it in. Slay The Beast. Spill its blood. Crush its skull. Do it in."

The Beast watches as Davis approaches. It has stopped struggling and doesn't scream anymore. That's a good thing, Davis thinks, it's accepted its fate, and this will be easier knowing the guilty accepts its punishment. Davis had killed a few of The Risen before, but that's it, and he has certainly never done anything like this.

He thinks of Javier. Javier was a good man, one of the best. This might be hard, but an example has to be made and as a community leader this is his duty, like it or not. It's a relief to know he won't shoulder the burden alone.

Davis looks down at the hammer in his hand then at The Beast. This creature deserves to suffer for as long as possible.

"Slay The Beast. Spill its blood. Crush its skull. Do it in."

He turns the hammer in his hand and holds it out in front of him, its heavy metal head poised to strike. The animal shakes, its eyes huge, wild and scared. Its chest heaves as it draws in sharp, shallow breaths. Davis draws back his arm and brings down the hammer on The Beast's shoulder as hard as he can. It screams.

The Mass is mad with euphoria and demands more. Davis lifts his weapon again, this time turning it on its side and lining it up with The Beast's head. Still a bit tentative, he swings, smashing the hammer into The Beast's skull. Scalp splits and bone tries not to break. The wretch cries out and struggles uselessly as blood pours over its face. The next hit will do some real damage.

The Beast moans and Davis draws back his arm for another blow, gathering confidence from The Mass. Behind him an unclear voice rises above the chanting. He turns, blood dripping from the weapon in his hand as an interloper pushes onto the platform.

"STOP! STOP!" Nick yells. "The boy is alive! He didn't kill him! Danny didn't kill him! The boy is alive!"

Mummers of discontent rise up. How can the boy still be alive? Hadn't Danny confessed? Concern quickly blisters the front of The Mass and eats its way back, breaking it apart. Some still cry out for blood, others are filled with instant concern.

There is shouting, anger. Those near Lot turn to her and she raises her hand, trying to calm the clamor of people, but they squeeze around her, besieging her with worry.

Davis is unsure of what to do. He can't see his leader through the throng of people. Someone shouts at him to keep going, someone else shouts at him to stop and he drops the hammer.

Danny's head rolls forward.

There is shouting, fighting, confusion. Lot is frantic, and can't get through the wall of people that surrounds her. Opie knows he has to do something before all hell breaks loose. He strides to the weapons cart and lifts a large serrated knife, the crowd following him with their eyes.

He quickly saws through Danny's restraints. The blond man slumps forward and, unable to catch himself, hits the platform with a thud. An uneasy hush falls over those nearby. Opie leans down and carves through the ropes that bind Danny's legs to the platform just as Lot finally pushes her way through the crowd.

Danny's head spins and he wonders briefly if this is a hopeful hallucination. He tries to lift himself—manages to push almost to his knees before his limbs give way and his body crashes back down. The pain is unbearable.

He hears Lot and she sounds distressed, but her words mean nothing.

Opie directs someone, but Danny can't focus on what he's saying, can't focus on anything. The room whirls, and his world makes no sense. He never imagined a human being could feel the amount of pain he feels right now.

Hands pull him to his feet. There is yelling, and he thinks it must be for him, but his legs won't obey—are no longer a part of his body. His mind separates, disconnects from events around him, and the clawing blackness that has been flirting with him since he was shot, finally drags Danny into its depths.

He hangs limply between Thick Marge and Davis. They stare at Opie, wide-eyed, unclear about what's happening. On the side of the platform, Lot and Nick speak heatedly. Fresh blood rides strands of Danny's hair, cabling downwards from his head, muddying the floor they stand on.

"Is he still breathing?" asks Opie.

Davis nods dumbly, his face turning green with nausea—hit with a ton of bricks by the fact the boy, Alex, may still be alive. What if it's true? His mind is already toying with the maneuvers necessary to alleviate his guilt and accountability. How could Lot allow this to happen? He turns his head, looking for his leader. She is following Nick from the room.

"That's something at least," says Opie. "Marge, we're going to have to lock him up again until we know what's going on. Get Julie to attend to him."

Thick Marge nods as she and Davis steady themselves under Danny's dead weight and begin dragging him away. They pause a moment, closer to Opie. Thick Marge looks over the crowd of people, worry creating turmoil at every angle. "Do you think it's true? Can he really be alive?"

Opie shakes his head, deep concern creasing his face. "We'll know very shortly." Opie raises his voice a little louder so those within close vicinity can hear him. "Please, don't worry. I'll get to the bottom of this as quickly as possible." His words are picked up and filter quickly through the crowd.

***

Alex sits by the fireside. The plate of food before him seems artificial; his hunger pangs a bad imitation of reality. There is only one concrete thing in his world now, the need to FIND DANNY, and there is only one person who might know where he is: Lot.

He remembers how the woman hovering over him is the reason CASEY IS DEAD and grief rakes her claws across him. With every blink he sees the bullet wound as it spreads across Casey's forehead, ripping it to pieces. He watches her body fall slack to the ground—feels each drop of blood as it hits the marble floor, like nails in his heart.

Lot.

The woman rubbing her hands on his shoulders with the same insatiable, demanding touch that guided him to her bed. Deceitful and misleading. Her fingers are like pins against his skin. Uncertainty and a secret shame still cling to him as he remembers what they've done.

Lot.

The woman speaking with Opie. She is the reason Danny is gone. Alex gently holds down the panic that Casey's successor is nowhere to be found. He still feels the grip of terror caused by realizing he might be alone.

Intense quiet surrounds him, punctuated by the sharp voices of hollow people nearby.

Opie looks over at the blank-eyed child sitting near the fire. He's struck once again by how similar his resemblance is to

Danny. Lot rubs the boy's shoulders and he can see a horrid squealing monkey once again saddles her back. It clouds her thinking and he welcomes it.

She intoxicated the people with her will, propelled them from their natural comfort zones and now a hangover is looming. The mental anguish caused by the knowledge they went too far will need a powerful poultice. What better cure than the body of a God?

There's a knock at the door and Opie crosses the room to open it, revealing Thick Marge and Julie. He motions for them to enter.

"Danny's locked in the kitchen cooler, still unconscious. Julie looked him over."

Lot's eyes dart to the nurse.

"Why is he receiving medical attention?"

"I asked her to see to him, Lot," Opie breaks the tension. "I was unsure how to proceed and thought it best."

"No. It wasn't best, Opie. He's a traitor, a—" Lot catches herself.

Julie speaks up awkwardly in the silence.

"I just looked him over. He's in bad shape. There isn't anything I can really do. The bullet wound is a real obstacle. I can't tell if there's internal hemorrhaging, but he probably won't bleed to death outright. However, there's no way he'll escape infection. If I give him antibiotics there's a slim chance—"

"No," Lot cuts her off. "Regardless if he killed the boy, he's still a deviant. He still attacked me, and he will be executed. We must conserve supplies for those who warrant saving."

Thick Marge glances at Alex. "Is the boy harmed?"

Lot shakes her head. "I'm unsure of the extent of his injuries. He won't allow anyone to examine him."

"I can try," Julie suggests.

"No," Lot says.

Opie rubs his face, seemingly ready to say something, but hesitant to speak. When he feels the women's full attention, he finally says what's on his mind. "Lot, I understand the delicate nature of the situation. I can appreciate the fact we have no clue what Danny did to this poor child before he was captured—" *what a crock of shit*, he thinks. "—but can we be sure the child hasn't been bitten? He could pose a danger to the entire community. I think it's best if he's inspected immediately."

Oblivious to the conversation around him, Alex plays with a strap on the tattered knapsack he holds on his lap. In his other hand, he still grips the baseball bat he came in with.

"He's under my quarantine," Lot snaps.

Julie discreetly locks her eyes on Opie's, concerned. Thick Marge digs into her front pocket and pulls out a padlock key. "For the cooler," she presses it into Lot's outstretched hand. "What should we do with the pris- Danny?"

Thick Marge can't stop staring at the boy and Opie can see doubt etching itself around her eyes.

"Forget about the prisoner for now," Lot demands. "I'll deal with him in time. Now please, leave me with the child. He's been traumatized enough."

Lot shoos away Opie, Julie, and Thick Marge, recklessly desperate to be rid of them. As soon as the door shuts, she locks it and turns toward Alex. On her way across the room, she tosses the key handed to her onto a small side table.

She sits down next to Alex and smiles, noticing the untouched plate of food.

"You must be hungry, Alex. If you don't want what's on your plate, maybe I can interest you in some of that special maple syrup instead? And you can let me check you over to make sure you aren't hurt in any way."

***

Opie, Julie, and Thick Marge tread the hallway in a small pool of candlelight. Thick Marge's feet carry her on autopilot, her mind still reeling from the implications of Alex's survival. A gentle hand on her shoulder pulls her to the surface.

"Don't worry, Marge," says Opie. "You didn't do anything wrong."

"I feel like we've gone nuts."

Julie nods agreement.

Thick Marge hugs herself as she walks. "That kid doesn't have a mark on him, at least not one that would come from having a grown man wrap his hands around the boy's neck."

Opie nods thoughtfully. "I see what you mean."

The three stop walking, as if the weight of the conversation is too heavy to bear while moving.

Thick Marge's troubled eyes seek solace from Opie and he shakes his head. "Don't forget Danny killed other people. Just because he isn't a child murderer, doesn't mean he's not guilty. And he confessed to you, told you he choked the boy to death. How were you supposed to know he'd lie about it?"

"But should we really be convicting one of our own without a trial? A *real* trial? I was standing right there, weapon in hand, like some sort of heathen. The crowd was screaming for blood and it felt good. I *wanted* to hurt him."

"Don't be so hard on yourself, Marge."

"It's just, I don't know, I feel like there's something else going on here we don't know about."

Opie and Thick Marge stare at each other. She's treading in dangerous water, and knows it.

"I'm not saying Danny is innocent," she backpedals. "I mean, why take the boy in the first place? But what I *am* saying is that we were overzealous, bloodthirsty, inhuman. We—"

Opie holds up his hand and Thick Marge swallows hard.

"Marge, you were led down a dark path—we all were."

Marge stares at Opie and nods slowly, then resumes walking, chewing on his implication.

Opie smiles to himself. Now that the mustard seed has been planted, it will grow quickly. If he plants a few more, he'll have a reaping.

Julie scuttles behind him. He peeks back and smiles reassuringly. She smiles back. If he's to spread his wings, he'll need all the support he can get.

21

The courtyard is silent, unmarred by the night's execution proceedings. Hannah sits in the dirt, her head resting against the wall, not asleep, but not quite awake. Dried tears mar her cheeks and her hypnagogic mind replays better times.

The soil churns at her feet. Earthworms and beetles rain from a rising corpse, tumbling dead from ears, mouth, and chest wound. Nothing lives long that has feasted upon the unsavory flesh of the living dead.

It turns dirt-smeared lenses toward the woman who sits on the ground. She flashes into awareness. *Jamal.* A bittersweet smile spreads over her lips. She couldn't let him die, but somewhere she knows he's gone—was gone hours ago. It's a fact she's unable to face.

Jamal's body crawls forward, one hand after the other, dragging him from his shallow grave. He is slow and awkward as muscles and joints crack loudly, like dried corn in a kettle. Hannah opens her arms, welcoming the rebirth of her only son, her eyes glistening. It took longer than she thought it would for him to rise.

Jamal stumbles, jerking to his feet. His bulging eyes lock in on her and he shuffles forward, an unholy grimace laced across his face. His lips are drawn back tightly, revealing a dying insect that clings to deadened gums.

Vertebrae crackle along Jamal's spine as he hunches down, arms outstretched. Hannah smiles at her son, fresh tears dripping down her cheeks, unable to look away. His jaws snap open and he leans forward to sink his teeth into her flesh. Skin and cartilage stretch and tear away as he rips her nose from her face. *Slishk.* Her hands involuntarily flutter beside her.

His strong, unflinching fingers push into her soft belly. They grip her pulsing intestines and jerk them from her body. As he stuffs handfuls of quivering meat down his greedy throat, Hannah can do nothing. He sits on her, consuming her still living flesh but she has no screams for the mindless eating machine, only love.

The courtyard door squeaks on unattended hinges. There's a small grunt as a pint-sized girl puts her back into pushing the handle. She holds the door with one hand and stretches out her arms, trying to reach for something in the dark.

Unable to find it, she wedges her foot in front of the door and stretches out her entire body until her fingers grasp their reward: a brick. The girl uses it to prop open the entryway then steps inside.

She isn't allowed in here, no children are, but that doesn't stop her from sneaking in on nights she thinks she can get away with it. A quick midnight munch and she'll be back inside before the grownups ever know. They are all at that meeting, or whatever it is.

Besides, tonight is supposed to be a bread night. The meeting took over everything, and she's hungry. They don't get to eat a lot of bread anymore. It used to be once a week, now it's closer to once a month. She heard her stupid uncle say, "Flour is worth its weight in gold nowadays." She doesn't see why anybody would want gold anyway.

Maybe everyone should start saying other things are worth their weight in flour. "That cookie is worth its weight in flour." It would be way more accurate because cookies are actually made out of flour.

She tiptoes over to the strawberries in the bright moonlight. She can make out where the fruit-laden plants are, but not whether they're ripe. As she plucks a piece of fruit from the stem, she wishes she brought a candle or something with her, oh well. She pops the berry into her mouth and chews. Ripe, yum.

Munch, munch, munch. Two more berries. They're good, but still, she misses cookies. Oreos were her favorite. She used to trade most of her lunch away for them in school. Her parents didn't believe in sugar, so Oreos were never on the menu. She showed them, though, she ate sugar every chance she got, without them knowing, of course. Now, she's stuck with stupid Uncle Jim who doesn't care what she eats, as long as it's food. God, she misses her parents so much.

A rustling noise from the corner grinds her munching to a halt and the unconscious smile of small pleasures drops from her face, replaced with curiosity. She had heard some squirrels lived in here once. They'd gotten into stuff, so the adults got rid of them a long time ago, but maybe they're back? The girl smiles again. Squirrels are so cute!

She would love to have a pet! She had a dog once, Maximutt. Mom named the dog. Dad told her mom's sense of humor was one of the reasons he'd married her—she misses her parents every second of every day.

She misses Maximutt too, he was the best dog, *ever*. She remembers when stupid Uncle Jim got rid of him. There was a gnawing hunger in her belly so bad it was all she could think about. They hadn't eaten in days, and it had been weeks since their last proper meal. Stupid Uncle Jim told her they couldn't afford to keep Maximutt around. Said they couldn't feed the dog anymore, that if they found any food, they had to eat it all themselves.

When Uncle Jim told her he was going to let Maximutt go in a field to fend for himself, she cried. She begged and yelled, cussed even, but his mind was made up, and she was honestly too weak from hunger to do anything about it. How she hated Uncle Jim for letting Maximutt go. Especially since that very evening, he was able to hunt down a wild pig and kill it.

She'd stayed behind in the car when stupid Uncle Jim took Maximutt to the field and he found the pig on his way back. He'd even cut it up and everything, so she didn't have to see. Poor piggy. There had been more than enough for Maximutt to have some too. She would have refused to eat if she hadn't been so, so, so hungry.

The noise stops and the little girl steps forward, straining to listen, the moonlight playing tricks on her eyes. She squints; thinks she sees something, and a cloud slides away from the moon, focusing her vision.

Five feet from her is a monster crouched over a woman. Its face is distorted, and it's covered in blood. Guts hang from its fingers and mouth and the woman reaches out a blood-slicked hand toward the girl. She moves her mouth slightly, but no sound comes out.

The girl tries to scream but the strawberry slides down her throat and lodges, allowing only a choked, raspy gag to escape. She panics, clawing at her throat. Her eyes bulge, and her face grows as red as the tomatoes in the garden.

The monster turns. Fresh meat. The girl runs. She trips, her face turning from red to blue and she crawls toward the door, gagging, the creature staggering behind. Its distended stomach, swollen from the feed, leads the way.

The girl's lungs ache. She needs air. Air! She tries to cough but can't. She feels a hand in her hair, and then suddenly she is weightless. The monster drags her toward its mouth. She kicks as sparkles of unconsciousness threaten her vision.

The kick glances off the monster and it pulls the blue-lipped girl up, its jaws wide and hungry. It tears into her exposed throat. For one brief, glorious second the girl can breathe again. Sweet, delicious air floods her lungs and her chest expands. With a second bite, the creature gashes open her jugular and blood shoots out over its face and body.

The girl is gone in seconds. Steps behind, Hannah's eyes blink in the moonlight.

***

Lot smiles at Alex and brushes dirt off his cheek, her fingers lingering just a little too long. His skin is so smooth, so young, so perfect. She feels that well-known, concupiscent zing ride through her body. It's been years since a boy this perfect has been at her fingertips, and having thought she lost him makes him all the more appetizing.

Ambrosia. Lot licks her lips and smiles. It's near torture to sit here next to him, waiting, his innocent eyes staring up at her.

Alex tightly holds the knapsack on his lap. It's hard for him to decipher people's thoughts from their faces, but he knows he doesn't like the look in Lot's eyes. There's something about it—it's the same look that was in the eyes of the pack of feral dogs he and Casey once crossed paths with. Wild, hungry, and dangerous. It's the same look Lot had on her face when she invited him into her bed. He hadn't recognized it then, but he does now.

She places a hand on his arm, and he retreats from her touch. "We'll have to get you out of these dirty clothes. I want to check you over, to be sure you're not injured."

Alex tightens his fingers on his knapsack, feeling each individual thread bending under his grip. He's afraid to take his eyes off Lot and his heart pounds. The room suddenly feels too small, as though the walls have jumped closer, and the bat, which Lot took and placed in a corner, seems too far away. She's watching him, and he has the distinct sensation he's being hunted.

"If you aren't hungry, why don't I remove these dishes, get them out of our way?"

The rumble in Alex's belly is distant as Lot lifts the dishes from the table. Her prodding eyes turn his blood to itching, burning lava. It smolders under his skin, threatening to incinerate his body. He can't stand her looking at him, and just when he thinks he may go up in a ball of flames, she turns away with the dishes.

Lot crosses the room, carrying Alex's untouched dinner to the hall. The moment she turns her back he sucks in a cooling breath——relief. With agile fingers, he unzips his knapsack. Inside, the Arnold-head rolls its eyes. Alex rips the balled-up t-shirt from the face and drops it back into the knapsack. The bag shakes as the head tries to bite through.

Alex holds it steady.

"What are you up to, little boy?" Lot's voice grates on Alex. She's back and flashes a smile down at him. It's too wide, too toothy, too bright. Her teeth are slightly crowded, her crow's feet deep canyons. Her skin is papery, quickly losing its glow, the fatty deposits of youth drained away from her cheekbones. Her face blazes in front of his eyes, every line, every hair, every pore shrieking at him.

Alex holds the bag up to her. She raises her brows, plucked a little too thin, and asks a question, but Alex can't hear it over her grotesque details. She reaches out to take his bag.

He pulls it back, away from her grip.

She says something again and Alex grips the bag tensely. He lifts it and her face pushes toward his, her voice dribbling over her lips.

"Yes?" She grazes the knapsack with her thin, worn hand, attempting to take it again. Alex wrenches it back. She smiles, but it's wavering, strained and plastic. She taps her foot. Impatient. Alex has seen that movement before, with many other people.

"Do you have something in there for me, Alex?"

The Arnold-head inside works its teeth against the fabric of the bag and Alex curls his fingers tighter around the outside. He holds it out for Lot once again.

She clicks her tongue and crouches down next to him. He shoves the bag at her. She sighs and nods and reaches her hand toward the opening, her fingers sliding in the top.

KNOCK. KNOCK.

She pulls her hand from bag and stands. Alex's face falls, someone is at the door.

"One minute, Alex."

The knock sounds again and Lot cringes. She storms across the room, throwing the lock in anger, but as she wrenches open the door she changes, becomes cool, calm, and collected. On the other side stands Patrick, a young man about Danny's age. He's scratching wax from his ear and holding the untouched dinner she left in the hallway.

"Sorry to disturb you, ma'am."

"Yes, it's fine. What would you like?"

"Odette sent me up to see if you needed anything else before she goes to bed. Are you done with this?"

"Yes. Thank you."

"But you didn't touch any of it."

Lot flicks her wrist at him. What's wrong with this idiot? She takes a breath.

"It's no longer needed, you can take it away."

"Okay." The young man stands there dumbly staring at her. She resists the urge to slap his hand away from his ear.

"Is that everything?"

"Yes, ma'am."

"Then have a good night."

Lot shuts the door without waiting for a reply. She locks it and is back with Alex in seconds. She slides in next to him. If he's done playing games, she wants to see what he has to give her. Danny used to bring her gifts all the time, anything he could think of that would please her. He worshiped the very ground she walked on. It seems Alex is on the same track and it's delightful. She feels like a kid at Christmas.

He holds out the bag again and Lot plunges her hand in without hesitation, groping for her prize. A sharp pain courses through her finger and she snaps her arm back, yelping. Her finger drips with fresh blood—her blood.

"What's in there?" she snarls.

Lot tears the sack from Alex's grip and angrily turns out its contents. The Arnold head hits the floor with a thump. No longer encumbered by the balled-up t-shirt, it bares its bloody teeth in a ghastly almost-smile.

Lot sharply draws in air. She backs away from the disembodied head as though it could leap onto her person and tear her limb from limb. Her face draws back in sheer horror and revulsion and she grasps at her chest with involuntary, anxiety driven movements. Her mouth sputters but no words come out.

Alex throws himself to the floor, scrambling, collecting everything that fell from his bag. The marbles, Danny's watch, his book, the aftershave... Where is the can opener...matchbook...t-shirt? He spins around, his eyes scanning the ground until he locates everything. He tosses them into the bag, leaving Arnold's teeth-gnashing head where it lay.

Lot stares down at her bitten finger, fish-eyed, as though it might not be true, but it is. She splays her bitten hand out for support, grabbing a bedpost and almost loses her balance; her other arm still confined to the sling around her neck. Her knees go weak, she doubles over and vomits on the floor.

Behind her, Alex snags the padlock key from the side table and pockets it. With a slight hesitation, he also swipes the bottle of maple syrup that still sits out, and throws it into his bag.

Lot turns her face, which is blank with shock, to Alex. He races for Casey's bat and while slinging his bag over his shoulder, then lifts it from the floor. Lot abruptly realizes what's happening.

"You."

Alex dashes for the door then fumbles with the lock. Lot staggers forward, her shock erupting volcanically into anger and her face contorting with pure rage.

Alex heaves open the door as Lot lunges for him, her hip catching a side table, spilling it to the floor. A lit candle tumbles to the ground where it rolls to a stop, right on top of the frayed decorative edge of a rug.

Alex sprints out of Lot's bedroom with her right behind him. She screams at the top of her lungs as he eludes her grip and races down the hallway, putting distance between them quickly. Lot pursues him into the darkness.

Back in her room, the candle's flame creeps from candlewick to rug.

22

Lot howls in the darkness. The little brat is gone! Disappeared into the bowels of the hotel. She screams, her vision red with fury, each step drawing her deeper into the corridor. She stumbles through the hallway, gripping the side with her bleeding hand and shrieking.

Bobbing candlelight rounds a corner and rapidly floats toward her. Another comes after it, and another, accompanied by the sound of feet pounding the thin carpet. There is shouting, and guards surround her. She clenches her bitten hand, concealing the dripping blood.

"Find him!" she snarls at a guard. "He's bitten! Find him now and kill him."

Surprised faces circle her, candlelight bouncing off their skin. Lot swats one of the drudges, veins bulging on her forehead.

"Did you hear me? I said the child is bitten. Find him and kill him before he infects anyone else!"

A guard stammers. "Want me to find Opie?"

Lot bites her lip. She wants to scream some more, wants to slap this peon's face, but she has to rein it in, has to save face. She takes a deep breath, holds it a moment, and exhales. All eyes are on her.

"I'm sorry. This is a very urgent matter, and it seems to have gotten the best of me. We must assemble a search party and go room by room if necessary. One of you take me to Opie."

Two of the guards dash away, lifting their candles high, trying to pierce the gloominess of the hall. The third stays and soon after, he is escorting Lot to find Opie.

***

It isn't long before news of the bitten boy spreads through the colony. He's a threat, a bio-bomb counting down, ready to explode at any second. Able bodies assemble rapidly in the lobby for the search.

Lot looks down at her hand. The bite wound on her finger is small, the skin barely broken. It bled profusely at first but stopped quickly and no one has noticed it yet. It may not look like much, but she can feel the inflamed pulsing of infection eating its way up her arm. Red tendrils of death spiral out from the wound and she can feel the corruption of her cells. They are giving in to the impurity that circulates through her bloodstream.

She keeps her hand low, careful not to use it too much. No one is paying attention, and it's hard to see by the single fire burning in the hearth, but the red spider veins are becoming more noticeable by the second.

There's discontent. Alex must be found before he turns, and no one knows how long that will be. For some of the bitten, it takes days, a fever building and breaking, infection spreading slowly but diligently. For most, it's only a matter of hours or less. The same holds true for the dead. No one can be certain of when a body will rise, all they know is that it always happens, without exception.

Lot shudders. Her joints ache, her head aches, everything about her aches and she feels as though she's coming down with a nasty bout of the flu. If only it were that simple.

Alex must be found. She will see him strung up next to Danny if it's the last thing she does.

***

Alex takes the stairs two at a time, his single shoe slapping each step. The stairwell is pitch black and he trips, his foot missing its mark. He catches himself and hurries on. There's muffled shouting and a floor below him, the light of a flaming torch breaks up the darkness. A man's voice shouts.

"I found him!"

Alex blasts through the door to the next floor and stumbles into the hallway. It's lit with candles and lanterns. Sitting in the middle of the corridor, a gaggle of children huddle around a tattered board game. Their sallow faces turn toward him questioningly. Alex stares back with a soldier-like expression, bloodied baseball bat in hand.

"Wanna play?" asks the oldest looking one, the boy is just about to throw a set of chipped dice. Voices fill the stairwell, riled up by the hunt and Alex darts away, narrowly avoiding the staring children and their game.

This hallway looks the same as all the others, rows of closed doors and nowhere to hide. His pursuers reach the top of the stairwell as he rounds the corner. Just up ahead and to the left, there's an opening and Alex dashes inside. Long empty ice and vending machines greet him in the cramped quarters.

He hears the search party coming and he scans the tiny enclave with distressed eyes. Alex drops to his knees in front of the vending machine where there's a four-inch gap between its bottom and the floor. He rips off his knapsack and stuffs it under the machine, along with Casey's bat.

As fast as he can, he climbs onto the top of the ice machine and uses it to launch himself onto the top of the vending machine. The gap between the machine and the ceiling is narrow, but he manages to jam into it. A split second later, someone steps into the enclave.

A flame reflects off the dusty glass of the vending machine. The person peeks beside it and lifts the lid of the ice machine. Above, just inches from the investigator's head, wide-eyed Alex holds his breath as he listens to the person's nose whistle. Satisfied the boy isn't nearby, the person steps away from the enclave.

The hunt goes room to room, tearing apart every nook and cranny Alex can hide in. Eventually, it dies down and the group decides he left the floor via the second stairwell. The light from the torches, candles and lanterns falls away and the children in the hall are herded safely into a room. They are commanded to play inside and not to come out unless someone tells them it's safe. Finally, Alex is left in pitch black.

His muscles cramp and itches dance across his body. The hallway is quieter than a morgue, but he's afraid to move, afraid the second he does, someone will round the corner and discover him. His heart pounds in his chest, skipping a beat every time he thinks he hears a noise.

After what seems like hours, he finally allows himself the luxury of movement and stretches from his hiding place, lowering himself to the ground. It's so dark he can't even see his hand in front of his face.

Alex gropes around on the floor, reaching under the vending machine until he locates his bag and the bat. Unable to see, he traces the zipper until he finds the tab and unzips the knapsack, then reaches his hand inside. He slides his fingers over the cologne bottle, begging to partake in ritual.

Try a little harder.

Alex forces himself to seek out the matchbook, forces himself to focus. Everything the outside world has to offer is like an icepick in his head and he wants to shut down, to leave it, but he knows he can't, he knows if he does, he'll never FIND DANNY.

He pulls the matchbook from the knapsack. He can't see it, but he runs a finger along the solitary stick that clings to the cardboard. The phosphorus-coated head scrapes against his dirty nail. He holds the match up to his nose and inhales, allowing his mother's last perfume molecules to embrace him. In two seconds, that scent will be gone forever.

Alex grasps the match between his fingers and plucks it from its bed. He turns the cover inside out and wraps it around the stick, trying to cling to its maternal aura as he draws the match against the sandpaper strip. The friction ignites it and the smell of burning sulfur infiltrates his nostrils, destroying the last relic he had of his mother.

Alex's pupils instantly contract with the birth of the flame and he fights the sudden impulse to sneeze. He stands carefully and holds the match up to illuminate something he saw caught in the searcher's glowing light: a fire route map. He studies it. Along with elevators and stairwells, the kitchen area is clearly marked.

The flame sputters, drawing his attention. He stares at it, looking away briefly to drop the empty matchbook back into his knapsack. He stands in the enclave, watching the fire as it burns slowly toward his fingers. Even when the heat becomes unbearable, he continues to hold onto the match, unable to let go. Finally, the flame sputters and dies, leaving Alex with nothing but an afterimage and singed skin.

From somewhere far away more shouting makes its way to Alex's ears. He can only make out one word: "Fire!"

***

For a while, there's nothing; the complete absence of anything, there's not even darkness. There is no knowledge, no feeling, and no being. All pain, fear, and despair have evaporated, existing no longer in the empty void of oblivion. Then, slowly, the darkness begins to unfurl itself, filling the void with great undulating shadows. Danny floats among the swells, knowing only the blackness that laps at his mind, attempting to disintegrate him, to carry him away.

The pain is what he is aware of first, only the pain, far away, like an ache that hasn't yet been noticed. It's playful, tickling his perception until it becomes a full assault on every last grain of his body. It's the pain that rips him from the lulling siren's call of darkness, shredding the fabric of unconsciousness and hurtling his mind back into his small, encapsulating body.

"Fuck."

The word squashes through Danny's blood-caked lips and pierces his eardrums. He moans, rolling over on his side, head throbbing and side on fire. The stench of his own clotted blood surrounds him, repulsive and nauseating.

Gingerly, he pulls his arms beneath him and pushes to a sitting position. He's dizzy, most likely from the loss of blood, he thinks, and wonders how long he's been here—hours? Days? Minutes?

He can't believe he's still alive, had resigned himself to dying. Had died already, several times over in his mind. Now, he lies here, strapped with pain and unsure of the future. Why did Lot stop the execution? Is this just an intermission while she preps for the main event? Everything after being brought to the platform is a blur.

There's a scraping noise outside the cooler and a shiver of fear runs through Danny's spine. The enduring grip of death holds him steadfast as the door opens. He squints against the light of an oil lamp, the person at the end of the cooler doesn't move. It's a long few seconds. Danny's heart threatens to escape his chest while his eyes take their time adjusting and bit by bit, a face becomes clear.

"Alex?"

The kid wears a smile, Danny wasn't sure he could even do that.

The wounded man climbs to his feet, leaning against the wall for support, his shirt crackling with dried blood. It pulls from his wound, and he grimaces. The bandage Julie put there must have fallen off at some point, but the bleeding is just sludge now, a minor leak. Still, the wound feels even worse than before. He stumbles forward.

Alex grins from ear to ear. It almost makes Danny laugh, except if he laughs the pain might knock him out cold. Hunched, barely able to stand, he guides Alex from the cooler and scans the kitchen. There's no one else. As they exit, Danny's accidently kicks the padlock and key Alex dropped to the ground.

"How did you get in here? Did anyone see you?" he croaks at Alex, his words almost unintelligible. "How'd you know where I was? Where'd you get that lantern? *How'd you get the key?*" And as the barrage of questions tumble from his mouth, he realizes he'll likely never have the answers. Alex looks up at him silently, still smiling.

"Where the hell is your shoe?" Danny shakes his head in

amazement and the world swims before his eyes. He reaches out to steady himself against a steel counter.

When he can see properly again, Danny points at the bat Alex holds in one hand. "Can I take that?" He's not sure he can use it, but he'll try if he must. The boy happily hands it over and Danny takes one more moment to gaze in wonder at the boy. "You're not as dumb as you let people think, are you?"

No response.

Nearby, a barrel of rainwater catches Danny's eye. He staggers to it, suddenly aware he's never been so thirsty in his life, then plunges his hands into the barrel and brings them up to parched lips, drinking deeply. Once his thirst is quenched, he splashes the cold water on his face. It stings as he rubs at his cheeks, trying to jerk himself into a state of readiness blood loss forbids.

Danny wipes water from his eyes and looks around the room, trying to collect his thoughts. Near his prison cell is a walk-in pantry where there are shelves lined with rows of neatly organized, nonperishable food items. He rifles through them, trying to grab a few high-calorie items. Smoked meat and a few cans of condensed milk go into Alex's knapsack. As an afterthought, he grabs a box of Triscuits and throws it in the bag too, then snags a canteen and fills it with water.

All the while, the boy follows him like a puppy.

***

Thick, poisonous smoke rolls along the ceilings and billows through the hallways. The bodies of those overcome by hot fumes already decorate the floor as the fire moves quickly, consuming everything in its path.

Anarchy settles in as people become aware of the situation. Many run, saving themselves, but those who would stay and fight find they are ill-equipped. Expired fire extinguishers spit and sputter, and buckets of water turn to sizzling steam. Lantern and candlelight reflect off the walls of smoke, creating a maze of patterns that lead many to their death. Those who do manage to find their way by touch struggle to breathe in the toxic air, each breath ushering in a myriad of chemicals, shutting oxygen out.

A few brave souls attempt to run deeper into the building, knowing loved ones are further back. They dampen shirts and hold them against their noses, hoping to create crude filters. Still others wrap themselves in wetted clothing to fend off the heat from flames they cannot even see yet.

In the lobby, still untouched by the fire, people gather, grouping in bunches, afraid, asking themselves the one true question: Do they venture outside? A woman in a tank top grips the hand of a small child and implores Lot to find an answer. "What do we do? We can't go outside! It's not safe!"

Lot's face is sweaty. She feels both hot and cold at the same time as her body burns with an infection it cannot resist. Amid this, she finds herself unable to concentrate.

Someone else answers the woman with the child. "Better to take our chances out there than to burn to death in here."

Another person puts in their two cents, "Maybe the fire will stabilize, you know, and burn itself out. We can just wait here until then."

"Are you stupid?"

"Smoke is filling the place!"

"What about the room with the gas storage?"

"I can't go back outside again! The Risen!"

Lot drifts away from the concerns of her followers and thinks instead about Danny, locked in the kitchen cooler with no way to escape, the ungrateful shit writhing in agony as he is cooked alive—her own form of the Brazen Bull. And Alex, choking on smoke and collapsing, trying to crawl further as he slowly asphyxiates, she hopes he understands he's dying. It lifts her spirits slightly and she raises a hand to the growing crowd around her. They need guidance, they need *her*.

"Calm down. Calm down, please."

They ignore her.

***

Danny creeps through the hallway, holding Casey's bat at the ready, every step taxing his will to endure. Alex follows cautiously, a few feet behind. The smell of burning insulation and carpets floats in the air around them. Shouting comes from far away and there is screaming. They carry on.

Danny's hyperaware hearing picks up on shuffling footsteps just about to round the corner and he pulls Alex into a bathroom that opens off the hallway. He hopes the owner of the footsteps didn't notice the light from their lantern.

When Danny and the others first took over the hotel, they had removed the main door of this bathroom and appropriated it as barricade material. Despite that, the room still serves its original function and buckets hang on the outside of every stall, their doors also removed. A barrel of dirty water nearly blocks the way in, its life as wash water long since passed. It now carries waste down the pipes, into the unattended sewer system below.

Danny stands near the doorway, bat in hand, just holding it up is exhausting. The pain in his head and side are excruciating. He is swollen and stiff where Davis crushed his shoulder with the hammer and his face aches with a broken nose. He'd gladly cut off a finger, hell two fingers, if someone could offer him a handful of ibuprofen to dull the pain. Behind him, he can hear Alex fiddling around with the faucets of the sink and prays the kid can focus long enough to get out of this hellhole.

The footsteps stop, and the only sound Danny hears come from the other hallways. After a long minute of waiting, he peeks his head around the door jam. Staring back at him is a face with bulging eyes and lips peeled back exposing blood-blackened teeth.

Danny gasps. "Jamal?"

The creature that was Jamal lurches forward. Danny swings the bat pathetically, his side screaming, and to his plain surprise, Jamal blocks the hit then rips the weapon from Danny's hands, throwing it to the floor.

There were stories of this, random creatures that hold on to something a little human. They have the capacity to react, are just a little smarter, it was said. He thought the stories were just old wives' tales.

The creature eyes Danny, hunger glaring in its swollen orbs. It screams demonically and its bulging belly jiggles like some sort of fucked up Santa Claus. Fresh blood drips from its jowls and it stands there, watching its prey as though assessing options. Danny feels for Alex by his side.

No longer hampered by the constraining effects of rigor mortis, the creature springs without warning. It slams Danny into the wall behind them, the mirror that hangs there cracks, and Danny almost crumbles to the ground in pain.

The thing bares its teeth and snaps at Danny's face. Danny swerves his head to the side, just avoiding a deadly bite. He shoves it away, into the barrel near the doorway, which tips, sloshing water everywhere. The creature and Danny struggle, slipping and sliding in the flood.

Fighting the unbearable pain in his side, Danny runs the ghoul into a toilet stall. The creature grabs at his arms, trying to drag him down as it trips back, over the toilet. Danny grabs its head and smashes it into the metal flushing mechanism that juts up from the back.

The ghoul struggles, trying to get a grip on Danny as chrome piping breaks off with the force of the blows, its jagged edges begging for more. Danny jams the creature's head down on the broken pipes. One of its eyes swells and bursts from its socket as metal spikes through its temple.

Wounds screaming, Danny hits a wall and his strength abandons him. He stumbles back, falling to his knees in a puddle of dirty water. The creature howls and flails. It rips the seat off the toilet and whips it at Danny. The seat bounces hard, bruising Danny's already battered chest, but the ghoul is held fast by the pipe through the side of its face.

Still trying to catch his breath, Danny looks over at Alex. The boy has barely moved, he just stands in the same place and watches everything, holding the lantern. Danny motions for him to come close and uses a stall side to pull himself to his feet. The creature screams.

Danny drops any effort at concealment, he and Alex beeline from the bathroom. On their way out, he searches the floor for Casey's bat, but it's nowhere to be found. Alex holds up the light, refusing to leave, his eyes scouring the ground too. The creature in the bathroom will be free quickly and they don't have time to worry about the loss of a bat. Danny grabs Alex by the arm and drags him down the hallway.

23

Opie is in the library, avoiding the big search for the bitten boy. At first, he dismisses the smell, sure he's imagining it, but soon it's hard not to recognize. Smoke and heat suck into the room as he opens the door to the hallway and he's stunned to see the glow of flames.

Odette and the children leap into his mind. This evening's events exhausted them, and she wanted to forget about it all, meaning they are upstairs and possibly asleep with no way to tell what's happening down here.

Opie sprints to the stairwell and looks up at flames that eat their way out of an open door at the top. He can feel the blistering heat from where he stands. He runs around to the second stairwell and it's filled with smoke too, but he dashes up anyway. Halfway, he's choking and his eyes sting so badly he can't see. Unable to breathe, he stumbles back to the bottom in a coughing fit.

It's difficult standing at the bottom of those stairs. Physically, he's capable of running up them, can possibly even get to the top if he holds his breath, and maybe into the next hallway, but what if that hallway is also filled with smoke? It seems likely, and it would be a death sentence. He wouldn't be able to last long enough to get back down the stairs.

Opie has spent his life doing things only for himself and every decision he ever made was one that would somehow benefit him. It's why he survives while others don't. Leaving Odette and the children behind is a hard decision, but one that has a well-worn path.

Years ago, when he met a young and amazingly charismatic Lot, he knew he could go far with her, and he did. They ran her crazy "religion" together, and it provided them both with a comfortable existence. Opie always knew it for what it was: a cult, a racket to separate people not only from everything valuable they owned but from the lives they knew, to inspire their devotion and servitude. There were days when it seemed as though Lot bought into her own bullshit, but still, he was well looked after, and that made him happy.

When the outbreaks began, he thought everything, all of his hard work, would be squandered. He had been living high, a loyal advisor with all the perks. People panicked, people abandoned, people died, but some believers remained true, and he was surprised to find things got even better for him after. Lot's people were willing to follow her to the grave, and Opie by proxy.

He can't understand that way of thinking. He isn't willing to sacrifice his life for anyone, it's all he has that truly matters to him. If circumstances come down to him or someone else, it's always someone else, and in the days and months following the downfall of society, he proved this time and again.

He is, he fondly likes to think, a self-preservationist.

Now, standing at the bottom of the stairs, the Gods of doubt and guilt smile down on Opie for the first time. He thinks of Odette and the kids. The only time he's ever considered risking his life for someone else is this moment. He envisions their peaceful heads resting on crisp, clean pillowcases, lying in the fluffy well-lined beds he provided for them. He knows even if they're awake, they are most likely doomed.

Bile foams in his belly, slowly eating away at the lining of his stomach as he turns his back on the stairwell. He really enjoyed having a family, he thinks, but he can't have one if he's dead either.

Opie runs through the hallway, ignoring the many people shouting and pleading for help. Smoke hangs thickly in the air, burning his nostrils and making it hard to see, but he knows these hallways like the back of his hand.

When he reaches the lobby, it's filled with a sizeable crowd and his heart grows hopeful as he scans it, looking for Odette and the children. They are nowhere to be found and his hopes are dashed; he'll truly miss them.

Thick Marge startles Opie from his thoughts. Her sooty face tells him she has already proven herself a hero this night.

"Have you seen Odette?" he asks. "The children?"

She shakes her head grimly and his eyes water, just a little bit. He can't remember the last time he got emotional like this, probably when he was just a boy.

Thick Marge leads him to a small group huddled in the corner where Lot sits facing a still blazing hearthside, her petite frame nearly engulfed by a large chair. She's surrounded by a few other advisors who wring their hands, waiting on their leader for word about what they should do. They welcome Opie, relieved to see him and the wall of advisors recedes, allowing him to approach.

He's taken aback with how sickly Lot looks. She stares silently at the glowing embers in the fireplace, a thin sheen of sweat standing out on her brow. Her eyes are bloodshot, her skin faded and gray. Even though she's sitting, he can see she trembles slightly.

Opie shuts out the lingering thoughts of his momentary family and puts on his most reassuring face. He moves into Lot's field of vision and her gaze, still acute, homes in on him immediately.

"The people are frightened, Lot."

She blinks but does not respond and he isn't sure she's hearing him. It doesn't matter, though. Speaking to her now is only a show for those around him and if he plays his cards right she'll be tossed aside like the senile old bat he'll make her out to be.

"You must make an announcement. You must reassure them, and we must get organized," Opie says.

Lot's face shrivels with disdain.

"Of what exactly shall I reassure them?"

He pushes down his shock and delight at Lot's uncharacteristic outburst. Her breakdown will ease his quiet seizure of power. He will be like a knife in the gut that slides in so perfectly she doesn't feel it until the blade is removed.

"Reassure them that with a calm and orderly exit, everything will be okay."

Several people around Opie nod, agreeing with him.

"Tell them we have enough weapons to keep them safe, tell them that—"

"Nonsense. These people will be lucky to survive the fire and those that do will be left to fend for themselves."

Thick Marge leans in closer to Lot, squinting in the dim, smoky light. "Are you feeling okay?"

Lot waves her off with an annoyed flick of the wrist. Opie can hear people coughing as smoke streams in even faster than before. "Lot, the calmer the people are, the better chance we all have for survival."

A dry, humorless laugh breaks away from Lot's throat. Her lips peel back from her teeth exposing the darkened and necrotic gums beneath them and her raspy laughter dances with the thickening haze.

Screaming from the other side of the lobby draws attention away from Lot and the tenuous peace preventing panic is suddenly shattered. People are beginning to run in all directions. They trip over each other scrambling away from a bedraggled and blood-drenched Danny, who limps into the room. He hauls Alex behind him, holding tightly onto one arm. The boy looks back, into the hallway, looking for something.

Lot bolts to her feet. "Them..."

The creature that was once Jamal tracks Danny, only a few seconds behind him. Half its face is falling away and its skull has been pulverized in places, exposing the black, gelatinous brain that clings to the inside. Its one remaining eye never leaves its prey as he pushes through the crowd.

Pandemonium takes hold. The armory has already been emptied, and with a flesh-hungry monster in their midst, those without weapons are now willing to fight for one. A brawl breaks out over a small hunting knife. People begin to push and shove their way toward the only exit in the building. The tank top wearing woman tries desperately to protect her fallen child from a stampede of people.

A terror-gripped man, who isn't watching where he's going, knocks the woman over. She tries to get up, but someone else steps on her. Feet rain down on her body, barely aware they're trampled a living being. A blow to the chest, another to the back, to the head, and more, until she stops struggling. There is no comfort for the child that sits on the floor and cries next to her mother's broken body.

Men and women claw at the foyer cage and the barricaded coverings of the windows. Only a few people at a time can funnel through the single door that opens out onto the warm summer night.

Danny drags Alex toward an area where the concierge used to sit. In recent years, the area has been used for many different things, but Poppy's desk is still there, overturned by the stampede.

Danny shakes Alex by the shoulders, the boy's hair flopping back and forth.

"You stay here until I can come to get you. Do you understand me? Forget about the damn bat and stay here. DO. NOT. MOVE."

Danny doesn't have time to drive home the point. He shoves Alex under the desk and dodges an attack from the Jamal-creature, then sprints away, drawing the enemy far from Alex. With every step his pain gets worse and he worries he might black out. The thing behind him doesn't miss a beat.

A deafening explosion reverberates off the walls. Drums of gasoline, hoarded in another room, launch metal and plastic through the air. Thick smoke and fire belch from the hallway nearest to Danny. The force from the explosion rocks the entire building, throwing a few people from their feet. Danny nearly loses his footing and the creature chasing him sprawls onto the floor, buying him a little more time.

Outside, the reinforced windows of a ground floor hotel room blow out with the explosion. The fire sucks in oxygen, feeding off it, and growing instantly bigger. A huge swell of flame spews from the window and into the night sky, illuminating the mob of pusillanimous people gathering outside the front of the hotel.

Attracted by the commotion and flames, creatures from the forest and surrounding field emerge one after another. Rotting bodies snake through the grass, preceded by the rancid odor from the flesh of their victims, decomposing in their bloated stomachs and smeared across their bodies. They snarl and gnar like the demonically possessed, their sights set on the huddled mass shivering in fright under the light of the moon.

BBQ TIME.

Cries of terror erupt, and people begin to push back into the building, fighting through those trying to get out. The Risen swarm, attacking the weak and defenseless, chasing after those who retreat back inside.

Fire eats away at the walls of the lobby. The hotel is like a tinderbox being greedily shoved into the open maw of flame. Paint and varnish bubbles and flakes away with the extreme heat. Wood paneling and support beams beg to be noticed by the growing inferno. Everything the fire touches is devoured, nothing escapes.

Danny dodges another attack from Jamal, too occupied to notice as the room fills with fire, or that a surge of The Risen from outside is pouring in. He frantically puts a table between him and his aggressor, trying to buy some time, searching for a weapon.

Jamal's gaze, aware and bloodthirsty, curdles what blood is left in Danny's veins. He fumbles around the table, staying just out of reach. The creature screams, as though in frustration, and whips the table out of its way. Now nothing stands between them and it lunges at Danny. Danny steps clumsily backward and trips, spilling to the floor.

The thing jumps for him. Danny rolls out of the way and with blackened eyes, spies a bright flash, light on metal: A hunting knife dropped by someone during the panic.

Jamal pounces on Danny and Danny deflects with a weak kick,

screaming as pain rips up his side. He reaches for the weapon and wraps his fingers around it, but the ghoul is instantly on top of him. It grabs Danny by the neck and pulls him toward its teeth. Danny jams his knife in the creature's temple and twists. Blade scrapes against bone, teeth clack together, and with a jerk, the ghoul stops moving.

Danny falls back, crying out in pain, tears spilling from his eyes. He rips the hunting knife from the ghoul's head and pulls himself out from under the corpse, crawling to his feet.

Across the room, Lot can't take her eyes off of the scene. She watches as the blond man drags himself toward an overturned desk, holding his side. She steps forward and Opie offers Lot a helping hand, always keeping up appearances.

"Get out of my way, you fool," she spits.

Opie and a few other advisors step back, parting like the red sea. Lot shoves her way through them, her feverish face set with determination. She tears her sling off and throws it to the ground and her arm complains loudly. She doesn't care, it's not like she'll need it where she's going.

Lot grabs Thick Marge by the lapel. "Give me your weapon."

"W-W-Why?" Thick Marge stutters. Lot already has her hand at her belt, drawing her machete, and she storms away without answering. As she leaves, Thick Marge and the others turn to Opie, seeking guidance.

"She's lost to us, my friends. The best we can hope to do now is to escape with our own lives," he says.

Julie, surrounded by her three sons, is the first to agree. After that, people fold like cards. The consensus is clear, if they can make it out of here, they'll have a fighting chance at survival. Opie leads the way toward the exit with one final glance back at Lot and Danny.

Danny reaches under the overturned desk to pull Alex out. Just as he grips the boy, Alex yanks, pulling Danny forward and to the side with surprising strength, almost bringing the injured man to the floor. A split second later, Lot's machete misses Danny by only a few inches and embeds in the wood of the desk.

Danny hitches away from Lot, dragging Alex with him. He shoves the boy behind him and readies his own, much smaller, knife. Lot wrenches her blade from the desk's grip and turns to meet Danny.

Danny is surprised by how horrible she looks. Sickness assails her body and her face holds the sheen of the dying. Her ashen skin is thin, allowing dark veins to create spider webs across the surface. Her eyelids have trouble blinking around her bloated, red eyes and her entire body quavers.

Lot hacks at him with her blade, missing. Danny wobbles away a step, and she swings at him again, forcing him back, feeding off his weakness.

She advances, and Danny raises his knife, scarcely blocking her with a counter-blow. It's just enough to force Lot's weapon to the side. He winces and thrusts his blade toward her midsection, but she sidesteps and chops at him again. He jumps back, groaning in pain.

As Lot advances, embers float down from the ceiling like wicked snowflakes, singing skin and burning tiny holes through clothing. People scream on all sides, the creatures inside attacking anything that moves. Danny stumbles back, trying to avoid another deadly swing of Lot's weapon.

"Leave us alone, Lot," he pants "There's no point to this anymore."

"Look at what you've done. This is all because of you! You've caused the death of all these people!"

Danny falters, almost taking Lot's blade to the face as he shakes her out of his head. It takes all his concentration. He's been manipulated by her one too many times and can now see her for what she is, but that doesn't make it any easier.

Their clumsy dance of death across the lobby draws little notice. Around them, people scream and cry. A few flee, but most stand or sit where they are, paralyzed into doing nothing. To escape the burning building will be to submit to the night and its many horrors. To remain inside isn't any safer, with flames consuming their shelter and creatures tearing asunder all they touch. It's lose-lose.

Most people are unable to decide, unable to try, and unable to save themselves. If Danny could take a moment to look around at the doomed faces that litter the lobby, he would recognize something—the same grip of death he felt not so long ago.

Lot flinches as Danny miraculously draws blood from her arm with his blade, but it's a short-lived victory. Before he realizes what's happening, he's being dragged down, falling backward. A man clings to his leg, Davis, from the platform. He's crying, his face burned, eyes blackened by the fire. "Please help me," he cries. "Please! I can't see!"

Lot pounces on Danny, cutting her knife down at his head. He blocks, and they become knife-locked, Lot straddling him from the top. Davis holds fast to Danny's leg, begging.

"You should have listened to me, little boy." Lot yells above the roar of commotion in the lobby.

She grinds her knee into Danny's side and he screams in agony, his arms wavering, almost giving out. Her knife skids over the handle of his blade, slicing into his index finger, severing tendons and digging into bone. He can't fight much longer: his body is giving out.

Suddenly, Lot pitches forward, nearly toppling over and her knife skitters across the ground. On her back rises Alex, biting at her face. He sinks his teeth into an earlobe and tears a chunk of it, then spits it over their heads, blood showering everything around them.

Lot reaches over her shoulder, rips him from her back by the hair, and slams him to the floor, knapsack and all. With a child's resilience, he bounces to his feet and scrambles for her machete.

Danny shakes off Davis.

Lot spins back around to face her son, teeth bared like a wild animal, and without a moment's hesitation, he plunges his hunting knife deep into her chest, through her heart, all the way up to the hilt.

Lot's hands fly up, and she clasps them around Danny's hand, still on the knife. She smiles eerily at him, her gray eyes coming to rest on his blue ones, trapping him with the last of her power. He can't look away as blood bubbles from her mouth, staining her lips and spilling down her chin. She attempts a laugh, but only a gurgle slips out as she slides from his knife and falls back, dead, into Davis's arms.

Danny collapses, death whispering in his ear once again. Alex, his hair mussed and tinged red from the fire that roars around them, steps into view. He stares down at Danny and Danny stares up at the boy, coughing raggedly in the smoke and holding his side in misery.

After what seems like ages, Danny drags himself to his feet. He squints his eyes against the thick, glowing haze and is about to rub Alex's hair when he notices his right hand is bleeding copiously from his index finger. It hurts like hell, just like everything else, but it's probably the least of his worries. He pats the boy's head with his other hand.

Alex, large machete hanging from one small fist, looks up at Danny, his eyes shining with the type of admiration only a child can muster. It makes Danny uncomfortable and he motions his head toward the door, "Let's get out of here."

They pick their way slowly through the carnage, Danny bowed forward, unable to stand straight. All around them, hungry creatures feast on the bodies of those who could not, or would not, fight. Gunshots ring out randomly as a few still try to make it toward the door, but for the most part, anyone who was getting out alive is already gone.

As they cross the lobby, Danny's foggy eyes pick up on something. Just ahead of them lies a man, shot in the forehead with an arrow. It's hard to tell at first, but as they near, he's sure of what he is seeing. Clutched in the dead man's hands is Danny's bat. He stops, crouches down painfully, and removes his bat from the man's hands.

Far behind them Davis weeps, Lot's dead body draped over him. With each breath he sucks in more and more smoke until coughs gradually replace sobs. His burned corneas can't see his Leader's eyes as they pop open.

Lot sinks her teeth into the chest of the man she lies on. She tears into the soft tissue and then rips out her devotee's throat, stifling the scream that pours from it. Blood sprays across the floor, leaving a fan-like design that cooks instantly in the raging inferno.

Danny and Alex head for the way out, trying not to breathe too much, or to be seen. The heat from the flames is beginning to sear skin and hair, but Danny stops, sensing something behind him. He peeks back over his shoulder as Lot emerges from the smoke. Her shirt is on fire, flames cooking the skin of her shoulders and neck, the heat so intense her necklace melts down her chest, bubbling flesh beneath it.

Hunched in pain, Danny stares down Lot as she approaches. He grinds his teeth, heart pounding. Every last ounce of adrenaline he has left surges into his body, taking over.

The world around him drops away.

He points Alex toward the exit, but the boy refuses to budge. Alex pulls on Danny's shirt, attempting to stop the judgment-clouded man as he turns to face off against a flaming Zombie Lot. Danny shoves Alex out of the way, hard.

Lot stops. Blood soaks her clothes and bits of stringy muscle hang from her bared teeth. The fire on her clothes chars her skin to a crispy black. She cocks her head to one side in an unnatural gesture, like an apex predator deciding on its prey.

Danny grips his baseball bat and readies himself for a showdown, feeling nothing but hatred. Behind him, Alex watches nervously and raises his machete, unsure of what will happen next.

Lot charges, but Danny only steps forward once. As soon as she's within striking distance he swings with everything he can muster, connecting with Lot's head. The side of her face crushes in, cheekbone and teeth explode outward with the arch of his bat and the force of the swing drives her to the ground.

Danny leaps on Lot, a madman. He pounds her head with his

bat, each blow spraying a little more skull and brain through the lobby. With tears coursing down his cheeks, he keeps swinging until she stops moving and there's nothing left of her head but a bloody pulp.

Heaving, taking in huge lungful's of smoky air, Danny spits on Lot's corpse.

A ceiling beam crashes down close by, pulled by the heavy chandelier made of deer antlers. It startles Danny, bringing him back to reality, and he stumbles away from Lot's body. Fighting off a coughing fit, he rests his bat on his shoulder and staggers toward Alex. Around them, the building is collapsing into a burning heap. Flaming creatures feed off the bodies of people he once knew, and the smoke is so thick it's hard to tell where they need to go.

Danny knows he doesn't have long. His side is bleeding again and he's completely empty, there's no fight left. Once he gets Alex out of the burning hotel, he's done, and he looks forward to returning to the nothing. Still, as they make a run for the exit, a sereneness he has never felt before embraces him.

Read on for an excerpt from

Purple Haze

The award-winning short story by
M.F. Wahl

For information on how to read more
please visit:

www.mfwahl.com

PURPLE HAZE

Adira sucked back on her cigarette, her first in nearly two decades. Jack Hatter's had been her favorite, but beggars couldn't be choosers, and she had bummed it from a colleague with an insistent hacking cough. He was dead now, almost everyone was. Only she and two others had survived the crash.

Long curling fingers of poisonous smoke caressed her lungs with the promise of an abusive lover. The cigarette didn't make her feel any better—but right now she needed it. Right now, more than any time in her life, she needed a crutch to help her stand.

Adam approached. The brief wrinkle of his nose, and the slit of his eyes on his weathered face, told her he disapproved, but she was the captain and he said nothing. He straightened the bleached lapels of his lab coat and swung his body down into the bucket seat in front of several computer LCDs.

Adira stubbed out the counterfeit Marlboro on the bottom of her boot. It tasted terrible anyway. She cleared her throat and rolled up the sleeves of her flight suit, then nodded at Adam. With a deep breath and a moment of hesitation, he tapped on the keyboard, shunting away the screensaver and bringing up rows of color-coded bars, each fluctuating slightly.

God, Adira hated this archaic system, but she knew it had probably saved their lives as they crash landed on Ningal. Which was the entire point. Everyone back home operated on nanotech, but out here they had no connection to the "hive." That meant nanites were practically useless. Anyway, the stasis chambers fried the little buggers, and having hardware that could easily be fixed with a solder gun and a screwdriver came in handy during times like this.

"It works!" Adira clapped Adam on the back, smiling.

Adam rubbed his face. His unchanging glower and his crew cut combined to make him look more like a drill sergeant then the acclaimed scientist he was.

"Yeah," he said. "But take a look at this." He pointed at the screen with a bloodstained fingernail.

Adira leaned in closer to the screen. A red bar flashed angrily at her from the display.

"The oxygen generator is toast," she said, crossing her arms. "Yep," Adam replied, continuing to stare grimly at the screen. "And so are all of our backup supplies."

"Yep. We're in a heap of trouble."

She had expected as much, and scratched absently at her arm as she thought. The ship was a total mess. Parts were completely broken off and scattered for miles around. Several huge gashes in the hull had already exposed them to the planet's atmosphere and it looked like, at least for the time being, that was unlikely to change.

"Well, we're not dead yet," she said.

"Perhaps we should consider stasis until help arrives?"

"And lose another ten years?"

"To avoid further damaging the environment here."

"The damage is already done. There's no way the crash avoided seeding this place. If we go into stasis, we'll miss our one and only window to study this planet; I mean *really* study it."

Adam sat back in his chair, conceding to her. They both knew that in ten years it was possible for the bacteria that were a part of daily human life to take over. While in orbit, preliminary tests had been unable to turn up any life, not even a single microbe. With the exception of the indigo-blue grass that nearly covered the planet's entire surface, the environment seemed to be sterile. But, just because they hadn't seen other life yet, didn't mean it wasn't there.

"What about us?" Adam asked.

"Did you say goodbye to everything you've ever known so you could get here and piss your pants at the thought of alien bacteria boogey-men?"

Adam reluctantly shook his head. She knew he wasn't the type to back down, none of them were. Hell, they were pioneers, cowboys in the Wild Wild West, but being the first to ever step foot on another planet with life, even if it was just grass, was a daunting proposition.

Across the control room, Jenna, the only other surviving crew member, limped in, carrying a few fire-suppression packs. She was probably walking on a broken ankle, but didn't complain.

"Bad news?" Jenna asked as she neared. Adira met her grey eyes with her own.

"Could be worse."

"Well, I've got some piss for your lemonade," Jenna said. "There's a fire in crew quarters."

Adira held back an exasperated sigh. She was trying not to think of her dead crew—people that were like family to her—or the disaster of a mission they had died for. A fire seemed like shit-flavored icing on a giant turd cake. Still, she knew it was imperative to set an example, to stay positive, focused, and motivated, for Adam and Jenna. She was going to make sure everyone left survived this.

Jenna held one of the fire suppression packs out to her, and Adira took it. Adam began to stand from his chair, but she placed a hand on his shoulder. "No, you stay here. See if you can at least restore communication faculties."

Adam gave a curt nod, and sat back down at the kiosk. "I might have to manually repair things, but I'll see if I can do something from here first."

"Good," Adira said, and looped her arms into the FSP to wear it like a backpack. She turned to face Jenna and motioned for her to lead the way.

The corridor was metal and lined with rows of emergency LED lighting on the floors, ceilings, and sides. The fact that the crew would probably be weightless in space with no "up" had been taken into account when the ship was designed. Even the emergency lighting reflected this thought pattern. Every little detail was accounted for, except the need to make the lighting bright enough to actually see by.

They were surrounded by stripes of glowing blue, and yet the corridor was still extremely dark. It made Adira feel as though she were walking through a carnival house. She expected the lights to begin twisting like a vortex tunnel, or the floor to become uneven and wobbly. As though to remind her of the severity of the situation, every few feet or so they'd come across dark spots on the lights and she knew it was blood on the walls and floor. They'd already moved the bodies, and bagged them according to protocol.

The corridor had never seemed so long as it did now, and to take her mind off it, Adira focused on the shadow just ahead of her that was Jenna. When the glow of fire seeped around a corner up ahead, she was almost happy to see it.

The corridor to the right ended abruptly in mangled metal. Adira couldn't smell much smoke, but she could see flames through the gaps in the twisted steel and sparking cables. Jenna peeked between pieces of the crumbled spacecraft. "Shit," she said. "The wreckage shifted. We'll have to get to it from the outside, before the fire jumps to the rest of the ship."

How Adira loved that woman's determination. She was as smart as a whip and never one to back down from a challenge. If something needed to be done, Jenna got it done, no matter how hard it seemed.

Adira nodded. "Let's do it then."

They jogged the corridor back to the control room, Jenna limping deeply with every step. There they saw Adam had opened a console and was shining a flashlight at a mass of wires.

"Any luck?" he asked, without looking up.

"We used all our luck when we survived the crash," Adira said, half-joking, and held out her hand to help Adam off the floor.

As she hoisted him to his feet, Jenna sat in a nearby chair, propping her injured leg out to the side.

"We're going outside," she said, wincing slightly.

"That's a bad idea." Adam shook his head. "If we do that, we risk exposing ourselves, not to mention the fact that we'll be further contaminating the environment."

Jenna pointed at a gaping hole near the now useless airlock. It started halfway up the wall and stretched partially across the ceiling, giving a view of a purplish sky outside that was otherwise similar to Earth's. "We're already exposed, Adam. We're exposed, and we've already contaminated this planet."

"The more we traipse around, the more we touch and poke and prod, the more we shed our own microbes. We have no clue how it will react in this environment. It could completely obliterate what already lives here."

"There's nothing but grass." Jenna threw up her hands in frustration. "This planet is sterile!"

Adam raised his voice a bit. "It's not possible for grass to have evolved here and live completely by itself. There has to be other life."

"Whoa," interjected Adira, sensing the pressure of the situation was taking its toll. "Let's just calm down"

She looked at Jenna. "The longer we're here, out of stasis, the more we contaminate the environment."

Jenna nodded. "The damage is done, and I don't want to lose another decade trapped in a pod while everything we've worked for goes down the shitter."

"I don't want to lose another ten years either," Adam said, his tone betraying his worry.

Jenna looked at him. For a few seconds he appeared to be struggling with his thoughts, and then he threw her a conciliatory nod.

Adira rubbed her face with one hand and wished she hadn't stubbed out that cigarette. She knew the protocol was stasis in an emergency like this. They could survive in it long enough for another mission to reach them. If they did that though, it wouldn't just be another ten years of their lives—it was twenty.

Twenty total, ten to get to Ningal, and ten to wait for rescue, rotting away in a stasis pod with nothing to show for their lost time but a contaminated environment and a mission gone horribly wrong. Twenty years, and four dead crewmembers.

"I don't want to go back in stasis either," she said.

There was silence for a moment and then, still wearing her FSP, Adira turned to cross the control room. Jenna and Adam shared a glance. After a few seconds, he offered a hand to help her stand. She accepted, and they followed Adira, ignoring the alarms and flashing screens all around them.

On the other side of the room, Adira grasped the lever that opened the hatch and pushed it down. Her stomach sank with the familiar hiss of the chamber inside depressurizing, its failsafe mechanisms releasing. Prior testing had indicated the air was hospitable to human life, but she still couldn't help but worry, even if they had already been exposed.

She stepped into the chamber, her heart beating so hard she thought it might crack her ribs. With a deep breath, she opened the outside door, releasing the triple seals that had once held back the emptiness of space.

The crew stepped into warm, humid air. It smelled horrible. Like a mix between death and what Adira assumed a hippo's breath would be like. She glanced at Jenna and Adam. They both had the same expression, faces pinched with disgust.

"This planet smells like shit," Adam said, eloquent as usual.

ABOUT THE AUTHOR

M.F. Wahl lives in beautiful Halifax, Nova Scotia, Canada where she can spend time in nature and raise a family.

When not writing, she enjoys a variety of hobbies, from raising moths to gourmet cooking, and studying Buddhism.

The written word is her first love (but don't tell her husband that).

Reach out to M.F. Wahl

www.mfwahl.com

M.F. WAHL - AUTHOR

www.ingramcontent.com/pod-product-compliance
Lightning Source LLC
Chambersburg PA
CBHW031942010726
47493CB00007B/2046